Little Friends

Kit Gilmore

Published by Kit Gilmore, 2024.

LITTLE FRIENDS

First edition. August 6, 2024.

Copyright © 2024 Kit Gilmore.

ISBN: 979-8227062789

Written by Kit Gilmore.

For Kellan (My most powerful light.)
For Danny (Who heard enough to fill several tomes, and still
supported my crazy ideas.)

. . . .

To everyone whose names I stole and personalities consumed. These
are mine now. The contract has been silently and secretly signed
since you were children.

I met a lady in the meads,
Full beautiful—a faery's child,
Her hair was long, her foot was light,
And her eyes were wild.
- La Belle Dame sans Merci: A Ballad
John Keats

Dear Mrs. Hernandez-Jansen,

Congratulations! We are thrilled to inform you that you have been selected to participate in the first-ever season of Peak Challenge, the ultimate wilderness survival competition.

As one of the carefully chosen contestants, you will be dropped off in the vicinity of Tenas Tilikum (Little Friend Mountain), where you will be required to climb to the summit while facing a series of grueling challenges along the way. Only the most determined, resourceful and skilled individuals will make it to the top and claim the ultimate prize of five hundred thousand dollars!

We were impressed by your application and believe that you have what it takes to be a real contender on this show. You will be part of an elite group of individuals who are pushing themselves to the limits and proving their mettle in one of the harshest environments on Earth. You will be required to use your wits and survival skills to overcome the challenges and outlast your fellow contestants.

Please keep in mind that participation in Peak Challenge is physically and mentally demanding. We recommend that you train vigorously and prepare yourself for the toughest experience of your life.

We will provide you with all the necessary information in a forthcoming phone call. But please consider this letter as your official welcome to the production!

We look forward to seeing you soon and wish you the best of luck in this ultimate test of survival.

Sincerely,

Miles Kovacs

Miles High Productions

Peak Challenge Production Team

The "Peak Challenge" acceptance letter all contestants received. This one was taken from a box in the attic of the parent's of Alessandra Hernandez-Jansen marked "Ally's Stuff".

Foreword

Peak Challenge was probably the best pitch Miles Kovacs had ever come up with for The Knowledge Network execs, in the five years it had been scraping by with the scraps and rejects it would accept down the line from Discovery and TLC. I remember early on at some crew mixer. Before things really kicked off, Miles was bragging about how he got the idea from being in Sweden for a shoot, and running across this show called Expedition: Robinson; pretty much the premise that we all know and love for the multitude of "survivor" shows now.

He liked to come off as being the one to bring the idea to the American masses. But most of us in the business knew that several shows of its type were being shopped around. During this period TKN caught wind of Burnett getting CBS to pick up Survivor. They knew once that hit the airwaves, they couldn't compete, but some cutthroat had the bright idea that if they could get the show out before the big S came along, then maybe they could jump ship with clout and knowledge of having done the "First" Stateside survivor show, and that they did it on an indie-film's budget.

Of course, we didn't know that last bit beforehand. Miles had a pretty standard track record with them before, had been the producer on Great Thinkers, Rise of Silicon Valley, and a hilariously bad Sex in the Dark (Ages) that he blamed on the director for it being "more like porn with fancy clothes" as he liked to say. So it was no surprise when TKN approved his idea, with some new conditions. A million dollar prize was definitely off the table. There was a good bit of back and forth on that, and it was settled at five-hundred thousand. Which, this is late nineties money, so even that for a few weeks of shooting for two people to take home was considered a pretty good payday.

Budgeting was the next concern. When isn't it though right? Again, we weren't going to match CBS at all on this, but Miles thought he could come close. So, it was a kick in the nuts to him when TKN stood firm with two million. It went from being a nice big production where we all get trailers and catering down to a skeleton crew, one trailer for all the hardware and a truckload of MREs. Naturally, we weren't privy to what the actual budget was, at the time. It wasn't until the trials started that these things came to light.

Most of the crew were brought in on the cheap, and frankly, most of them were happy for the paycheck, and to get their names credited on a network show. I was the PA (Production Assistant) for the base camp, and had been working under Miles for a couple of years. How I made it that long, I don't know. In retrospect I was merely a dumb stubborn kid, and I assumed that all producers were the smile in your face, bad mouth you behind your back, work you until you dropped type. Miles knew people, so following him around gave me what I thought were the connections I'd need to keep moving forward. In spite of him having a big ego and empty personality, he at least delivered and always got the job done. The four other PAs brought in to work with the field crews were pretty recent hires at minimum wage. Basically interns with pay, and unless the show became a hit and actually got a second season, were probably going to be let go once it was all said and done.

Now, I know you're not here to learn the ins and outs, ups and downs of making a show. If not for some temporary entertainment, then maybe you're here to learn the "true story" of the Peak Challenge Massacre.

Okay...That, was a bit sensationalistic, I know, but it falls under the "funny because it's true" purview.

Or maybe you remember hearing about the events, how producer Miles Kovacs pushed people to a breaking point, then when he didn't get what he wanted, he and a loyal band of followers decided to bring things to a whole other level.

Or saw that shitty 2005 slasher flick "based on a true story" with Jared Leto playing Miles where he and his "satanic cult" drug everyone with magic mushrooms, and Heather Matarazzo, playing Sound Tech Megan Phillips, comes running naked out of the forest, covered in blood, screaming her head off, only to be hit by a logging truck (that didn't happen).

I don't know, maybe you're bored, picked up the book, flipped through, saw a few words that really caught your eye, and now you're wondering why this is under "true-crime" or "nonfiction". Clearly, it should be listed under fiction. Right? It's because I managed to convince the people that mattered, that this happened. It was real. It will sound insane, outlandish, fantastic even. But people died. People I knew, they deserve at least this.

According to most authorities, back then, and now; a lot of it should be considered fiction. What I've compiled here, is the absolute most comprehensive accumulation of accounts from those few of us that lived, and from those that didn't make it off the mountain. For the family members that have wanted better explanations than that short shitshow of a trial ever could have provided, I think I have them. While I understand that I am in no way unbiased towards the events that took place twenty-four years ago I have done what I can to preserve the voice or words of the other people involved. Trauma, and a wish early on to be taken seriously have done a great job at making me do this in private for as long as I have. There were other factors too, like having to wait twenty years for moratoriums to finally run out, and tracking down people who didn't want to be tracked down. To those I bothered, I'm sorry, I know it was hard, and you have my utmost eternal gratitude for all the help you were able to give. All I ask is for you to go into it with open minds. I don't know how much time will be left after this goes to print, hopefully I haven't delayed it too long. What matters is that the information gets out. That you understand what is out there. Time is almost out.

    -RM

Taken from the 1999 deposition of Lucas Manning, Location Scout. Edited for smoother reading:

• • • •

Lawyer: Good afternoon, could you please state your name for the record?

Lucas: My name is Lucas Manning.

Lawyer: And your profession?

Lucas: I'm a freelance Location Scout.

Lawyer: Mr. Manning, can you describe your role in the production of the reality show that was shot in the area of Tenas Tilikum?

Lucas: I was hired to locate a suitable area for the show. My profession then was to find a place that met the requirements of the production company. For the size and duration they were looking for; I was able to go in and camp over night. Took some beautiful shots of what I thought they would like from certain times of the day, then a day later I mailed off a brochure package to them.

Lawyer: How were you hired for this job?

Lucas: The production company had my name on file, they contacted me.

Lawyer: When was this?

Lucas: Sometime in August, around the middle of the month.

Lawyer: How did you choose the Tenas Tilikum area?

Lucas: I found it during my research of available locations. It had the right mix of scenery and isolation that the production was looking for. Have you seen that place? It was like a dream. First it's plains, next a marsh area, then a forest, and spanning up in the middle of all this is this picture perfect mountain. You could slap it on a bottle of water and call it a logo.

Lawyer: I'm familiar. The land is listed as privately owned by a lumber company, [name stricken from records]. Did you contact them directly before camping on the land?

Lucas: Of course I did. For something like this, you always need permission. Usually there's compensation in it for the landholders too. The more desirable a location is, the more money the company that hired me is willing to throw at it to get it.

Lawyer: How did you contact [name stricken from records]?

Lucas: There was a billboard on the side of the only road going into the place, it had their number on it.

Lawyer: Are you aware that during the investigation, no billboard, or evidence of a pre-existing billboard ever being anywhere on the land has been found?

Lucas: No, I was not aware of that.

Lawyer: Who did you speak to, to obtain permission Mr. Manning?

Lawyer: Mr. Manning? Please answer the question, who did you speak with?

Lucas: I'm trying. It's really strange actually, I don't remember. It was a woman, she sounded older, that grandma kind of voice you know? I swear, it's at the tip of my tongue. It's, it's...

Lawyer: What about the agreement? How was this made? When you were subpoenaed, you were ordered to bring any and all pertinent paperwork as well.

Lucas: There was an agreement faxed to me, but my home was broken into a few months ago. It was stolen along with other belongings and almost all my scoutingdocuments. I filed a police report and have brought that with me today. *(Author's note: this was attached to the original deposition, but not included here.)*

Lucas: I sent a copy of the agreement to MHP as part of the packet I put together. What about that?

Lawyer: It has conveniently gone missing along with the rest of the packet as well.

Lawyer for Lucas: Come on Jim, we're cooperating with you, Mr. Manning did his job like he always has for the past four years. These events have happened outside his control. There's nothing for mud to stick to here.

Lawyer: Alright, alright. Moving on then. How was your stay for the duration when you were examining the location?

Lucas: At the beginning of the day it was like any other. It was strange though, the area is owned by a timber company, but as far as I can tell they've never logged it. They didn't even have offices or machines there that I could ever find. If I hadn't known better, I would have said it was a national park. It did get a little strange once I got into the forest though.

Lawyer: Strange? How?

Lucas: Well, the birds for one, there were a lot more ravens than regular. Usually they tend to outnumber the crows anyway in mountainous areas. But when I say there were a lot more than usual, I mean like triple the amount.

Lawyer: Okay, I see where this is going. Let's stay away from the X-Files stuff please.

Lucas: I'm not making this weird stuff up. It really happened, I took photos, I had video. If it hadn't been stolen I would've brought it with me. I had pictures of a clearing with thousands of glowing mushrooms at night.

Lawyer: Glowing mushrooms? Can you elaborate on that?

Lucas: Sure, lots of types glow. Look, I study about the areas I scout. I don't want to recommend a spot that's known for having nothing but death-caps or destroying angels. But that night out there, I saw a clearing full of what looked like Chanterelle mushrooms, but a sickly bone-white color not the usual orange. And they were glowing just as bright as a light bulb. And these weren't like the Jack-o'-Lanterns, I know the difference.

Lawyer: You seem to know your mushrooms pretty well Mr. Manning.

Lucas: Like I said, I study what I scout. I don't want to end up being responsible for poisoning people.

Lawyer: Like some of the victims were?

Lucas: I'm sorry that happened, aside from the weird mushrooms, I didn't see any others that would have set off alarm bells for me. If I saw anything that I would have thought would be dangerous I would've made a note of it. I mentioned the glowing mushrooms as a selling point, but I definitely cautioned them as a just-in-case to in no way eat them, in the packet.

Lawyer: So you say. Anything else you noticed during your stay at the location?

Lucas: Yes, I heard some strange noises during the night. I woke up approximately around three in the morning. I don't know how to describe it, a guttural high-pitched noise I suppose, like a raven but more nasal. It sounded a lot like "call" or sometimes "gall" maybe? It went on for about ten minutes. Then one of those ravens finally made a noise from right above me and the other noises stopped. I didn't sleep anymore after that and left as soon as there was enough light. I've never been that spooked before.

Lawyer: Mr. Manning, I have to admit that I find your story a little hard to believe. Are you sure that the noises and mushrooms weren't normal occurrences in the area? Or maybe your imagination getting the better of you at night?

Lucas: Look, I've scouted many locations before, and I know when something is out of the ordinary. It was creepy, and maybe then I did write it off as my imagination. After everything that happened up there, I'm willing to admit that it was definitely real.

Lawyer: Alright, I think we're done here. Thank you, Mr. Manning.

. . . .

So you were able to get that huh? Suppose that means the records aren't sealed anymore. Yeah, it was short, not so sweet, and to the wrong point. And I definitely remember how awkward it was, trying to explain a few details.

It came as a surprise when I was subpoenaed though. I wasn't even trying to dodge anything, dude walked in to this little coffee joint I stopped at a lot and gave me this thin-ass envelope. The lawyer they got for me for this told me not to worry, that they were throwing mud to see what would stick. Like I was some henchman to that psycho movie-maker guy. Sorry, the producer. Doesn't really matter. See, they tried to make it seem like this whole thing was, what's the word, premeditated? Yeah, that it was cooked up to sacrifice some virgins on top of a mountain. I was a freelancer back then. I had scouted several other spots for TKN, and the chick that put the word on the wire that they were looking for places to film a revolutionary reality show, so happened to have my name in a Rolodex as first notice. So she called me up, asked if I had something they could use. I said maybe, and to give me a few days, and I'd get a packet overnighted to them. Hell yeah I wish I had gone somewhere else. Maybe it would've played out differently for those people.

My lawyer was right by the way, don't get me wrong, I don't blame them wanting justice for their family members out there. I would've done the same, but they were going after anyone they could get their hands on. I don't think my deposition was even used during the trial. I think the TKN guys knew they were done, they tried to fight for about two seconds, then saw all the hate they were getting and decided to settle before things got worse. And then just like that, TKN went defunct. No one got any jail time. They had a problem and threw money at it. I was hoping they'd use my deposition, call me up to take the stand. There was so much more to say. The weirdness in that location. I remember the lawyer guy cutting me off a lot. The deposition makes it look downright conversational, but it wasn't. He was getting pretty annoyed with my "story". Trying to make it out to be like an episode of X-Files from back in the day. I remember thinking during it, I wanted to give this old-white-guy the biggest "fuck you" possible. But my lawyer and I had gone over it a lot, he didn't want me going into the "strange" territory either. But for me, that's all it was. I never had any contact with, what was his name? Miles. Yeah, I never had any contact with Miles, so there wasn't anything to go with there. It really was the girl that called me up, I don't even remember her name.

Firmara Lumber. Shit no, that name I didn't forget. Why it was stricken from the record is beyond me. I don't remember anything controversial with them coming up, they had their own money to throw around. Also the fact that even before I was there in August, no one had really set foot on that land in about a hundred years, far as I could tell. They never even built offices, or a sawmill on that land. I'm not an expert on lumberjacks, or what their business is, but you'd think if you were in the business of cutting down trees for as long as that sort of thing has been going on in Washington. Then wouldn't you have cut down a tree or two? Which following that thought, leads me to wonder where their money came from? It's like the weirdest non-reason for a cover-up. Although the woman I talked to seemed pretty fine with giving me, and then TKN the run of the place. And this here, where I don't remember the old lady's name. Again, you can't tell on some court reporter's script here, they like to keep it all "just the facts ma'am", like Dragnet you know, but I was trying hard to get this name out. It fucked me up for a while, because this information was fresh, and I had been on the phone with her at least twice. I'm good with names, I don't usually lose them on the spot like that.

We never had long conversations, the first time was my usual type of call for that situation. "Hey I'm Lucas, I'm a location scout, for like movies ya know? I like your land and want to show it to some big-wig t.v. show executives, how about it?" Well yeah, it was a lot better than that. I mean, I haven't done that in a long time now. After my girl got pregnant, I needed something a bit more steady. So hello office sales, and goodbye camping and hoping I'd get paid for it. But the pitch went smooth like it usually does. It normally takes a little bit more convincing when the production wants the site to shoot a crime scene on, then the older folks get a bit worried about what their neighbors might think. Since this was for something new and rarely seen or done, especially on American soil, I remember her jumping at the chance for it. I thought maybe for some publicity. Then I went, hiked around, stayed for the night and saw that they appeared to have never even attempted to log anyway. It was all just so damn weird. What would publicity ever do for them?

So, for scouting out the location. I have my handycam, that thing was a miracle device. Remember those big-ass shoulder mounted ones we had in the early nineties? Yeah, the handycam was incredible. I had a Canon film camera too. I don't remember what type it was anymore, but I made sure back then to get a wide angle view attachment. I actually have some shots still framed in my office. Nothing from Tenas Tilikum, those are all gone, never recovered. But yeah, I got some good shots of it too. The entrance, the plains, nice and dry, a little rugged, but I was able to get through it in about an hour. After that hour, you realize your feet are getting wet, and you've walked into a marshland fed by a nearby river. It was pretty cool around the time of the month I went in, I don't think the temperature went over sixty-five, or possibly up to seventy. The marshland was pretty slow-going, I had hiking boots on, a camping pack on my back, cameras around my neck. Looking every bit like a tourist lost in the middle of nowhere, and that place really is the middle of nowhere. You can kinda drive in there, and with a hefty enough vehicle you can make it through the marsh too, but walking all that, I remember it took me about three or so hours to finally reach the forest. By this point in time I think it was reaching noon.

No, there wasn't any road or path to follow at that point. The road itself going in wasn't even really a "road", it was a driven path in the dirt that didn't make it far off the main road. I think it kinda petered out right after the billboard. The forest wraps nicely around the mountain like a skirt, or like Friar Tuck needing a trim. Tall old pines, the ground under them was crunchy and spongy, years upon years of needles building up. I'm snapping photos at this point all the way in. Filming in little minute long bursts. I might spend several days in a location getting everything, but what the studio people get on their end usually isn't longer than maybe ten minutes at the minimum, twenty minutes at the longest. I've heard sometimes these guys wouldn't even look at the tapes I'd send anyway, they just wanted the photos to lay out on a board. I liked making the videos, so they got those too.

Anyway, I'm about half an hour into the forest. The quiet, it felt near absolute. It was a cool, sunny mid-August day. That forest should have been alive with noise. All that ambience adds up to this natural presence. And when it's not there, you may not notice at first. But yeah, bit by bit it pecks at you. And yes, that pun is my intentional segue for the lack of bird noise. When you go into a forest, the crows and ravens are nature's little tattle-tales. They let everything else in the forest know you're there. Song birds are doing their thing looking for a mate, there's probably at least one woodpecker knocking away on a tree. Yeah, That didn't happen here. It's like the forest knew this, because when I noticed, like really noticed and said "huh, that's strange". That's also when I saw the first raven. It was a big fucker, beautiful though, like one day oil decided it wanted to be a bird, pure black and sleek as can be. It's up high in this tree looking right at me. And I'm like, yeah I see you too big guy, and I have my handycam pointed right at it. Then it glides off smoothly through the trees. I definitely remember commenting on that to the camera. That's when I notice a few more around me. And more. And more. I tried to impress upon that damn lawyer how strange this was. I didn't exactly get a head count, but I'm guessing there were possibly well over a hundred up in those trees. Don't get me wrong here either, I'm not a superstitious guy, I go to church with the family on Sunday and say my please and thank-yous before a meal. And back then I wasn't much different, minus the family part is all. So, strange for me was thinking I stumbled upon a roost, and that this was pretty much the middle of the day. They should've been off in pairs or smaller groups, looking for food or whatever else they're gonna do during the day. Not sitting around waiting for me to come walking up on them. To hear some noise, I asked them what they were doing, having a town meeting and then some stranger comes walking in? At least we were all the same color, so nothing to worry about there right? But don't mind me, I'm merely there to record the meeting, make sure everyone stays on the up and up. They were a pretty stoic crowd though, not a single one made a noise. Sure, sitting up there in the tree observing, they might be quiet, but these guys are smart you know? They communicate with each other fly to another branch and make a call, tell their neighbor they're coming over for tea or something right? Again, not these guys. That intelligence was there, but it felt singular, like they were all one mind up there deciding what to do with me. No, I wasn't really thinking all that back then. It's pretty easy to look back on all this and wax poetic about it. I mean, I wasn't thinking anything too far off either. It was weird. I was weirded out. But no, not enough to turn around and leave. As red flags go, this one was pretty minor. I had other sites

I could go to, but this one called to me. It was scenic, someone was going to get great B-roll shots, it had this obstacle course going into it... I can't express it any better. This was the place, it had to be that place. Maybe there was something extra going on there. One of those great mysteries to life. The studio would never have known, or cared, if I had gotten spooked and went to another place. But that's not how I reasoned it, I remember thinking something like what kind of location scout would they think I was, if I had this amazing spot for them, and then balked and said nope, can't do it. It's got spooky birds and glowing mushrooms, and weird night animals..... Sorry, got ahead of myself, again it wasn't exactly like that or course. I had my pride, and I wanted to get paid, so I wrote it all off as strange but nature whatever. Hindsight of course is twenty-twenty, I wish I had balked, I wish I had gone somewhere else. I'm pretty certain now that those birds followed me the whole time I was there.

Where was I? Yeah, half hour in, lots of birds, I say it's strange, but I soldier on. For the most part it's sloping up more as I go, though mostly it feels pretty even, there's plenty of nooks and crannies, big-ass rocks sticking up out of the ground, some ravines and glens here and there. Good places to shelter at when you don't have proper camping gear, or to break an ankle in if you're not paying attention. I was coming up to the top of a rise out of a small glen, and ended up with this perfect view over the forest, straight to the mountain sticking up out of it all. At that point my plan was to camp pretty much right there. I was on this narrow spot of the rise jutting out. But ten good steps back into the trees, was a flat area with enough space between them for me to put my single sleeper, eat some lunch, hang the bear bag and take it easy for the rest of the day. Which is more or less what I did, I think a little too well. See, I like getting to places like this nice and early, set up the tent and then have a little siesta. The day-time part of my job was pretty much over. And while there isn't much to see in a forest at night, I knew they'd want some shots of that too, I was going to nap for a couple of hours, get a campfire going, eat a hot meal, then get to work. The sun didn't go down then til I think sometime around eight, eight-thirty, so I had plenty of time. I kicked my boots off, crawled into the tent and laid on my sleeping bag looking up to the blue polyester ceiling, and I blinked. It was the simplest and craziest thing of my life. I'm telling you I laid down on my bag, and it wasn't even like a slow lazy blink, I literally blinked like I am right now, and then it was pitch black night. Oh, it was definitely pretty confusing that's for sure. I didn't feel as if I had slept seven hours straight through. My body clock was telling me it was still two in the afternoon, but my watch was telling me it was sometime around nine at night. I've had some pretty crazy nights back in my college days, you know, go out to the bars, then hit a house party to finish off the night, sleep for half an hour then stumble home feeling like a zombie. And one nasty illness in my childhood where I thought I had been asleep overnight, but turned out I was out for almost two days.

But nothing ever as bad as what felt like a physical shift in my reality. I didn't have any of that waking up sleepiness, no soreness in my joints or muscles from not moving for seven hours. I crawled out of the tent pretty quickly, and standing up gave me a strong sense of vertigo. It wore off as fast as it came on, and I double-checked my watch. Back then, I chalked it up to the hike, and possible the ham in the sandwiches at lunch gone real-bad. I still don't know though. Maybe a roving vortex like those crazies down in Sedona go on about on The History Channel came through and took me from the afternoon and into the evening. Sorry, I know, I'm trying to keep "back then" separate to how I feel about it now. Because all those little things that happened then, and you coming along now wanting to know about it, feels like maybe I should start being a little more superstitious than I am. So what I did next, I shook it off. It was around nine, I'm in the forest, it's pretty black in there, it's cold, and

I don't have a fire. I had a heavy-duty camping lantern right there, I flicked it on and set about getting some wood and trying not to think that I had traveled through time in the literal blink of an eye. I've got my camera with me, and it's set to a low light mode, it takes some great in the dark pictures that kind of makes it look like a night scene in a movie, the studio guys loved that. So I'm snapping some pictures here and there as I'm gathering sticks. Which, the ground was surprisingly bare for that, so I'm going further and further from my little camp site, but I'm not worried because I left another light on there, so I can see it pretty well. And of course, since this is turning into the weirdest trip of my life, that's about when I notice the glow through the trees a ways off. It was something out of an old sci-fi movie from the sixties, you know the meteorite hits the earth and that crazy glowing rock is lighting up the area. Glowing away like nobody's business, attracting farmer Bob to his doom. Well I was farmer Bob, and you don't see glowing like that in the middle of nowhere unless it's coming off a fire. Except this was blue, a nice cool blue. There was no way I was going back to my tent and without investigating that. Maybe I was about to reenact a scene from Close Encounters and get to meet some aliens, it's not too much farther away from me, so I set down the sticks, switch off the lamp, and start sneaking over. I'm joking about aliens, but aside from the light being blue, I was pretty worried I might have stumbled on some redneck's hemp crop. I'd have rather run into aliens than Bubba and Jim-Bob with shotguns. This glow was strong enough the closer I got to it, that I could hide in the shadows it was casting. But it's also pretty quiet. There were bugs at least, which weren't present during the day, some crickets doing their thing communicating back and forth with the chirping. I peak around the side of a tree, and there's this glade full of the weirdest, brightest, glowing mushrooms I've ever seen. They're lit up entirely and emitting this blue light. They looked similar to Chanterelles from a distance, but up close they didn't have the gills underneath, they were a smooth one, and this sickly white, almost like a bleached bone. Its head was flared more too. I plucked one at the edge, and that blue glow died in it the same instant. I ended up getting the video camera, and spending maybe two hours there, freezing my ass off snapping pics from different spots, and filming too. And looking in awe at it. I didn't know if the forest had more clearings like this, but I figured the studio guys were going to love it. There was a lot of potential for some cool night shots in there for sure. I was so distracted by it, that I never did get a fire going that night. Which, that at least wasn't anything strange. I had the pile of wood there, ready to go in the morning though, gotta have my morning coffee you know? I'm not sure what time I turned in at, I know I was pretty damn excited about those mushrooms. Sure, there's glowing mushrooms all over the world, but not filling up an entire clearing and lighting up the area like these did. I knew then that if nothing else got them to pick that area, it would be the mushrooms that did it. This time, I fell asleep much more like I usually do. Only to wake up later to those damn noises. Reading the deposition helped remind me what time it was.

So yeah, around three in the morning. The birds and silence was strange, the mushrooms were magical, and this part, this part was scary as fuck. I did a safari trip with my wife for our fifth anniversary, and our third night out, the camp was visited by hyenas. The guide told us that it would probably happen, and all we had to do was stay in our tents and stay quiet. They'd come in and check things out, and then they'd leave. What he didn't say is that they would sometimes do that laugh they do, and when you're less than ten feet away, and all you have between you in a thin-ass tent wall, it chills you to the bone. I told my wife then that I was right there with her and had never been so scared in my life. Mind if I say this right to the mic? Sorry Brenda, if you're hearing this, or reading it, I may have lied to you a little bit. Okay, see, I've kept this to myself, only told my lawyer, the other lawyer, and now you. I'm sure Brenda would believe me, before our vacation, it just never came up, I had changed careers, she was a city girl and so vacations were to other cities, there never seemed to be a good time to talk about it. And then after the trip, I don't know, I guess I was worried how crazy it would sound. Laughing hyena's when you expect them are one thing. Being woken up, alone in a forest where things had been getting stranger and stranger, just felt too much like a campfire story, and she didn't need that. So I kept it to myself, and had rarely thought about it until you called me up. They sounded like raven calls. But there was just something else to them.

"A guttural high-pitched noise I suppose, like a raven but more nasal."

I remember saying this, and it still holds. Yeah it sounded like they were saying "gall" even that was a lot like a Raven and the noise it makes. There was definitely more than one, it was like they were saying it to each other. One direction would be like "gall, gall" and then from behind me another would repeat it. And this was all around me, and it was at varying volumes, one would yell it or scream it, and another would whisper it. It absolutely felt like they were all there for me, because of me. Like I was very much the reason this was happening, and not that this was a nightly occurrence that I happened to be in the middle of. I had the handycam going from the get go with this. So at the time it was easy to say it was about ten minutes, that's what the readout said. None of them sounded like they were getting closer to me, but being in that tent, I couldn't tell you how far away they were, could have been twenty feet, could have been ninety. Somewhere around that ten minute mark is when this fucking raven "spoke up" right above me. The only time one of those fuckers made a noise the entire trip. On the video its what sealed the deal for what a raven sounded like compared to these other animals, like they were imitating it and coming up short. The raven let out the biggest fucking squawk right above me, and how I didn't shit myself right there, I don't know. I made a noise, I remember that on the camera, it scared me bad, as tense as I already was, then this thing ambushes me with a much closer and louder noise. The other things must have been scared of it though, because it put an end to them. I sat there for a bit, and then about as slow as a snail, and as quietly as I could, I went over to the zipper on my tent. It was the kind that had that curved cave-like door, you know, where you close it from the bottom left on the ground, then up and over to the right, then down to the bottom right. Now, one of the coolest features on that video-camera at the time, actually caused some trouble for the manufacturers, when it came out. It had like this super-powered night vision mode on it. It turned out that this thing was so strong, that some fucking creepy guys figured out they could point it at girls in swimsuits, and it basically rendered them see-through. I don't know how that works, that it apparently means it was pretty powerful. There was a recall though, and they made some changes. I happened to be one of the many consumers that had this original camera with a crazy strong night vision. So I'm moving as slow as I can, I reach the zipper on the bottom right, and I raise it up just a couple clicks, and of course it is the loudest thing since Mount Saint Helens blew her top. And I had also seen more than enough horror movies even then to know enough not to unzip that door all the way. I mean, I know if anything wanted in, it was going to get it, that tent was about as much protection to me as a piece of paper. But still, I felt safe, and I wasn't about to unzip the door all the way, a couple more painfully slow, painfully loud clicks, and I had enough space to stick the lense through. I had the display closed, the green tinge from the night vision on the display was too much light in that tent, and I didn't want to risk anything seeing that. So I stuck it out, angled it left and right a bit, and hoped that maybe I got something on there. I never sent that footage along with the rest of the packet. It's also the only footage I took to a guy I knew down in Portland who could get a screen grab from a video and print it out, it was that freaky. At the start when I turn it on, you hear the noises, turn up the volume a bit more, and you can barely hear them moving around, they were stealthy little fuckers, like that raspy noise a snake makes when it moves through grass. But they weren't small. Remember I told you how strong that night vision was? Well, it was strong enough that it could "see" through the tent fabric, not clearly unfortunately, it was kinda like having a clouded over window. It's enough though, this little clearing I was in the center of, the trees were probably about twenty, maybe thirty feet away, somewhere in that range, big enough to park a few cars in it. And you can see them, the trees I mean, these green tinged shadows, and kinda behind, next to them, in front of them, fucking everywhere, are these very fast, agile shadows, it seemed almost feline, they had that flowing grace that cats have. It's hard to tell if they were on two feet or four though, some were moving low to the ground, but some were also up higher, like they were on two feet, as weird as that is. And the amount of them, I don't know how it's possible. Animals don't group like that in North America. If they had not been so graceful in their movement, I almost would have thought I was surrounded by a horde of baboons, seriously man, there were a lot. Counting them was out of the question, the blurs and shadows melded together, although with the different "voices" and amount, it was at least easy to tell that only a few of them were being vocal, the rest were silently stalking around the perimeter. Well, if I had to guess, maybe one-hundred? Maybe more? I was surrounded, and even watching that video again safe in my apartment was terrifying.

That went on for ten fucking minutes, with me in the center. I'd rather have the hyenas again than go through it again, at least for that I wasn't alone. Then the fucking raven deafens the world and maxes out the microphone on the video camera. I didn't even notice it then, but I do let out a little shout, and video goes a little janky, so I must've dropped it a bit. I get it stable though, then it's like you're looking at a wall around the edges, but it's them, holding still. It's a pretty solid looking mass probably about four feet high maybe? At least somewhere in that range. Of course, I don't know any of this at the time. I'm glad I didn't. I would've been shitting myself into a heart attack. I assumed whatever they were had run off because of the bird. Then the camera starts going pretty shaky while I'm finding my way to the door, and you can see me unzipping it very slowly like I said. Then the camera starts going towards that opening, pushes through like a baby's head and then it's out. It's pretty low to the ground, a little obscured by grass and pine needles, not a great shot. I angle it up a bit, and it's doing its sweep from left to right and there's this weirdly strong reflective light coming back at it from that perimeters edge about four feet up. I bring the camera back in, and then shut it off. It was terrifying, I didn't go back to sleep. Just sat there cross-legged trying not to make any noise. Making all the usual promises to God about becoming a better man, doing more with my life, blah, blah, blah you know? It started to get light sometime close to six I think? I get out of the tent, and it's clear out there. With the coming of the light I began to get myself worked up, getting angry about being spooked by whatever it was out there. I told myself it must have been a prank, like maybe a boy-scout group stumbled on my camp and decided to fuck with me. I don't know, I was grasping at straws and looking for a way to get my courage up, so I could get out of there. Holding onto that kid theory made it easier, I came out of there ready to fuck some kids up. But it's clear, like nothing was ever there. There wasn't even bird shit on my tent. Only two things were really different from the night before. One, my bearbag was gone, the rope, the bag, the food I had in it, gone entirely. I don't know at what point they did that, but it was like it was never there. And two, all the ravens were gone.

I packed up the camp and got the fuck out of there. I didn't stop for more pictures or film and made great time getting back to my car. Afterwards, back on the road, then in civilization, it was easier to rationalize. The only thing that made sense to me was that it was a prank, and with pranks, the punchline doesn't always make sense to the person being pranked. The only people that knew I would be out there were my girl, Brenda, and the woman with the logging company. I wasn't about to call her back and ask if she was messing with me, that would have been like admitting defeat. And Brenda never would have done something like that. So I tried really hard to get good and angry that it was the logging company, like maybe they had changed their mind about letting a film crew there, and they were trying to scare me off. I know, I know, it doesn't make sense like that either. I was grabbing at what I could. Because what's the other possibility? Monsters in the woods? Tiny hillbillies trying to keep me away from their crop? Aliens? Hell, let your imagination run wild because it could be anything. I do know something though. Watching that bit near the end where I'm waving the camera around through the little hole in the zipper. Scared as all hell, so I can't even keep a steady hand while I'm doing that. That's when I thought of the guy I knew in Portland. So I take it to him to see what he can do with his tech setup, he was starting to make a small fortune converting rich people's VHS home movies to DVD, and knew how to do all sorts of tricks. We get to the end, and he's able to get it to go frame by frame, and there must've been one spot where I was holding still for a hair. Just long enough so that reflective blur that streaked across the top part of the video stopped being so blurry. And we both were a bit surprised, and he asked if I wanted that bit printed out, and I said hell yeah I did. I actually wanted to get it framed, but didn't get around to it. I mean, it wasn't very big to begin with, not much bigger than a postcard. We tried printing it bigger, but there was only so much that he could do, and anything larger got more distorted. At some point I folded it in half, and stuck it in my wallet. After the break-in, it was all I had. And for twenty some odd years. Twenty-four years? Okay, for twenty-four years I've been carrying it in my wallet like some damn secret holy relic. Because look at this, how would you explain this to someone? They'd probably think it's fake. All those great big eyes.

Wow, look at that. Barely sit myself down, and you've already got the recorder going. No small talk then? Straight to the point? Fine, whatever, it's your dime. Oh s'cuse me, your boss's dime. Look, I don't have long alright, my daughter is supposed to be bringing my grand-baby by the complex soon and I wanna get back before that. How about you order me a couple of something from the tap, and we get this trip to hell started yeah? Yes, my name is Jodie Foster, I'm aware of the irony. Gone my whole life with jokes about it. I don't know why I changed it back after the divorce, shoulda kept that dumbass's name. Guess I hated him more for sleeping around than I did my maiden name. My role? I didn't have a role, they had me listed as the assistant for Ryan, but he was my boyfriend, and it was an easy way for me to get a paycheck. Oh, yeah, okay. I was the official assistant to director Ryan Davis. That better? I mighta brought him his coffee or tea, or a bit of Jack when he needed a kick, but he had other people to do the paper running. I didn't touch that. Most'a the time I was either by his pool getting some sun, or on set watching him work. I liked watching him, sure he was a bit older than me. I was twenty-three, I think he was pushing forty-five. He was a good man, he was good to me, I knew I thrilled him something good too. Balding and pudgy with a pinched in face and a long nose. But he made me laugh, and that went a long way with me back then. We had walkie-talkies on most sets to keep in touch, and he'd call over going "I need Contact, where's my Contact at?" And I'd get all riled up with him for it, 'cuz I knew he was talking 'bout me. That alien movie with the other Jodie came out a year or so before he went off into the woods. He loved that stupid movie, all the more with me along because I was his very own Jodie Foster. So after that my "call sign" as he put it, was Contact. I'd put on the cute pouty face for him and act put out about it give him a slug on the shoulder. And he'd grin, and then I'd laugh and all was right in the world ya know? I think I loved that man.

He was excited about the project. Mind if I smoke? I need it, can't do it around the grandbaby and after this I'm gonna need all the relaxation help I can get. When I got with my ex later on, then had Alicia in ought-three I put Ryan and all that other shit behind me. Oh sure, helped that I got some of that payout since I joined the suit against the studio. I was smart with it too. My daddy found me an accountant to get some invested, then later on got some put in for Alicia's college fund. I see that look you're giving me, I know what you're thinking. I don't give a shit. My kid had a good life because of that, so don't you sit there in your nice suit looking down your nose at me. I was a good momma and that's what matters.

Yeah yeah, well, Ryan, He wasn't so thrilled to be working with Miles again. Those two had been going back and forth at each other's throats for that damn dark ages sex show. But Ryan also had the experience of working with MTV and their reality stuff, Miles didn't know shit. Ryan told me he (Miles) had a good idea with the mountain survival thing, but that he didn't know how to pull it off, that he wanted to get some people struggling and getting some drama. But Ryan knew what to do, the TKN guys liked him, so Miles had to go and have a tantrum in the corner.

Ryan told me when they were flying out there, Miles wouldn't even look across the aisle at him. Sat there being this big cry-baby about it. No I didn't go out right then with 'em. About two days before we're gonna go we had this party at his place. He had a nice big place up near Buffalo, I mean, nothing like the Hollywood guys have, but Ryan's was nice, and it had the pool. Some of his friends and working types usually hung out there. You want me to drop some names? I can drop a few, Chelsea Green was there showing off her fake tits to about any guy she could. Goldblum showed up swaggering in looking sexy as ever. Alex Jets was there too, he brought the coke that wasn't as clean as he said it was, because I ended up in the hospital for it, that asshole. Well yeah, sure, I guess it saved my life in the long run. It was Ryan who told me I should take the time and join NA. That was him, looking out for his Contact. I wanted to fly out to him, I was fresh out of the hospital, it was still that first week. But he wouldn't have it. Said I partied too hard, and seeing me overdosed was too much. So I went and got clean, and he went got killed.

Did I mention he was excited? Well he was, CBS hadn't gotten their thing going yet, and TKN was making it a race against the clock. All gung-ho and let's go out and film some people freezing their asses off on a mountain in the fall before the snow's supposed to move in, yeehaw! D'you know Ryan even suggested trying to get them naked? He sure did, but TKN wasn't having that bit. Miles about flipped his shit at that too, started ranting and raving that it wasn't going to turn into another dark ages sex show. Ryan told me a couple of those actors were actually having sex on camera, it was supposed to be simulated, but they hit it off pretty well, and with all that frilly stuff everywhere you can't tell. If only he could see the shows we have now. Naked people all over the place, he would've loved it. What, no, this wasn't for his gratification. He was a professional, he knew what people wanted, he'd always say sex sells.

Peak Challenge was really gonna put him on the map though. The budget wasn't all that great, but he had a plan for that. They agreed on keeping the teams small, each group would have a camera, sound, and a PA to relay messages back and forth. The day before they started, he had this wilderness survival guy come down from Canada and give everyone a pep talk, made sure the contestants knew their shit, how to start a fire with sticks. General knowledge stuff. I know they had a medic too, but I think when the bad shit went down, they lit out rather than stay and help, you track them down yet? Bet they might have something interesting to talk about, damn coward. Ryan and Miles had a satellite phone between them when they went out there. Ryan told me they were getting along a bit better then, they would've had to, crammed together in the trailer like that for most days. They had some big tents they set up too. He said it looked more like he was gonna do a shoot for an army movie. They got all this stuff on the cheap from a depot supply store. Old army tents, a full truckload of MRE's. Oh sure, no catering out there for them, Miles didn't want anyone making any runs to whatever towns might have been nearby. It was gonna be twenty-four seven surveillance, so they got boxes and boxes of those food packs for the crew. One of the guys, I think it was Spider, Jason something or other, I don't remember his full name anymore, only that his nickname was Spider, no idea why. He and Ryan had worked together before too, and Spider had a reputation for being a pothead, so he had some joints to pass around before setting off into the wild with his group. And Ryan was pleased, everything was set to be a great time for him.

Then they actually got out there, and it turned into one headache after another. He said there wasn't a path going in at all, not like the scout described it for them. Just this fenced off opening going into some pretty rugged land, tons of bumps and dips, said it shook their trailer all over the place, they had to stop and make sure all the equipment was staying in place. He showed me on a map before they left. What they wanted to do, drive in a bit, stop before the marsh, they'd need a tank to get through that mush, then setup camp. Only, the ground was so uneven and all over the place. He said it was like the left-overs of a war zone out there, not a single flat space, and only one shovel that just happened to be on the utility truck that was with 'em. So they had to spend about all day taking turns flattening out a space to set up the tents. He was so tired that night, talking to me about it all, about broke my heart that I couldn't be there for him.

I think it was a couple 'o days later when I heard from him again, and he was not a happy camper. Said rats or mice or whatever were chewing through their cables, so they had to be replaced constantly. Shit was turning up missing, little things here and there at the start, but two days in, and they had somehow misplaced an entire box of the MRE's, and these things weren't exactly small. I think it was something like twenty to thirty of them in a box, way more than what the army kids get out in the field. But they looked high and low, and it was plain gone. He said Miles didn't give a shit, was all so what, they got them on the cheap and had thousands of them apparently. So they feed some of the local wildlife, get 'em fat for a hunter or something. He only complained about the pests chewing up their cables, never mentioned anything about birds. Ryan couldn't believe the stupidity, but like he said, Miles didn't give a shit. He was only concerned about what they could pull out of the contestants. One group couldn't even get a fire going at this point, so they were getting the treatment from Miles. Ryan said he'd be on the walkie-talkie with the PA for their group, telling them to ask "how do you feel without a fire", getting the reaction shot on the camera, taking one of them to the side away from the other and trying to get them to blame their spouse or friend, I don't know which one of the groups was having the fire trouble. Wasn't enough that those people had to get their own food, and then to start getting pestered about the fire and doubts.

It got worse for him, and them, from there. Each day was a new complaint, the generators they brought went and quit. All at the same time. I don't remember how many he said they had, but their camera tech guy, that was Tyler Lee, he did some trick or something and wired up their trailer's engine to the main tent. It wasn't pretty, but it did the trick, for about a day. Then the trailer stopped working too. No one could explain it, but then he said that Lee was about the only one there who knew how these things worked, and he couldn't find anything wrong with them. Ryan was as angry as ever. Miles seemed to thrive in this helter-skelter atmosphere. He'd have the PA's report in for anything. The camera guys out with the teams were doing fine, but Ryan needed to be able to see what they were doing, and no one was gonna start taking field trips to each group to direct the action. So how was he supposed to direct, when there wasn't anything for him to direct? I don't know how much ground they had covered in there. It was big enough to be an inconvenience to him though. He said he wanted the groups far enough apart from each other, so that there wouldn't be any overlap. They'd have these assigned tasks, or challenges, they were supposed to complete for the day. Each day they were supposed to move a little bit closer to the mountain when they finished whatever it was they were supposed to do. I don't remember too terribly well how that part of the game was worked out, but it was supposed to eventually end with one group getting up to the top of the mountain or something, to be the winners. I remember how the studio guys and Miles had a lot riding on this one thing. If it worked, it would put them on the radar, ahead of everyone else, and they'd have this shiny new toy to ride into the new century and beyond. Someone pulled some strings though and got 'em some brand spanking new gennies. Ryan must have been going through the worst emotional roller-coaster ride. But with the new stuff on its way, he was optimistic. They'd hook it all back up, get some power going, and then be able to know for sure what teams were doing what. That optimism lasted for oh about five minutes when their PA told 'em that the walkie-talkies stopped working. Exact same power stuff as before, they had their's torn apart damn near the moment it happened, batteries were fine, the insides were fine. But they went all useless on 'em. I don't know how the satellite phone was still going when it seemed like everything else was slowly dying. Ryan didn't know either. Kept saying each time might be the last phone call for a bit. I'll tell you this though, he was starting to think it was Miles.

With all these problems, they weren't getting on so well. Ryan thought Miles was doing all this to push him out. Either through pure frustration, or to tell the studio that it was Ryan doing it as some sort of revenge on their old show not working out. I told him he was being paranoid. Miles might have been a pretentious ass, but he was also a professional. There was also no way they could get another director in there on their schedule. So him being forced out wasn't gonna happen. I remember what the lawyers said, and I went along with it, but Miles wasn't some cult leader, his PA's weren't his followers. He was a pushy asshole who didn't care enough. I wasn't close with them, the other assistants, but they were out there to do a job, they wouldn't even have had time to plan on sacrificing everyone, they were worked to the bone just keeping up.

Well, so that's the million dollar question, isn't it? If it wasn't Miles and his cult, then who was it? I don't think they were alone out there at all. Ryan was starting to suspect that after I talked him down from the sabotage idea. I mean, when a box of food ups and vanishes on its own, or other small things go missing, and stuff goes and breaks for no good cause. Not to mention when almost all of them got drugged. Well, it stands to reason to me that there was someone there fucking with 'em. That's what scares me, whoever did all that, killed all those people, they're still out there. Everyone was convinced it was Miles, that once the blame set, they didn't bother to look to see if anyone else was around.

Those generators were dropped off for 'em down at the road, and had to be hauled back up. So at least then they were able to get the power up and running. He said that he had a plan, what's that word for it? A contingency? Yeah, that, for in case they had technical difficulties. The teams were supposed to keep filming, if they hadn't heard anything for a while, like a few days, then the PA could hike back to make contact. So the monitors start to come back on, and everything looks like it's okay. The teams look pretty worn out like he expected them to. And this part, I remember him telling me pretty clearly, it was like the weird things at the camp you know? Those moments stand out and last longer, funny how your mind does that isn't it? So, he says that two of the teams were together, I think the Detroit and Arizona guys. They weren't supposed to do that. The camera guys, they were filming, but they didn't seem to care about who or what, but he had two separate angles of one place, so he was getting a pretty good view of everything. The sound people didn't have their boom sticks up either and were mingling with the contestants. He said someone pointed out that there were only eight people, counting the two guys off camera, there should have been ten. He told me who was missing, I don't remember their names anymore, just that it was the PA's. With the main sound off, and relying on the camera's mics he couldn't hear them too well. Guess those weren't so great for much outside of ambient noise. But He and Miles kinda figured that with the groups together, something obviously happened, and the PA's were doing what they were told to do, come and make contact. He didn't know when they left or when the groups came together. It had been about three days since they lost power and the squawkers went out. He was expecting them just about any time from a bit before he told me about it.

We didn't have much more contact after the last call. He had a lot going on of course. One problem would get solved, another would crop up. He was stressed and tired, but determined to see it through, that's just the way the entertainment industry is. There's all sorts of stories about shoots being absolutely terrible, but they still always seem to finish you know? That was Ryan's world, the ones who quit are the ones who aren't remembered. The very last calls kinda blend together, maybe even were in the same day. He had called real early in the morning, sun hadn't even come up yet for me, I remember that was the only time he called so early. The connection wasn't the best either, it was mostly a lot of "what was that" and "sorry I didn't hear you". But I think it was around the time that they got dosed with something. That girl at the trial had talked about it. When she and the other one fought while the little green men were watching. Whatever that was about. Yeah, I think it was shrooms, pretty sure aliens didn't go out there to watch people fight. Would've made for an interesting twist on the show's format though I tell ya. Ryan never said anything about aliens, at least, I don't think he did connection being what it was, it was only that he was feeling pretty sick, and things looked a little funny I think he said the tents were bleeding. But that was during the bad call, and I couldn't get much out of it. You know what, I think it was later in the day, when the other and final call came. Connection must've been even worse then, the first minute or so was a choppy collection of noises, but then he said my name all quiet like, and then it disconnected. I tried to call him back, but it wouldn't connect, and I never heard from him after that.

It was almost a week later when the studio finally got concerned and sent someone out there to check up on them, and they found what they found. I had been worried sick, pestering just about everybody I could, but getting the runaround. See, I knew they were in Washington, but I didn't know where exactly. TKN wouldn't tell me, I never even got through to anyone except for the secretaries, and then it was "So and so is in a meeting" "So and so is not available" "Would you like to leave a message?" I called a couple police stations in Washington too, but without knowing where they were, and that they weren't in a national park or anything, they weren't much help either. They said that someone from the shoot would probably get into a town wherever they were, and to wait for them to call me.

After that, it turned into a missing group of persons for what, a week? Then they found the bonfire spot with the bones. And sometime around then those survivors started popping up. Then I got a call from the Phillips family, they were gonna sue TKN for negligence and liability, and whatever else they could get 'em for. I think they were from Spokane, it was their girl that was one of the survivors. Even got made the main character in that movie some years later. Based on a true story. My ass it was. They didn't even let her live at the end, let alone anyone else. They didn't even put Ryan in the movie. Made Miles the madman doing everything. Producer and Director. It was ridiculous. I tried to get in touch with the people making it, told 'em I knew stuff and I could come on as a consultant, but they turned me down. Then that fictional mess came out, I was glad I wasn't a part of it.

Oh shit, my kid's texted me a couple times now, I gotta get going. Got my grandbaby waiting on me, and she's gotta work. Thank you very much for this, and for the beers. Shit yeah, I'm fine driving, it's gonna take more than a few to put me on my ass. Hey, you need anything else, you just give me a ring, bring another one of these envelopes, and I'm all yours again mister.

I met Caitlin outside a general store, hauling food into a trailer with a big sooty gelding hooked up to it. She was small and struggling, her voluminous tresses of black hair constantly getting into her freckled face. I saw that she was paid no attention by any passerby. Being taught to avail myself to any person in need, I approached her.

'Don't you have no one to help you miss?'

'If I had, would I be doing thus such as I am?'

'Reckon so. Where are they?'

'Who?'

'Your Pa? Your Ma?'

'Never had a Pa. Haven't seen my Ma, in many a year.'

'How old are you?'

'Seventeen.'

'And you're out here all by yourself?'

'Perceptive of you to notice.'

'You should not be out on your own.'

'Why? Do you wish to save me?'

'No. I do not think its right for a young lady such as you to be on your own. May I offer you some help?'

She stood a moment eyeing me. Taking measure of me, and coming to the conclusion I was of good nature. She gave to me a smile as such to bring the angels down from the heavens above.

'You may.'

Afterwards I inquired where she lived, and she pointed to the South. Stating she is several days away from home. She had come to Seattle to await for my arrival. I scoffed at her and asked how this was possible, I do not know her, and most certainly do not have the ken of any Irish girls at all. A fire lit in her eyes at that, she stated very firmly that she was not of those people. She said I come to her in a dream, and that I would help her with anything she so desired.

I told her I had no money for her. I had heard of such scams from beggars and the like. I had no wish to be tricked. She said she knew I was there for the gold rush North. I told her over half the men in the state were there to go Northwards. She countered that if I came with her instead, she knew for a certain I would make my fortune. I thought she had lost her mind. But her countenance was unlike any other. My companions going North were a sullen lot. Caitlin with her tresses, freckles and green eyes was surely not as dangerous a sort as these men, who to tell the truth, were as desperate as I to make our claim. She told me no one lived on the mountain where she resided, and here she leaned in close to tempt me further with a secret, she had seen signs of gold in the land.

I told her I knew her game. I was a crack shot with my long gun, and I would dispatch of her compatriots waiting in ambush before they thought of coming near. But then she said my name. I had not told her this, and was stricken with surprise. With my name, came a promise.

"If you come with me, you will have all you ever want in the world, if you go North, it will be to your death."

And I tell you, the hairs on my neck pricked up, and a cold wind crossed my face on that hot dusty day. I made a jest to say that she was bewitching me, for I was accepting of her offer. Her aspect became grave as an undertaker, she said if she were to beguile me, thereupon I would not need convincing. To becharm me, would be to lose me, and she so desired me as I am. I understood then, that for something said so with wit, she had much more learning and perspicacity than I.

Thus, two days hence, I find myself on this long trail with her to her lonely mountain. She sees me at this journal, and is appreciative that I know my words. I say my ma put more importance to learning than scrapping about as my pa had done. She says my mother is a smart woman. That there is a power in words. To put the spoken assertion to paper is to make it real for everyone else to see for time to come. I divulge to her I do not understand. And she tells me to do thus. To take my pencil in my hand and write:

> *I will find gold*
>
> *I will be married with this woman*
>
> *She will bear me a boy.*
>
> *June 23rd 1895*

She made me record today's date, and tells me now to scrawl no more. Simply stated is simply done. There is much work to attend to, when next I write in one years time, it will be to say she was right.

Text transcribed from audio from the audition tape of Ally and Eric Jansen.

AHJ: Hello! This is our submission video for The Knowledge Network's reality survival show. I'm Alessandra Hernandez-Jansen.

EJ: And I'm Eric Jansen

AHJ: I'm a thirty year old Special Needs Teacher. I have a Bachelor's of Science in Special Education degree from Arizona State University. Go Sun Devils!

EJ: And I'm twenty-nine with a Bachelor's of Science in Computer Engineering, also from ASU.

AHJ: Our family's lived close to each other when we were kids, so we went to the same schools together. Although growing up we probably said about 5 words to each other. We graduated in 'eighty-six and started at ASU later that year at the same time. There were several of us all going there together from our old school. We'd hang out, or study together in our first year there. I got to know Eric a little bit better, but I was way more interested in those foreign exchange students back then.

EJ: I was pretty nerdy back then, it wasn't cool to be seen around me too much. I had a crush on her in high school, but I think most of the guys did.

AHJ: Oh stop, they did not. Anyway, once we got settled into or college life, the group kind of drifted apart, and we lost touch. It wasn't until our ten year reunion in '96 that we met up again, and I don't know, we just really hit it off.

EJ: We definitely did, I proposed to her two months after we started dating. And now here we are about to have our two-year anniversary and still going strong.

AHJ: We found out when we started dating, that we're both pretty active people.

EJ: By then I was assisting in ASU's computer engineering department, and saw this flyer on a board for a rock climbing group. I took it to Ally, and by the end of the week we were climbing up a wall together.

AHJ: Now we've been all over the state, Cochise Stronghold and Mount Lemmon are pretty popular spots for us. Last week, we spent a weekend in Yosemite National Park in Cali, and in about three weeks we're making another trip to Enchanted Tower in New Mexico.

EJ: We think we'd be great for this upcoming show because we work so well together. We have no trouble camping outdoors, and we're both competitive enough that we'll definitely give the other people a run for their money.

AHJ: If we win...

EJ: When we win

AHJ: Of course, when we win, we're planning on putting the winnings into starting a family, we're coming into our 30's now, and feel like it's the next natural stage to our life.

EJ: Yeah, it's time to start the next generation of rock climbers!

AHJ: For sure!

• • • •

On August 15th 2020, I sat down for a joint interview with Alessandra Millsner formerly Hernandez-Jansen and Andre Millsner. I have once again omitted my questions for sake of page space. This section is to cover team Arizona first, but I have left in statements made by Andre "Dre" during the course of it.

Well would you look at that. I haven't seen our audition tape in years. We were babies ourselves then. How corny we were about it all. That enthusiasm was completely for the tape. Oh sure, we wanted it, but we weren't like that in our day to day. And I was so, so angry with Eric. I don't know what we were thinking, trying to get on a t.v.

show so we could win some money. Why was I angry? Well, I caught him in our rock group's locker-room with another man. Oh sure, that was upsetting. That thing about starting a family was true for me. For him…I think he wanted to be caught. The signs were there, but I was young, and it wasn't like it is now with better support structures and a culture that is a lot better at embracing people coming out. And like I said, I was angry with him, I was so damn selfish about it. I didn't give a damn how he felt. I was awful to him. I was the one who forced him into the reality show. I told him he had to do this one last thing for me, and he better work his ass off for us to get that money, then he could have a divorce. So we put on these happy faces, and made the tape. It wasn't too much longer after that and we both got letters accepting us.

It was two months later when they flew us up to Washington to start the show, and I had cooled off a bit by then. I was still upset with the state of things, but we were still living together, and I loved him. We were keeping up appearances for our families, for the show, for the whole damn outside world. But there was a change in him, he was relaxed. I think it was a big weight taken off his shoulders. This almost always tensed up man had this serenity that I could only see after a good climb. I got a chance to apologize to him, before the show started, he apologized too. If I could go back, I'd be more understanding, more accepting, less selfish. But, could have, would have, should have, never did.

The show, that fucking awful show. As soon as we got there, it felt like an accident waiting to happen. The guys running the thing had this weird fake friendliness with each other. Miles and Ryan? It's been so long. We were flown in, shuttled to this steakhouse, it was a pre-getting-to-know-you thing. They gave speeches, then we went to some cheap hotel for the night. Early in the morning the next day they took us out to the site. We were thrown into it quick enough. I was excited and ready to go. I had never been in or around anything like this. I had no idea how shows were made. Those first few hours ended up being a complete slog. About a hundred yards from their main camp we all came together in this group, from slightly different directions, like we walked in on our own. Then we have to act like we didn't all just meet the night before and do introductions. And then we had to do it again, and again, and again. Each time with someone calling out "now stand here, do this, make this face." It was tiresome and annoying. I thought they were going to turn us out and let us go. We didn't even get to choose the direction we were starting off to. All this at the crack of dawn, and no coffee. Oh they had coffee, but we couldn't have any. Finally, after what felt like the entire day of repeating the same thing over and over they pointed us off in our respective directions then they let us go.

The challenge bit was that each day the crew with us would have this like list, of jobs we were supposed to complete. I think that first day's job was to make a shelter and fire. If those tasks were successfully finished, the next day we could move a certain distance closer to the mountain. If we failed, then we had to stay and do it until we got it. It was fairly simple. Eric was pretty good at rubbing two sticks together to get a fire, well, it might've taken him half an hour, but I never could do it. That first night out wasn't too bad. Eric and I weren't allowed to split up very often though, there was only one camera out there for the two of us. When it came to us needing to build a shelter, and gather stuff for a fire, they had to radio back to the base to see if we could separate for that. I heard the first response of "can't they do that together?" That whiny nasal voice grated on me. Yeah I think that was Miles. But I didn't want to rock the boat, said fine, whatever, let's go. We found what we needed though, and got set up before it was dark. We were supposed to forage on our own too, I saw the list later on, and it was a task for one of the days, to come up with a certain amount of food. After we had our shelter and a fire going, the crew guys stopped filming and set up their tents.

Then it wasn't us and them, it became all of us. They shared their food and water with us. Eric asked if that was allowed, and I think it was the camera guy, Brandon, he was like "fuck those guys". We had a good laugh, and it was a pretty good night. There were a couple times where Miles would come on over the radio, not to check up on us, but to get reaction shots. The amount we faked, well, there was a lot. They'd do these mini-productions with us. Like, we'd act like we'd been sleeping for hours, they'd douse the fire, then I had to "wake up" and tell Eric the fire was out, and we'd have to huddle together on our bed of pine branches and complain about the cold. Of course right after they'd spray the wood with some lighter fluid and get it going again for us. Just stuff like that to really disenchant you to the whole t.v. thing.

There was an element of danger to it, we were miles away from the nearest town. There was only one medic with a four-wheeler on standby at the main camp. The tutorial we were given by some survivalist type before we set off gave us the basics, like don't eat any mushrooms, the type of noise bears make, what to do if we fall in a river and get soaked. It was cold enough hypothermia was a concern. And check your footing if you go over any rocky ground. It was all pretty standard, and nothing to make us question our safety. Eric and I had scaled cliffs with each other and no hope of backup at all, so a hike in the wilderness was child's play. And we made friends with the crew, and they were like our silent support system. When the camera was on it was all professional and business like. Then when it was time for a break, or downtime, whatever, then they were people again. Oh I said something like that a little bit ago didn't I? Sorry, I sometimes repeat myself like that now, tendency of old age I suppose.

Dre: You're not that old yet Honey.

Not compared to you yet, Teddy. Where was I? Yes, no we didn't feel like we were in danger. It honestly didn't even feel like much of a challenge. More like a half-baked idea that someone liked enough they wanted to make it happen. So we felt pretty lucky to be in it. That first night went well. Then the following day, I don't remember what the task was then, but we did it, and moved on to the next point. They couldn't say how the other teams were doing, so there really wasn't much of a competitive edge to it. We had to assume they were doing the same as us, and to keep pushing as hard as we could.

So here's the thing, it was so subtle, so insidious. By the time we realized something was wrong, we were already deep in it. These little things would happen, but they were easy enough to write off. Not finding food at one point was because we were in the wrong area. Same with not finding enough materials to make a good shelter for the night. Then one of the bear-bags of the crew got raided in the night. But we assumed they didn't tie it off as well as they thought, that a raccoon tried to climb the line, and that added weight made it come undone where it was tied off at. It was an annoyance, all these things were. But it wasn't anything to make us worry. Hell, it wasn't even enough to make us question if someone was playing a prank on us. Not then anyway. When the radio stopped working, we thought, huh, that's strange. I don't know when that happened, maybe several days into it? Miles was talking to Brittany, she was the go-between for us, and then he cut out mid-word. The way she explained it, these things were brand new, and had a battery that would last about forever. She still had an extra pack with her as the just-in-case and when that didn't work either, well, she had no clue. Neither did the rest of us. There was a plan for that too, it was something like just keep filming anyway, if they still hadn't heard from the main camp after a few more days, then they'd have to set out to find out what the problem was.

That night, when the radio stopped working, that would be when it went from bad to worse. We wrapped up filming for the day, the crew said it was actually kind of nice to just be able to do things without the constant nagging from the main camp, so we were feeling pretty relaxed. Eric was getting pretty good at getting a fire going, but we didn't really find much lying around to make one with. It probably wouldn't last the whole night. So we, all of us, not just Eric and I, decided to play it safe, and we'd all cram into a tent. Then in the morning we'd film a bit about how cold it was that night, and how we were freezing and didn't get much sleep. Before we turned in though, we were all huddled around the fire, getting nice and warm from it. One of the guys said they had a joint in their bag, and that sounded like a good idea to the rest of us, I think it was the camera guy, Brandon. And he got up to go to the tent, and I remember the zipper noise coming from behind, and then he just went "What the fuck!?" So we all look, and the backside of the tent is shredded to bits. It was like a bear had torn into it. I'd heard they can be pretty stealthy when they want to be, but not like this. It had been quiet at night, every night since we had been there. Sometimes there would be a little bit of wind, but otherwise it was usually quiet. The sound guy still had his stuff with him, and so he puts his headset on and does something with this set with dials and buttons on it, and starts moving the microphone stick thing around. And then he stops moving and is standing there with it pointing off a little bit away from the tent, but still in the same direction. He was making this confused face, like he wasn't sure what he was hearing. And we're asking him what it is, is there a bear nearby? Do one of them have bear-spray? tell us what the fuck is he hearing. He shushes us and stands there with it a bit more. Then he's unplugging stuff and plugging other things into it, I had no idea what he was doing. I've never been much of a tech person, that was Eric, I don't think he said much then, but I'm sure he knew what the sound guy was doing. Anyway, sound starts playing from these things, and it's like all the little noises are made into really big noises, and you can hear the whooshing from when he was moving around, and then there's this weird noise and the wind sound stops. And you can hear what sounds like someone with the worst smoker's voice ever laughing like a crazy person. Eric switched then from not saying much, to what the fuck, what the fuck, what the fuck. The camera guy yelled off into the night I think something like "we know you're out there." Nothing was taken though.

Brittany still had her tent stored away, she had her own to stay separate from the guys, it was smaller, we packed into it like a can of sardines. We talked about setting a watch for the night. Eric, ever the logical and stressed out one, over-road the rest of our fears, saying it was one of the other teams trying to psych us out. And really, what was the alternative? We had our own Wicked Witch from Oz out there? They shredded the tent, but we weren't going to give them the satisfaction of thinking they had us freaking out. Laying there that night, all crammed together in this small tent meant for one or two people, I didn't sleep much.

Dre: Tell him more about that silence.

It was creepy, and surreal. The ecosystem that is a forest is very diverse. Plants, trees, bugs, animals, they all come together to create the living system that works in tandem with one and another, and it's rarely silent. I didn't notice it when we first got there, and during the days when we were kept busy. That night lying there wondering if there was some crazy axe murderer stalking us. That's when I noticed how quiet it was outside our tent. We could've been sleeping in space for the lack of noises. I relaxed a little, because of that silence, we should've been able to hear the person laughing if they were close enough. Because a microphone was needed to really pick up the noise told me they were pretty far away by then, and maybe going back to their camp. At least that was the conclusion my tired mind came to. I was able to sleep a little after that. We woke up cold, cramped, and grumpy early in the morning. Our grumpiness turned to anger when we discovered someone had come back again at some point, and took a very large shit over the remains of our fire. One of the guys yelled out pretty loudly that this wasn't funny. Brittany had, had enough and said she was going back to the main camp. Brandon offered to go with her, but she told him to stay and film everything. If they were nearby, and we could catch them on camera, then it would be a lot easier to get someone fired. Plus she could move pretty quickly on her own, so it shouldn't take her too long to get back to the camp. She figured it would take her about a day to get there, and then a day to get back. So to sit tight. I admired her courage. We told her to be careful, and then she was marching away with her pack over a shoulder. We were the last people to have seen her. I heard, later on, when all the police people were sweeping the surrounding area looking for survivors or remains, a dog found her pack. On the other side of the mountain, miles away in the complete opposite direction from where I told them she left us from.

There wasn't much for us to do from then on. We spent that day scavenging for anything we could burn, but the surrounding area had been picked clean. It added to the creepiness. I paid attention that day, and sure it was pretty cold then, so it's not like I was going to see butterflies and grasshoppers everywhere, but it was so empty. I couldn't even find so much as rabbit or deer poop, I feel those are common for a forest, you're going to see them if you look hard enough. We ended up, gathering up a lot of "green" material. Not much of a woodsman are you? You want dead, dry things to burn. Pulling live branches off trees, or tearing a live bush up, those are "green" get it? They still have a lot of moisture in them, so they don't burn as well. Makes a ton of smoke.

Dre: Which is how we found you.

We ended up with a nice smoke signal and unintentionally broadcast our location to Team Detroit. That was I think the day after next when they came stumbling in. We built up the fire bigger than before. Brandon still filmed us like we were filming for the show, but Brittany had the task list. We managed to get a lean-to built up against a tree using the ruined tent for building materials. And some rocks stacked around the fire to make a shield wall. No one was going to be sneaking up on us that night. And that night we were fine. Brittany did leave her tent with us, she said she would be back at the main camp before she would need it anyway. With our extra bit of work that day, we didn't have a use for it. We did take turns at guarding the fire. They showed they could be stealthy enough to come right up to us awake or asleep, but we wanted to be ready this time. I took the first watch of the night, the fire was making enough noise that I didn't feel the surrounding silence as being so pervasive. Tim was the last watch of the night, before dawn, I don't think he was much of a morning person to begin with, so waking up around 4 or 5 was already a struggle to him, and he dozed off. I don't know for how long, he claimed it was only for a few minutes. I was woken up by their arguing about it later. I told them to shut up about it when I saw what had been done this time. A little ways out were two, long straight branches shoved into the ground, at an angle to each other. Tied together with some of the shredded tent in the middle, forming an X. It looked like one of those ancient crosses that Romans used to hang people on you know? Albeit done very roughly. I think that was the message they were trying to convey "we're going to crucify you".

Eric was taking it hard, put some obscure computer problem in front of him, tell him he had twenty minutes to solve it, and he'd calmly and methodically get it figured out. Put a difficult climb in front of him, and he would proceed to send it the same way. But to put this chaos in his way, stressed him to no end. He was done with everything then, yelling to the trees that they would be sorry to show their faces. I remember he paced a lot, going from random point to point, quickly turning around to catch someone taking a peek at us. The pressure was too much like that and his internalized paranoia came flowing through. I got him to calm down and lead back to the lean-to. And that was our day. Brandon would film what he called B-roll, Tim left the sound on, but we sat around our fire all day waiting for Brittany to return with a new plan, or orders, whatever.

Dre: A fucking helicopter would've been nice.

Absolutely. But, that's not how it played out. By night, we were ready for whichever team it was trying to force us out. After Eric had a chance to cool off, he began thinking. I know it sounds silly, but he had one of the sharpest minds of anybody I knew. And being a stressed out problem solver he came up with a way to maybe bring some stress back to "those assholes". It was already pretty late by then, and we only had so much for resources. He laid the plan out to us, and we worked as quickly as we could to set up what we could. It was simple, the sound guy, sorry. I told myself I'd never forget these names, long as I live, and here I am remembering them by what I called them back then. Tim, he had a lot of cable with him. So we made one end into a snare, hung up the bear bag about at a height where if you stretched up to it from underneath, you'd grab it. And beneath that, we covered the trap on the ground. The line for the bag was strung back to our lean-to, with a pine-cone of all things acting like a bobber. All we had to do was wait for someone to make a grab for the bag, then Tim would pull his cable, and we'd "land us a big one" as I remember he said. It wasn't foolproof, but it's what we had. So yeah, we were ready.

Author's note: I feel it worth mentioning that at this point in the interview, Mrs. Millsner fell into a melancholic silence, swept away by memories of the traumatic events. I respectfully waited, giving her time. A glance towards Mr. Millsner had him raise a hand to me in affirmation of my waiting. He then placed that hand on her back, asking if she needed me to leave the room. This brought her back to the present. She in turn gave her husband an expression of such love, I couldn't help but smile myself. She then excused herself to make some tea, which I accepted an offer of. While she was away, I told Mr.

Millsner that we could stop at anytime he or she needed, they could take as long as they want, and I could come back later. He shook his head at this, and said that while reliving these events was hard on her, she was very strong. They had tried all those years ago when they were finally found, to explain what had happened, but with no one believing them, and with the constant pressure, they changed the story to fit what "they" wanted to hear. Now with someone coming to them, corroborating what they knew actually had happened, they couldn't keep it in anymore. She was strong, he reiterated, just needs a moment. She came back shortly after, fully composed and setting drinks down in front of us, continued.

I guess I got a little ahead of myself there. That night, we made it look like the same as the night before, I was on watch, sitting with my back to the rest of them, a little towards the extra smokey fire, a little out into the darkness. Eric, Brandon, and Tim were pretending to sleep, and then it was a waiting game. You know how it is like that don't you? Like waiting for water to boil. It may take only a few minutes, but it feels like hours when you're looking right at it. I'd look from the pine-cone, to the fire, to the edge of the light. Over and over willing that damn thing to shake and for this to be over with. The guys had even selected sticks they would use like switches just to really teach our catch a lesson. And there I was, nervously waiting, wanting something to happen, but at the same moment, maybe two nights was enough for them? But then the pine-cone started shaking on the line, I don't know when or what time it was. I didn't have to do or say much, a little quiet "hey" was all it took.

Tim sat up pretty quickly, "gotcha fucker!" was his battle cry as he pulled the cable tight. And it did go tight and something made this garbled angry noise, and Tim went flying face-first into our fire shield as he got pulled to it instead of him pulling it to us. The others came out shouting, I stood up yelling, I don't remember what. Tim had the cable wrapped once around his hand for a grip, so he didn't let go when he bashed into the rocks. He was holding his face with one hand, while the other was sticking straight out to the taut cable. Eric reached him first and grabbed the line too, pulling as hard as he could. He went "what the hell" because it didn't budge, I was worried we actually had caught a bear. Then it started going up, like it was climbing a tree, and I could tell Eric was angry, he was at the point he didn't give a shit if it was a bear, or person, he wanted to hurt them. By then Brandon had a hold on it too, and Eric said to yank as hard as they could. It didn't have such a good grip up in the tree, it was maybe ten feet up, but another of those garbled noises came from it, then the line immediately dropped, and you could hear a thump at the edge of the light.

All around us came the worst sort of screaming noises I have ever heard in my life then. One time, when I was young, one of my cats caught a bird in the backyard, and all these other birds went crazy around it, they recognized one of their own had been taken down, and they were not happy about it. And that's what this was like. We took something down, and it had friends, and they were not happy. The guys stopped pulling, I remember Tim looked up at me then, and had blood streaming out of his nose. Then the cable went tight again pulling all three of them forward. Tim yelled about it going too tight around his hand, and they're slowly being pulled over the shield, and into the night. Those screams around us continuing, all these other weird birdlike noises were going on too. And in the direction the guys were being pulled to, was that demented laughing we had heard before. There wasn't anything they could do, they were straining hard, but that line was being pulled off into the night. I screamed at them to let go. Brandon tripped over something then and let go to break his fall, this was enough of a surprise to have Eric and Tim get taken off their feet. Eric let go then as well. The amount of strength used to pull three men was enough to have Tim sliding away pretty fast. Eric made a mad scramble to him and caught him by his feet. It wasn't enough to stop them, and Eric was just getting pulled right along with him again. Then, just for a second, the line went slack. Eric got up fast, and got Tim's hand freed. It all took no more than a few blinks of an eye, but I see it in slow motion now. He's scrabbling up Tim's body, unwrapped the cable, and not even a second after that the line just zips away into the dark. That evil laughter coming just as hard, like it was some cruel joke. Eric helped Tim up. Brandon was already up and moving to them, and they're running back to me. When, at the time what I thought were black arrows, come flying out of the darkness into the ground around them. There weren't many, and I think they came from up high, from the trees. It was their angle, they were sticking at a good slant up out of the ground. The guys came tripping back over the shield wall and collapsed in a heap just past the fire. I was right there next to them, thinking for sure more arrows were coming any second. But nothing came, and that's when I noticed that all those screams, laughter, and angry awful noises had stopped. Like someone flipped a switch and turned them off. I'm certain now, that's just part of how they played with their prey, their food. Taunt, scare, hurt, kill. With all that adrenaline flowing, and in the excitement, Eric wasn't aware that he was injured. I didn't even see it till he stood up, but he had one of those arrows stuck in his back.

I said something like oh no, or oh my god. Some of these things I feel I'm remembering perfectly, what had happened, who said what, just a clear scene from a movie. Then there's other small moments where I know something might have been said, the feeling is there for it, but the exact words aren't. I suppose it doesn't really matter. It wasn't an arrow though, it was a porcupine quill, and it was black and greasy looking, and smelled terrible. He became aware of it in that moment too, and it was obvious the pain came flooding in. We, Brandon and I, got him to sit, I tore his shirt open on his back and there it was, just going right into his left shoulder blade. Brandon produced a first aide kit, but it was pretty rudimentary, a little bit of alcohol, several rolls of bandages, and then a little baggy of like q-tips and tweezers. With the black stuff coating the quill we couldn't get a grip on it, it was just too slippery. I used his shirt to wipe it off the best I could, then we used the alcohol to clean it even more. I got him to bite down on one of their switches, and Brandon counted to three before trying to pull the quill out. The pain must have been excruciating, Eric bit down on the stick so hard he bit through it. The only problem was that Brandon hadn't managed to pull it out, it ended up being so brittle that when he pulled and squeezed on it, it just broke off into pieces. That's when we noticed that the inside was filled with the same stuff as the outside, this bad smelling sludge. Honestly, I think it was their shit. Just black and foul, poisoning whatever they hit with it. And now Eric had this jagged piece leaking that stuff into him. He did pass out when I poured the alcohol over it. I'd like to think he didn't feel the rest as I used the tweezers to get what I could out of him, and then the remainder of the alcohol to clean it further before we wrapped it up. The sun was coming up by then, a thick fog had come in at some point, so even with the sun, we still couldn't tell if we were safe or not. We moved Eric into the lean-to next to Tim, who up to then I had actually forgotten about. His nose was definitely broken, we weren't sure about his hand, he couldn't move his fingers, and it was pretty swollen, so we thought it probably was. We were so exhausted though, I just curled up next to Eric and fell asleep.

Brandon woke me up later in the day. You gotta come see this he said. As if I wanted to see anything else after that night. But I got up and went with him. The fog was gone, and he led me to where they had gouged a path into the ground being pulled. In the night it had looked like they were being pulled such a long distance into the darkness, in the day, it was a short path the length of two or three people. About the same distance further was where the trap had been set. The bear bag was still where we had left it, but the bottom was shredded, at least we had taken the food out and just put dirt in instead. Beyond this in a straight line was a tree, the base of which had a rock sticking out through the roots. The rock had this black tar like stuff on it, and splatters of it were around the area too. I asked if it was blood, Brandon was pretty sure it was. But we didn't even know if there was anything that had black blood. He pointed up to the tree, and up high were these deep furrows in the wood. Claw marks where it had been when they pulled. So it fell, hit this rock, and was hurt. Then they tried to pull the guys off into the dark, and when that didn't work, shot those quills at them. I went around the tree, walking further where these things may have been. Looking for any more signs, but nothing was there. They didn't leave any gouges in the dirt as they pulled. I think it meant that they were strong, much stronger than any of us. On the way back to the camp, Brandon asked if I noticed anything else. I told him no, and he asked what happened to the quills they shot at us. At some point they had come and taken them. Aside from the havoc they caused, they left almost no trace. The claw marks and blood being the exception. At the camp site, I began looking for the broken quill Brandon had taken off Eric, I asked him what he did with it, and he said he just threw it by the fire. I searched for it, but it was clear by then it was gone too. They had come right up to the fire to remove their evidence, but did nothing to us? It didn't make sense. I just could not, could not understand why this was happening. Tim was sitting up by then, but Eric was still sleeping, so I went over to check on him. He had a fever and was sweating a lot. Before I left he had seemed fine, and now just twenty minutes later he had gotten so much worse. He was on his stomach, so I pulled his bandages aside to look at the wound. It was bad, it was really bad. It smelled terrible, it was this dark angry red around the edges, and spreading out under the skin were these black trails like spider webs. Tim was watching and asked if infections were supposed to be red, not black.

I told him that's what I thought too. I think I was crying then. Sometimes I remember it, and I'm angry and stressed and ready to fight. And sometimes I remember it, and I feel like this helpless child, just crying her eyes out for help. Maybe it's both of those things? I certainly didn't know what to do for Eric, I cleaned it as best I could, but the little bottle of alcohol had barely lasted his "surgery", so I had no way to disinfect it.

Brandon was somewhere behind me, I think maybe at the fire? Maybe even right behind me? I don't remember, I know he yelled something then. Hey? Or just some noise that sounds like "hey". But I remember thinking "jesus, now what"? I thought maybe he was yelling at me, to get my attention, but when I looked, he was gesturing with this big stick towards something. I come out of the lean-to, and look and through some trees, team Detroit is coming our way.

Dre: I bet you wanna ask me about how I lost my leg now?

V. The Prospector

June 23rd 1896

She was right.

June 29th 1896

She says her foretelling and my writing made the events manifest. That I am to tell of my arrival, and what I have accomplished in this year of time. To make the past real for the future.

We arrived to her, to our, homestead on the twenty-eighth of June, through a singular path following along an easy dale. She had a simple cabin with a wide stoop. On the deck, stood the tallest and ugliest man I have ever laid eyes upon. I had my gun shouldered and was fast ready to put an end to him, but she bade me lower it away. It was her man-servant Bres. I asked how this giant creature could be anything civilized, above all as a man or servant. She said that in another life, he broke the rules of hospitality, and was cursed for it. Now he served out a penance with her, to be rewarded greatly when that time was complete.

As we arrived at the stoop, she called out a greeting to him in a language that caused a shiver between my shoulders. This Bres creature raised a great hairy arm in return. She ordered him to begin the delivering of goods from the wagon to their proper places. He passed us by on her side, and my first up close look of him was that he was possibly worse than I thought from a distance. I asked her if he was of the Chinuk from the area, as his head was flattened and elongated as is their custom, his skin was darker in color, and his bearing was most surly. She said he come with her from their first home and had no relation to the peoples of this land. He had the sickliest smell about him as well, as if he had spent days mired in a pit of refuge. His teeth were large as to almost protrude from his mouth, and his height was so enormous that he made the horse appear small. She said for me to not worry, as he lived off in the woods behind the house, and had his own doings to attend to. He was there to serve her as she needed, and this he did to satisfaction.

The next day saw the three of us going up into the mountain, to a place similar to any other. She pointed to a spot of moss covered rock and bade Bres to dig with his pickaxe. I have seen dynamite do a worse job of clearing the way than what this creature did to the area. We stood uphill as to be away from the destruction, and shortly he had a pit dug around him. With a sound of finality, his pickaxe pierced down into the center of that crater producing a clear ringing tone of something other than dirt or rock struck. Giving a great heave of his shoulders, the beast exposed a boulder of gold. My shout of excitement was met with a smile from Caitlin, and the surly look from Bres which I would come to see was the only face he had to wear. I estimated that this "nugget" must weigh upwards of two-hundred pounds. She said it would do for us quite well. Bres conveyed it with his arms as easily as Caitlin carries our Lou. Caitlin and I returned home, whilst Bres and the gold vanished into the forest. He shewed himself the next day with 7 solid bars. I asked where the remainder was, he met me with the sullen silence, I then repeated the question to Caitlin. She said it was being worked into something special, I must wait to see.

Some days after there came a curious knocking to the door and walls of the cabin late into the night. Like hundreds of knockers were repeatedly rapped against every surface. I was up and to my gun as quick as coming from sleep would allow. But as with Bres, Caitlin bade me to lower it. She said it was her Fir Glas Brecc with the something special. But for me to stay inside and not look out through the window. I told her the mysterious surprises were beginning to weigh heavily with me, and that she did not seem as alone on these steeps as she said. On her way out the door, she gave me such a look as to make me regret my words, and exclaimed that she had always been alone on this mountain.

I did as she asked, and took a seat in a chair ruminating on her words, endeavoring to better myself for her. When pressed, she would only relate to me, a few bits of her past. She was the last of her people, with Bres being of an unimportant relation. There had been some form of upheaval in her land and she had fled. I often wondered if her family had done something to provoke the ruling British, and seeing that, had been exiled to this land. I did not wish to be a cause of distress to her by questioning her thusly and would let the matter lie.

By and by she returned, carrying with her a spear of the like I have never seen. It was, to my reckoning, as tall as the doorway, being slightly taller than myself. I being of average height. The blade was long, about the length of my fore-arm, and carried the cross guard of a boar spear. I was told the metal was crafted of silver remnants she had fled her home with during the catastrophic event. Gold was set into every surface from the tip of the spear, down to the haft of the ash-wood pole, in the most curiously fine script. I asked her the meaning of it, she said it was not time for me to know, that later she would teach me the power of these words. I asked of her glass men, to which I was met with a most disdainful of looks, and was given the correction of the phrase. Her Fir Glas Brecc are a diminutive, secretive people that she has bestowed a home to, further up the mountain. I will ever be a stranger to them, and they would prefer I have no interaction with them. Let it be known, I am not a domineering man, nor am I weak in my standings. Caitlin bade me to trust her, and this I shall.

Later in the week, after completing preparations, I set off back to Seattle with the first of the gold bars in my satchel. The seven together made for some hefty weight, nor are they without a hefty risk. It was decided that I would carry one, for now, to the Assay Office for receipt. She gave me leave to take Douglas with me, as with no wagon attached to him, he can travel as swiftly as a horse ever could. He was a good companion on that first ride and I have no complaints toward him. We have been friendly ever since. I was met in the Assay Office with a great amount of surprise and minor furor by an agent of the company, a Mr. Johnson. Not being attached to a mining assembly, and coming in with my own sizable claim was cause for some celebration. I was treated never so well as I have before, and found their terms most agreeable. I left then with a receipt which I promptly set to a bank for, and set up an account therein with excellent standing. After some small inquiry, I was directed to a land agent by the name of Janicke in order to purchase in its entirety the mountain and surrounding acreage for us under the distinction of Firmara Lumber. Requested as such by Caitlin, this way we were able to keep our anonymity, registered instead as a company. While in his office I discovered that our mountain has a moniker, Tenas Tilikum. I asked Mr. Janicke about this, he knew it was a Chinuk name, but not to the meaning of it.

Purchase complete, with a record for me to take home, to be folded into this page, a copy for him to keep in his books, and one for the bank for safekeeping. I left his office with a nice spring in my step feeling as accomplished as I could for stumbling upon this perfect life. I have since made the same trip three more times, each instance carrying another bar. Mr. Johnson exclaims I have become his Midas. Well-read enough am I to have replied that fortunately my golden touch was only in the ground, and not to my food, for else I would have no end of serious of problems. The most recent trip I am returning from, bivouacked for the night in the valleys that will lead me home in a half day ride.

An item of interest from my return trip, as I was encamped by St. Helens with wood burning and pan a sizzling, I sighted a pair of sad eyes across the way at the edge of the fire. The cooking smell had attracted a critter, and feeling generous I threw a hot biscuit to its place. The eyes vanished for a few minutes, and I suspected I had scared it off, thinking I was tossing stones rather than victuals. It did not take too long though, for the eyes returned, this time coming closer into the light and shewing itself to be a much malnourished Labrador. I am ever an ally to animals, particularly those in need, and set to coaxing the poor beast closer to the fire. She cast about wary eyes to me, and to Douglas, who seemed not at all worried by this intrusion. After some slow moving she made her way to my plate on the ground, gobbling up the entirety leaving it freshly shined. I could see by her manner that she was in a great state of mistrust, and I set about with soft words, slow movement, and an extra coverlet next to the flames for her to relax at. Given the choice of meandering back into the night, or a chance at a warm fire and a nice bedding, she rightly chose the blanket. Trying to get closer met me with a warning noise. It was with a truce that I bedded down for the night. The next day she was still there. Sitting on the saddle cloth waiting for me to wake up. A good morning to you sis, was all the further reassurance she needed, and she was on me with tail wagging and licks all about. I was not by no means prepared to leave this civilized creature alone in the wild and was determined to have her along. She did not at first appreciate the ride on the back of Douglas, but she managed it after a time. I believe she saw the correctness of the action due to her malnourished state. Now we sit together, the dog attached at my side, I am making use of her head as a rest for my writing hand. I have not seen fit to give her a name yet and wish to leave it to Caitlin to decide.

Yeah, we made the one tape. Ty showed it to Momma, she said it was good. Off it went, and then we got the letters too. Ty was a little shit though, waved it around saying thank you affirmative action. Hell no, we were a couple 'a badasses back then, only good thing those idiots did was letting us in. Got me to meet my Mrs. here. Well, by day we were your mild-mannered citizens, at night we were superheroes. Leaping from roof-top to roof-top, fighting crime, all that fun shit.

Ally: Stop messing with him, just give him your backstories.

Ty, he was finally at the local trying to get a degree in Fine Arts. Seriously, that kid could draw. He was good at it, when he was young he turned the wall of his bedroom into this mural of half Superman half Batman. Didn't tell Momma 'bout it, just went and did it. Did it real fucking good too. I was living with them then, and he come runnin' into the kitchen and says come look what I did, all excited. Momma, and his dad, who was around back then, would usually let him be, in his room figured it was better there than out on the streets. Now, I knew what he had been doing, but I wasn't going to say shit about that to nobody. So, they go on back to see what he did, and Momma, she goes "Oh my word!". And Dad, he claps, and rubs the top of Ty's head and says "looks good little man". Ty was so damn proud. Every right to be too, it was a good mural. Still there even.

Then I fucked up, got put away for a few. Girl I was running around with at the time was getting harassed. I lost my cool and walked up on him while he was at work. I was a big guy back then, even tried out for The Bears. Guy went down harder than I expected, he didn't get back up. I didn't kill him, don't think I'da been released if that had happened. No, ended up with a pretty bad TBI. I knew then and there I'd made a big mistake. I didn't run from it though. Got put up for, oh what was it now? Assault with intent to cause great bodily harm. I did the time, worked my ass off as much as I could to show I was a changed and better man. I got out early because of that. My parole officer was a hard but fair guy, became a good mentor to me. First day we met, he sat me down "Don't fuck with me, and I won't fuck with you. Now that's outta the way, you want a donut?" I wanted to be like that, so I became a Social Worker. I seemed to have discovered a calling for incarceration community programs. Basically I was a go between for inmates going through the release process, and helping the ones who needed an extra hand getting started up again. It was good work, I think I helped some, I tried to anyway.

While I was locked up, Ty's father passed, one day he was working under a car at the shop, got out, stood up too fast, and a vein burst in his brain. Wasn't anything anybody coulda done. So it was just Ty and Momma at home. I didn't want him to come visit me, he didn't need to see me in there like that. Momma'd come though, tell me how he was doin, maybe pass a note or picture from him. But, anyway, I was out. I was gonna make a difference to the little part of the world I lived in. And Ty was very much a part of that. He'd grown up fast, almost as tall as me, wiry like his pops though. Early nineties he gets into photography, saves up for this real nice camera. Decides his subject matter will be "the lost places". Yeah, I asked him "what the hell does that mean?" Well it meant that he wanted to go wandering around abandoned places and take photos of 'em. I told him as long as he never had to break in to a place to get inside, never stole anything, never left any sign he was there, then that was fine by me. Now, bear with me here on the next part. Ally here isn't a fan of it, but you ever have a religious experience? Well Ty's walkin away at that point, and knowing him when he gets something in his head like this, he's goin straight out to do it. And I get this voice in my head, just say's "Go with him". Sure as shit wasn't my voice. But you know what, something else I picked up on in prison was God. Only once more in my life have I had a moment like that, and it'll come up later. But right then, I did what my learning told me to do, I obeyed. I called after Ty, told him I was coming with him. And next thing I know we're urban explorers.

Once a week, he'd have a place in mind to go to so we'd go, spend the whole day and night there if we could. Most of the time it was some long abandoned industrial site. They were the easiest to get into, they usually didn't even have doors on them, so we could just stroll on in. Sometimes there'd be some homeless, lots of times there would be evidence, but no one around. When we ran into people, I usually had an over packed bag of food and water just for that occasion, just in case I could help 'em out for a minute. Normally I'd give 'em the address of a shelter, or a buddy of mine in the VA who would make an effort on their part. You'd think in the several good years we had doing it, once a week almost without fail, we should'a ran into trouble at some point. But you know what, just never happened. No crazed out junkies with knives, no cops givin us shit, nothing. I'd often wonder about that "voice" I heard, and I'd think on it for a bit, because I always assumed it meant for me to go because there'd be a problem, and I'd be there to save the day. Then I'd recognize the pride in that, because if there's a plan and a reason for everything, it probably wouldn't matter whether or not I was there. So maybe it was just a "hey, go with your brother and have some nice bonding time." Which seems a little silly to get a message like that from the higher up. But, who was I to question that anyway right? We always had a great time, he was really good at taking pictures. I'd always tell him he needed to set up his own gallery, but he was too shy for that. He knew some people though, and he'd shop his pics around, and make a good buck off of 'em.

I knew he was making some money that way, but I didn't know what for until he showed me an acceptance letter into The School of the Art Institute of Chicago. He'd applied, they loved his portfolio, he had enough cashed saved up, he damn near was able to pay that first year of tuition from it. He was so damn proud, I was so damn proud, Momma was beyond proud, she was over the moon. Her boy was going to a prestigious college. Sure, it was in Chicago, but that really wasn't so far away. I had a car, Momma and I went and saw him every chance we got. This changed up exploring a bit, but there was plenty enough around Chicago for us to go take a look at when we could. One weekend, this would have been around the time that TKN was broadcasting their casting call I suppose. Momma was feeling a little down, told me to take the trip over on my own, she'd be fine. So I went, and Ty had a camera he was borrowing from the school, said we were gonna do something a little different. We went to this old, massive rundown factory, It was like stepping into a time machine to like the early nineteen-hundreds, give us some ole-timey clothes and shovels for coal, and we would've been part of the scenery. Anyway, Ty's being a bit goofy, I asked him what he was playing at, and he just told me I'd see, just do what he told me. So I roll with it you know. It's one of those big ideas that I'm not gonna stop him from doing even if I wanted to. So he's got a script he's scribbled down, introductions for both of us, tells me to play it big on the whole getting locked up, and then reforming myself to this awesome person. He's talking about how after his father passed, I stepped up and became the figure for him to look up to. It was kind of him, we'd never really talked about that, and I was always a little worried he'd be mad at me, thinking I'd abandoned him somehow. But no, this whole thing he's doing is just talking me up, making me see through his eyes how he's seen me. By the end of it, I'm not afraid to say, I'm crying my head off. Big guy like me, people always thinking I'm gonna bite their head off and chew 'em up. But I'm just a big softy.

Ally: That's why he's my Teddy Bear.

Sure am baby, sure am. So, I'm sure you see it now, but he was making our try-out tape. Had us doing other stuff, got me doing some jumping and climbing. And then we finish up and spend the rest of a weekend together. I don't give it much thought after that. Until the next weekend Momma and I were there, he brings us up to his room, says "watch this" and sticks a tape in a VHS player. He'd spent that whole week editing the video into this ten minute adventure show. He did a great job at it, I'd love to see that tape again someday, but it's been so long now, whoever stole all that stuff from TKN probably just tossed it anyway. But it was pretty damn cool. I asked him what he was gonna do with this tape now, and he just says "this" and then rewinds it, takes it out, puts it in it's own case, puts that in a box from the post office, already marked up and everything to get mailed out. He seals it up, and gives it to me and tells me to drop it in the mail, and then lays out the plan. I tell him he's crazy, but if, and on the off chance they actually accept us, I'd do it. I didn't think we'd have a chance in hell you know? I mean, what are the odds of that? I never knew how many people applied for it, but it had to have been a lot right? And from all over the country too. We joked about it a bit, fantasized a lot. What if we got in? What if we won? What would we do with all that money? When I asked that last question, we both burst up laughing and said "give it to Momma!" I mean really, what else were we gonna do with it? She'd done good by us our whole lives, if we got it, we were gonna finally do good by her.

Then like I said, we got our letters. Could not fucking believe it at first. Kept thinking they were gonna get in touch and say "woops, we made a mistake, this was supposed to go to someone in Montana." But nope, they called later on, got more details from us, and for us, and then that fall we were off to Washington to actually do this crazy thing. It didn't hit me until we got out there to that fucking mountain. That's when I finally accepted that this was happening, we were a part of it.

It went the same for us as it did Ally and her group at the start. Except our guys were assholes. We had Nick, Sam, and Josh, couldn't tell you what the jobs were split between them, but I still remember their names. Told myself I'd never forget that. But they drank the producers Kool-Aid all right. Ty and I might as well have been animals in a zoo for them to observe. Stoic ass motherfuckers. Josh did most the talking. He had the radio and the plans. Kept trying to pick away at us that first day. Andre, don't you think Tyrese didn't get enough wood? Tyrese, what do you think of Andre's shelter? Looks a little bare to me don't you think? And that shit was constant. Ty got pissed eventually just at being full named. He was never really fond of the whole thing, just wanted to be Ty, and that was it. He was getting the fire going with a lens he claimed to have "found". Josh had this stupid ass ear-piece wired to the radio, he was in a tiff about that lens, and called back to base about it. We could tell when Miles was talking to him, that shithead would puff up his chest and put his hand upside his head acting like he was talking to the President. Then he opened his mouth and out came this spoiled brat attitude: Tyrese, Miles said to lose the lens and try the stick method like you were shown, it'll add to the authenticity. When Ty gets mad, he goes quiet, and he won't look at you. And that's what he did, just sat there staring at the log pile, and the little trickle of smoke coming up from the bright spot he had focused. And yep, Josh thought he was ignoring him, and that sure didn't go over so well. So he went and crouched down next to him, doing this buddy buddy thing as if he didn't just tattle tale on us, and was all, "come on Tyrese, you gotta play ball here buddy. We're all here to make a show. Blah blah fucking blah." I'm sure you can add in whatever you want. You know what? He was like Grima Wormtongue from Lord of the Rings. Huh, never thought of that till now. Ty would've seen that connection. Man he would've loved those movies. Sorry, anyway, yeah, so our very own Wormtongue is trying to slime his way into Ty's ears, invading his personal space, calling him by his full name over and over. Little shit never saw it coming. Ty had a good sized branch in his hand, and just whacks Josh right in the fucking knee with it. Josh fell over going "what the fuck man?" and Ty stood up over him all six-foot-three of him and yelled "My name is fucking Ty you dumb motherfucker. Call me Tyrese one more time and see what I do. Fucking call your daddy Miles on me again and I'll stick that radio up your ass. Fucking try me." And I'm just howling, it was hilarious. Ty was angry, but he was all bark, that crack to the knee was just to get the attention he wanted. Josh sure as shit didn't know that, he's laying there on his back, completely out of his element. Did the trick though. He said "okay, sorry Ty." Ty still needed a moment, he went off mumbling something, I think it was about getting talked down to by somebody his own age. I helped Josh up, but I made sure to let him know what we were about. I might have given his hand a bit of a harder squeeze than I needed to, but I told him we were there together. He needed to stop this shit of trying to turn us against each other. All it was gonna do was lead to something worse than what he just got now. The point got across to him, and he didn't bother us so much after that. Kid had an inflated sense of ego, and Ty and I helped to bring him back down to Earth a bit is all. I don't think it helped bring us all together any closer though. But, Ty and I weren't even thinking about making friends with the crew, we were there to do the tasks, and to get to that summit.

Now, here's where we're getting to that freaky shit. It didn't start small and insidious for us. Ally's camp had silence, remember? Well, ours, that night, we had noise. Fucking raven's came swooping in, apparently decided we were trespassers on their land, and decided to have a word with us about it. For the entire. Fucking. Night. From sundown to sunup they squawked endlessly. We tried screaming at them, throwing anything we could get our hands on at them. Ty tried to scramble his scrawny ass up a tree after some, but they'd just fly to another and make more noise at him. The crew was fucking eating it up. Miles had told them to film it all, it was gonna make for some fun viewing. Couple brothers out in the woods fighting with noisy ass ravens. We tried ignoring it, tried to sleep. But it was like as soon as we closed our eyes, they would turn up the volume and become even louder. Like that movie ya know, they turned it up to eleven. Sun started coming up at some point, we were tired as hell, I had a headache from that constant alarm clock blaring they did. Then it just stopped. We looked up, and they were just sitting there, beady little black eyes staring down at us from all around. And then as one they took off. Ty didn't believe me then, but I saw one in there that was a lot bigger than the others. I'm talking eagle sized, maybe even bigger than that? My memory might be making it bigger. And, yeah, that's not possible for a raven. Which is what Ty told me too. But I saw something that looked like a very large, very black raven.

After we got over the shock of the night, and the weirdness of that morning. We said fuck this place, and got to moving. Got to the new spot, did whatever it was the challenge was, and got set up there for the rest of the day. And, from what I remember, the day was fine. The night ended up being okay for us too. The birds didn't come back. I told Ty it was a test, and we had passed. I think I said it just a bit too preachy, his reply was to tell me to "shut the fuck up." And please don't misunderstand, he didn't say this with animosity towards me, it's just how we talked to each other as brothers. It wasn't until the third night that something happened to us, not that we were aware of it. By this point we were just writing the ravens off as a weird fluke of nature. Josh was still behaving, and we were getting nudges here and there from the show people that fit a bit more in line for us. We didn't know about anything going on at the base camp, so for us, it was all smooth sailing. We had just bedded down in our shelter, the crew had a nice big tent to themselves set to the side of us so they could shoot around it for night shots and early morning stuff and make it look like nothing was there. They were taking a break inside, getting ready to sleep for a bit themselves, but they were chatting, not quite at a whisper level. They must've been thinking their tent afforded them a bit more privacy. It did not. Because I had overheard them say that we were in the lead. I remember nudging Ty, and told him what I heard, we were pretty excited of course. And I fell asleep feeling pretty pleased with myself.

I woke up with the Sun, a weird habit I've had for as long as I can remember. Sun comes up, I'm up. I got up, stretched my sore ass back as well as I could, and took in the world around me. It was a mess. Trash was strewn all over the place. Plastic bags, chip bags, the MRE bags, basically the remains of the crew's food scattered about. I was thinking "The fuck?" Crew went on a food bender or something while we slept. And off by their tent, where they had hung their bear bags up and away off the ground, well, those bags weren't there anymore. So something else had gone on a bender with the food, and was kind enough to leave the trash behind. I hollered for them to get their asses up, they weren't gonna be happy about this. And of course they weren't. Lots of 'what the fucks' going around that morning. That food was meant to last them a while, and it was totally cleaned out. So Josh gets on the radio to let Miles, or whoever was up, know what had happened and that someone would need to make a food run for them. Except his radio wasn't working. Same thing that happened to Ally and her people was now happening to us. Except Josh wasn't going to wait around a few days first to see if the radios came back on. Their loss of food was a big enough issue he decided he had to get back right away to get that problem sorted. I don't think it was even noon by that point. He didn't even take anything with him, just his, and one of the other guys' canteen of water and that was it. He said he was gonna get there and back as fast as he could, there wasn't too much rough terrain between us and the base, and the amount of food would excuse a ride on the four-wheeler. This unfortunately meant for us that we had to stay put until he got back. I tried arguing with him about that. Knowing we were ahead definitely played into my pride there. I wanted to maintain that. It wasn't my fault that something snacked on their stuff. And besides, if he was coming back on wheels, he'd have a much easier time finding us a little further ahead. But, he didn't want to take the risk of not finding us. This setback was already gonna put him into deep shit with the boss, he didn't want to make things worse, by then losing us too. I admit, I sympathized with him a little, so I gave in. Just like Ally with their person, that was the last time we ever saw Josh alive. I did see him again, fuck, but by then it was much too late to do anything but say a prayer for him.

But, again, there's an order to this, don't wanna be getting too far ahead of myself now. With Josh gone, and no food left, Nick and Sam went through a change. One of them had a candy bar of some sort stashed away, but that was it. Ty and I were barely foraging enough for ourselves, so the dynamic of feeding them too was about to get interesting. They both agreed that if not for a paycheck, they would've been out of there in a second. But they didn't even try to keep up the semblance of doing work. If anything, Josh would be back sometime the next day, and with t.v. editing, no one would any wiser to a missing block of time. They wanted to just sit around and wait, but I said no, that wouldn't do. What if Josh didn't come back tomorrow? What if it took him longer? Not to mention, he took their water, what were they going to do for that? I said no, gentlemen, this just turned into a survival trip for you too.

We had a stream not to far from us, so we had water. That was fortunately the easy thing to mark off the list. Food was harder, a lot harder. You know what a game trail is? Animals are a lot like people, in that in a forest, often times seeking the easiest path and sticking with it. A few trips back and forth, and you get these nice little routes meandering about in the woods. Now, what you do is, you find one of the smaller, more narrow paths, usually this means it's rabbits that pass through. Then you take a rope, loop it and tie it so that it's like a simple noose, and put that somewhere in the path and hope Mr. Bunny sticks his head through it. Have that rope tied to something and the rabbit will be stuck waiting for you to come and claim your prize. Well, there weren't any game trails. No tracks, no droppings, nothing. Like they knew we were coming and cleared out months ago. We thought maybe we could get a fish out of the stream, but Ty had studied for that part, and said it wasn't big enough. So that was a bust too. That just left scouring the bushes for edible berries, and anything with a large meaty root. And those options were almost slim to none. It was like they specifically chose this place just because of how fucking bare it was, just to really mess with us. You really want to mess with a person's head, take away their means to food. I don't think Nick and Sam were taking it very seriously. Why would they? They'd gone their whole lives never having to worry about where the next meal came from. If they were hungry, they'd simply get something to eat. When that is the status quo for as long as you've been around, why would you even question it? So, we foraged, and foraged, and foraged some more, and barely had a handful of anything between us. So we ate what was there, and then boiled enough stream water to fill our bellies with. They had a pot and stand just for that, so we made good use of it. While I was out in my selected bit of the woods, I came out onto a ridgeway. That mountain was more or less to my back, so I would've been looking out East over a small bit of the forest, back the way we had been. And wouldn't you know it, just a bit off to my left was a nice column of smoke coming up out of the forest. It wasn't too far away, a few miles as the crow flies. I made a note of it, sorry, a mental note I mean, and went back to camp.

That night I got Nick and Sam to agree to Ty and I joining them in the tent. It really wasn't that hard. I think being the oldest one there, and the physically biggest, they decided to look up to me. I always was good about being a leader in any given situation. It was pretty nice falling asleep in that tent, compared to our poorly constructed shelters from the past few days. I slept like a baby, until I wasn't. It's hard to explain. You ever wake up, but not know you were awake, then you come to and realize you're sitting up and your eyes or open? That's maybe the best I can describe it. There I was, in this pitch black tent, and just noticing that my eyes were open and I was aware of not being asleep anymore. Everybody else was still out. Ty was even snoring. The way we were positioned in this tent, okay, so here's the door in the middle, come in and turn right and there's Ty, laying parallel to the wall the door was on, then a gap, then me laying parallel to the back wall. Our feet going to the middle. Nick and Sam were on the opposite side, laying the same way. Got that picture in your head? Okay, so put yourself in my spot, sitting up, you can't see a thing. You can hear your brother next to you, but those other guys might as well just not be there. And from my right, outside the tent, I can hear some whispering. But it doesn't sound right at all. It was too high-pitched, like it was coming from a kid. But it was raspy. Smoker's voice to the extreme, like there was a layer of phlegm they had to push through to get those words out. I'm thinking "what the fuck is this now?" Trying to make out that whispering, it's coming closer though, and right fucking to me. Gives me goosebumps just thinking about it. I had them then too, every hair went straight up on my body. But I didn't dare move. Whoever was out there, was doing a great job of scaring the shit out of me. I didn't think it was Josh, he was way too much of a square for that you know? And this came right up to the tent, right up next to me. This fast whisper, pure gibberish as far as I can tell, something like, here, let me write it down for you "Sama led mid ko, tavirt tooda gall." Over and over. Raspy and guttural, and childlike. Fucking creepy as hell. I reached over and started hitting Ty, somewhere on his body, I needed him to wake up, no way was I going to be alone in this. And I hit him, and hit him, and he would not fucking wake up. I hit him hard enough it hurt me, gave him a fucking bruise on his bicep, he showed me later. But nothing. When it touched the tent, that's when I finally lost it, or found my courage, I don't know. It dragged it's nails, claws, whatever the fuck they were along the tent just right there next to my head, and I jumped up yelling at it to go away. It fucking cackled. Make it sound like a male version of the witch from The Wizard of Oz, and that would be what it was. By then I'm screaming at them to wake up. Guys wake the fuck up, please wake the fuck up. And they wouldn't fucking wake up. This just incensed whatever it was outside more. It wasn't alone either. I should've known it wouldn't be alone. More scratching started up behind me, then to the left, and right, all around the tent. You know that "zippy" sound something sharp makes when you run it over nylon, that's what they were doing. And laughing, mocking me. I didn't know what to do. So I kicked at the tent wall and hit one. It felt fucking solid, like I just hit a tree. It didn't like that though, it fucking hissed like a cat. A moment later I have this searing white-hot pain in my ankle. I reach down, and I feel this, thing, like a fucking arrow stuck in me, and I didn't even think I just pull it out, and that hurts just as bad. So bad my brain can't even handle it, and I black out.

It's light when I open my eyes next, and it feels like I'm on fire. My eyes burn, every joint hurts, my leg feels like it's too close to a broiler, and my foot is encased in molten metal. Ty is sitting there next to me, looking like someone hung the wash out to dry in a storm. I try to move, his hand, and an intense wave of nausea keep me on my back. I try to talk, but my throat is sore and dry. It's a strange feeling though, what my body was experiencing, all that pain, but my mind was clearing. I was able to get "drink" out of my burning throat. He gave me some water, and it helped. After a few more moments of just catching my breath, I asked him to help me sit up. Doing that made everything spin around me and I had to turn to the side to retch up the water he just gave me. I had to take another breather after that. I sat there looking at my legs, and saw my left bundled up in bandages from a first aid kit.

Ty said he did that. He had woken up with the dawn, and I was just laying there across his legs. He woke up the other two, but they couldn't figure out what was wrong with me right away. Then they saw how much more swollen my foot was, found the wound in my ankle and got to work cleaning it out as best they could. That alone probably went a long ways to saving my life. Wasn't enough to save the leg entirely of course. After it was all said and done, a doctor in the hospital told me that the wound developed a type of necrosis that just ate away at everything around it. They had seen something similar in spider bites, but not to the scale that happened to me. I felt then, that telling them it was the result of a porcupine quill filled with monster shit, would have been met with some disbelief. But there I go getting ahead again, where was I?

So Ty patched me up, told me what happened during the day. Then told me that I had been out entirely until the next day. And they had gone through one hell of a night. When he said that, he spaced out a bit, went away to the night before and looked around. I hadn't even been aware of my surroundings yet, I was still in the tent, but there was a breeze moving through it. Looking around I saw that the walls were just shredded. It was about then that Nick came in with a long sharpened stick, and said it was time to go. It was not easy getting up, the severe aches to my joint, and the overall feeling of being on fire everywhere just got worse as they got me to my feet. After the attack they endured, staying another night just wasn't an option. When I put it together, I realized that Josh hadn't come back by then. I asked if there had been anything from him, or the HQ, but they said no to that. I told them about the smoke I saw in the distance, thought maybe we could go to that, maybe they had a working radio, food, shelter, some sort of safety.

July 10 1896

My Caitlin, never to be surprised by anything, was wholly taken aback at the appearance of the dog. When questioned, I gave account of our meeting, and this seemed to settle her. I told her I had not named the poor dog, thinking she would wish to do so herself. She replied it was very lucky to have found a kind soul such as myself, and should henceforth be known as Sona.

August 1st 1896

Lammas Day

She imparts that Lammas is no more. That the holidays of the God of the East are not to be entertained here. Today is not a good day for her, but tells me not the why of it. Last year we laid together under the night sky, afterwards it was with great joy for her to announce that this was our union of marriage, its after effects would bring about the birth of my son nine months later. To the day, our son Louis was delivered to us on May the First. What she called Cétshamhain and taught me to write properly, as its letters do not rightly match how they sound. As are most of the words she has taught me with our time together. With this day being our one-year jubilee, I presented her with a bundle of darkly red coloured cloth of the highest quality. In turn, she revealed a finely twisted bracelet of gold strands so thinly spun, they shift about like a coil of horsehair. I asked if her forest men were of a relation to the fabled Rumpelstiltskin, able to spin gold so well to make it feel as if it were alive. This amused her greatly, and she said she would pass on the compliment to them. She seems to be in a better mood, and is already set about, to turning the cloth to something that she fancies. I also had plans drawn up to expand our small home into a proper house. Caitlin has said so long as it keeps the look of a logged cabin, that she so prefers, then I can expand upon it as I wish. I have stated my intention of beginning construction, and finishing before the first snow fall come this November. Babe at her breast, she gives me leave with a gentle wave of her hand. I will set out near Portland tomorrow to hire a team, my man Johnson, in Seattle has received adequate word of.

August 25th 1896

I am returned from a productive spell in Portland. Accompanied by a score of union team carpenters, hired at satisfactory terms, for an agreeable span. In my time away, Bres has felled enough trees to accommodate the creation of multiple homes. He is to remain hidden for the duration of construction as I do not believe these men will be as accepting of him. The men wondered at who had been hired before them, to only fell trees. I found it necessary to lie to them as such to reply that a family of missionary settlers on their way north had sheltered with us for a spell, and as repayment offered to log the trees for us. Sufficed by my explanation, they proceeded to set up a small working village for themselves. The appearance of Caitlin and her ever youthful beauty mystified the men. And they set about with many a yes ma'am to her questions, and to a demand to not venture too far away from their local environment as there have been grizzly bear seen in the area. This of course another lie, her Fir Glas Brecc have the capability to be quite savage when encountering strangers, and we did not wish to have trouble befall us, or them. Caitlin assures me, the weather is in a perfect state for them to make excellent time with their labors. She keeps a sly look about her, when given inquiry to this appearance, she will not admit to any such thing. With her proclivity to prophecy I can only guess as to what future she envisions heading toward us, and hope that it leads ahead as it has so far.

August 28th 1896

Damn the man-creature Bres for his temerity. The men, having erected a privy, simply a rough construction set a ways off from the housing with a deep pit in the ground for their earthly offerings. A man by the name of Bald Jake was seen to be running from said location in a great panic and bellowing for the men to take up arms. I, the team foreman, and a few curious onlookers not currently engaged ran to see what the fuss was. Cursing this man to be demanding we take up arms on my land, I asked him what he was about, but inwardly guessed the reason. Sure enough, he has seen what he described as a tall hairy beast, watching him from a distance through the trees. One of the other men with us, being of mixed-blood, and I believe by the name of Charles, exclaimed it to be the Skookum. If the land was his, then we must leave it, he had heard stories of it from his mother's people. The Skookum was a fearsome powerful creature that could lay waste to us all if we went to war with it. Panic welling amongst the men, some clamoring to hunt and kill this monster whilst others wished to follow the advice set forth by Charles, to run and leave this land be. I shouted both groups of men into a nervous submission, I put to them reason, that this monster Bald Jake had seen, was no more than our native man-servant. Owing a life debt to the family of my wife, her and my child being the sole remainders of. He was not one to live under the roof of a house, and much preferred the open sky for his home. I proclaimed further that his appearance being that of one so beastly was an unfortunate birth deformity, he wished to serve my family, and exist in relative obscurity, he would be no cause of detriment to the men. This seemed to settle the men further, with some more of the vulgar types calling for me to present this man to them, so they could believe me. I put forth that he was not an attraction to be viewed at a carnival, and if they wished for such entertainment to put in there. The foreman agreed on this, and set about to the men with shouts and threats that this show had ended and to return to work. I apologized for not disclosing this man to him. He speculated a man's troubles and life were his own, to do with as he sees fit, and being hired men, I was not required to inform them of any of my goings-on I did not wish to. He did however call for Bald Jake to join us again, and so doing demanded from him an apology. I accepted it with a sense of overplayed eagerness disingenuous to myself, but seemed to satisfy and put a close to the situation.

Later I had words with Caitlin to again order her man-servant to stay away from the laborers as I am not sure if I can dissuade them against the chance to posse up to hunt down a monster. There were those in that group that seemed displeased to not be out chasing prey no matter what manner of quarry it were, another sighting could prove most disastrous for us all. I saw the fire behind her eyes, but the words from her lips were amicable.

August 29th 1896

This next day has greeted me with the headless body of a large elk upon the back stoop. Caitlin tells me this is an apology from Bres, to have the laborers come take it for their fires. This pleased the men greatly to have fresh meat delivered to them. The team cook set about butchering the animal straight away. After finishing a cold lunch at midday, a heavy knock came to us from the front door. The foreman, his name being Mr. Farkas, brought forth the skin of the aforementioned animal, claiming it to be in excellent condition. Unfortunately they were not equipped to tan such a pelt as this one. Not wanting it to go to rot and ruin he presented it back to us. He furthermore wished to proclaim how no one else, but he, mind you, found it curious that the hide had no wounds to it. Caitlin spake from my side, her man-servants size and cunning knew better tricks than the white hunters to claim a prize, Mr. Farkas had most keen eyes for his observation. She accepted the fur from him and was away. I recognized the look of covetousness upon his face, and instead of feeling threatened as might most men, I felt a sense of pride.

Before coming here, I would not have said I was a vain man. I came from meager beginnings, and was taught well to treasure what I have, to never begrudge another for what they do or do not have. That those who want for nothing, and sneer down on others for being less, were a disdainful folk not to be given the time of day. When I set forth to join the gold rush in the North, I knew that if I managed to find that precious metal, my life would henceforth change. Discovering my good fortune with these, strange as they may be, events, has led to great alterations I am still ever in awe of. I do not find this extra vanity as well fitting and fear it may lead me to become a cruel man. I will express myself to Caitlin later, and seek a suitable reprieve through her. Though she is a perfect example of the Mysterious Woman, she is ever my rock, to cling to through the fiercest of tempests.

VIII. The Survivor

First interview:

Do I thank you for coming? I don't know. You're the first outside visitor I've had in years. You know my parents are dead right? First my mom, ten years ago. I think that was ten years now, feels longer, maybe it was. Then my dad. Three years ago. They said it was while he was sleeping. The nurses at the hospice called to tell me. It was just the three of us for the longest time. Now it's just me. Here, in this place. Did you bring it? I haven't had one in so long, the food here is so bland. If there was a motto stuck above a door here, it would be "Blandness is Our Specialty". But those nut-rolls were something else. You actually did it. You're kind, thank you. Did you try one too? You should've. It was a pretty easy deal to make wasn't it? Get me a donut, and I'll tell you all my lies. Everybody says they're lies. "Oh no Megan, it didn't happen that way. You were drugged."

I wasn't drugged the whole time. I remember it all. All of it. Fucking all of it. And it's been so long, and no one believes me. My parents didn't believe me either. That's why I'm here. As long as I take my meds, and be bland, and smile and say everything is okay, then everything is okay. It's all just fine and fun here. But if I leave, then they'll get me. They come to my window at night, and they whisper at me. But they never come in. They come and whisper and tell me they're going to get me. And I sometimes I scream for help. But no one comes. There's a camera in the corner, and someone sitting comfy and safe in their room watching. And I'm not hurting myself. Why would they come, when there's no problem? I'm safe in here. When my mom died, Dad came and took me to the funeral. I didn't want to. I told him we had to be somewhere safe before dark. They come at night. Only at night. Always at night. They can't during the day. And Dad made them. He made them put me in the car. They're not supposed to. But it was my mom's funeral. And it was my dad's money. Why would they listen to me? I'm crazy. It's not a jail, I'm not a prisoner, I'm not an inmate. I'm a patient who's scared of the dark. If I'm back before dark, then what's the problem right?

Order, order, order order order order. If you say it enough it stops being a word. It's just a sound you make. It's a sound you can make if you get hit in the face enough and can't talk. When your teeth are broken, when your tongue is swollen. When your jaw is broken in several places and you don't have a nose anymore. It's just gibberish. That's what she did. When I hit her with the rock. I hit and I hit and she just made these noises that can sound like words if you hear it enough. But then you hear the words too many times and it's just gibberish. Then they start laughing at the gibbering mess of what used to be your friend. *End of interview one.*

October 1st 1896

The carpenters were worth every penny I put forth to them. Mr. Farkas assures me they are on track to a full completion by the end of the month. Caitlin has made for me the most dapper of vests from the elk hide, the backside being replete with the silvery sheen of the elk's hair. For Sona, she has created a very fine collar. For Lou a pair of mittens for the coming cold. I put to her my fears, of growing into a vain man, to look down upon the masses with this life of ours, so full of wealth. She tells me my very acknowledgment of the fact, shews that I am not a bad man. That I shall grow as a powerful man is only natural to my station. I am a descendant to kings of ages since passed, being now the ruler of my own demesne. As long as my mental faculties remain intact, I shall strive to conduct myself with honor and dignity. It is high time I have my first of followers. She has made a gift, for me to dispense, to the foreman, of wolf hide bracers, and a belt of the same. I am to wait for him to complete a task worthy of them. I inquire to what this feat may be, and as usual am met with her cunning smile, like that of a fox. I must simply wait and see, but it shan't be long. Afterwards in giving these items to Mr. Farkas, she proclaims he will be my man of the land, to always be counted upon.

October 20th 1896

Mr. Farkas and I have slain a bear.

October 25th 1896

Forgive my simplicity, I believe I was in a mild state of disconcertion. We have unfortunately lost several men to this bear before it was slain. A Mr. J. Jefferson, Mr. M. Davidson, M. P. Dubois, and Bald Jake being viciously set upon by a true monster of a griz. I will see to it that their families, if any there be, are compensated heavily for this sad loss of life. Now to the events, as I bore witness to, from beginning to end.

I have made it a habit to break my fast with the men in the early hours of the morning, this day, of the 20th, being no different from the others. The men had heard bellowing from bear the night prior. The sound having travelled from further up the range, was oddly more vocal than expected, the men having surmised that two males were having it out over a lass and the loser was sorely bitter. Enlivened by the morning's bacon and biscuits, the men commenced their daily labors, the bear being of no concern. I returned to the nearly finished cabin to discover Caitlin at the window, being up and about much earlier than she is wont in the day. I commented towards the morning chatter at the fire, being out of ear shot to the cabin, and told her of the nightly noises. She made no reply, continuing to look about as if waiting to see if the bear would pass us by. I joined her at the lookout, finding her quietude queer, and inquired as to what she could see. She proclaims, shortly I will be wanting the spear. I stand with her a moment longer, when a great shadow passes the window by. The speed of which, makes the falling drizzle appear at a standstill, I do not comprehend how something can move so quickly.

Mr. Davidson coming up the way to the cabin, was the first to be set upon. The bear, seizing the entirety of Davidson's head within its massive jaws shook him about, much the same way a dog will savage a rabbit. Flinging him aside immediately after, it's next victim was Mr. Jefferson stock still, I presume not believing what had happened so suddenly right in front of him. I did not see how the bear brought him down, witnessing later the terrible aftermath thereof. I had exclaimed in my panic only for my gun. I was already starting out the house rifle in hand, Caitlin crying after me to take the spear. Coming up behind me from their points of labor on the cabin sides, Mr. Farkas was on my right a mere hatchet at the ready, and M. Dubois being on my left shouting in his patois. I fired into the expansive rump of this shack sized monstrosity at our front. It spun quickly on its hind quarters, a massive paw snapping the rifle from my hands and continuing into the face of

Dubois, who for if only he had not taken three steps further, would still be alive. The bear was then standing above us, towering over us in a way to humble us as fragile insects to be crushed at the whim of an angry god.

I do not know the how of it, I can say that it is most likely to be Caitlin stepping up behind us, thrusting the spear into my wanting hands. But how she could make entrance to our impending demise, and be seen at the door of our cabin at the same point, I do not have the ken. In that moment I was not in the state to be considering her whereabouts. The spear in hand, and looking to Mr. Farkas to lend his, we thrust upwards, into the bear's chest. It fell to us with a great roar. The butt-end of the spear hit onto the hard granite beneath us with the booming sound of thunder. A rich font of blood erupted around the blade, drenching us. The bear, huffed down to us, trying but failing to rend me with its claws, the light left its eyes with a curiously confused look, it's brow furrowed together. Coming to a stop at the guard, propped at such an angle to stay up right. Thus, the bear was fully impaled upon the weapon, its last, fetid breath gave out into Mr. Farkas' bloody face.

The spear itself was clean of blood. Whether as a repellant to the gore surrounding it, or a drinker of it I am not satisfied to know. I have examined it twice now, there is certainly a warmth to it, but no blood is to be found in its golden inlays. Mr. Farkas and I did not escape the ferocity of the bear either. As the behemoth settled and the moment began to clear, I saw that his face had been raked by a fumbled weakened paw, the damage being only on the surface. My shoulder receiving a much similar treatment. Being patched up by Caitlin, she assures us both that the scars from this attack, will serve to give us a rugged handsomeness most men cannot lay claim to.

The aftermath of this attack, has shewn what fragile creatures we are. The bear worked ferociously in the time it took us to rally against it. Mr. Jefferson was split near in twain at the midsection, we have found debris from his ribs and entrails some distance from his body. Mr. Davidson's head was discovered to be crushed completely, and separated from his neck. M. Dubois was struck with such speed, that while his neck was broken, his face was carved away in a series of furrows. We located some of his teeth, and other various pieces, so that he too may be buried as whole as could be. We are all shaken by this, Mr. Farkas and I are lauded as heroes for saving us all from a grim fate. With all the men hauling, and a team of the horses, we were able to move the beast away from the cabin, stretching it out in full upon the ground. Some men being in the business of hunting brown bears exclaimed it was nothing like they had come across, it's face being much shorter and more stout. It's limbs are also reported to be longer than usual. A freak of nature said a man, and it has caught. The length of it being about fifteen feet, teeth four inches long, and claws being almost ten inches in length. Upon further examination, long blackened quills, were discovered punctured into its thick hide. I overheard a man say it must have taken a tumble with a family of porcupines before coming to us. None of this should be possible, but the evidence presents itself in front of many witnesses. Mr. Farkas has dispatched two men to Portland, a two days ride from here, to bring back a photographer. Work was understandably cut short this day, with the only wood-crafting to be the coffins for those we lost.

Panic was in the air the following morning, with us awakening to find the beast entirely gone. Some expressed fear that the monster was not fully dead, and managed to escape in the night, Mr. Farkas quickly put that concern to rest. A search was undertaken, with further bad news, as Bald Jake's body was discovered, it was then that we were to become aware that he had not been seen since even before the night prior to the attack. Most likely set upon by the bear in the dark as he made his way to his own forest privy, not wishing to use the one that had been espied by Bres. I have given the men leave to return to Portland with the bodies of their friends. I have placed my concerns to Mr. Farkas, that the men who do not wish to return, shall be paid in full, with an extra bonus in addition for their troubles, and have asked him to make any new hires he feels the need for. Before leaving, I made the gift of the wolf fur bracers, and belt to honor him with. Caitlin having formed words to the leather inside being Krall and Slack. Seeing them and repeating them cause no issue, but as when she uses her speech with Bres, a certain uncomfortable feeling trembles through my head and chest at her utterances. She tells me this means Bear Slayer, the same words being embroidered by her into my vest with gold threading. It will act as a ward, and to show our mastery over nature.

Mr. Farkas has proclaimed himself to be my brother, and I to be his, blooded and baptized together under the shadow of our awesome kill. He assures me of his, and the others return. I have been a most satisfactory employer to the laborers, and now I am as family to him. I bade him and the men to take the time they need, and to rejoin us with the advent of the new month.

Second Interview:

I'm sorry. You came all this way to talk to me, you brought me a gift. And I handle it by losing my cool. That happens to me sometimes. I was just having a bad day yesterday. I talked with my doctor, she helped me process through better. I'm broken. It's okay, you don't need to be concerned. I've been broken for a long time now. So, how does this work? You have the basics down yes. I suppose we can start there. I'll do what I can for you. I guess I don't have to say "you're going to think I'm crazy" do I? I mean, here I am, locked up in a place specifically for people with the crazy. So it's convenient. I never changed it. I told it how I told it to the cops, to my parents, to the news, to anybody who would listen. It was real. They tell me all the time that it was real for me, but that reality for one person isn't always that for everyone else. I see the platitude they're giving me. I liked it more with my parents early on. Before it was too much for them. Before I was too much. They told me it wasn't real. There's nothing out there in the dark. What happened was a nightmare, but I came home from it, I was safe. But I wasn't. I'll never be. Did you talk to anybody else? You have to tell them how dangerous talking is. If they hear you talking about them, if she hears it. You have to tell them. They need iron bars on their windows. They need salt on their doorstep. They're not safe if they've talked to you. I'm only doing it because I'm in here. Okay. Deep breath. You said there is an order to this right? Like the King said to Alice, "begin at the beginning, then go on till you come to the end, then stop.

Okay. My name is Megan Marie Phillips. I was hired as a Boom Operator to work on the production of Peak Challenge. I was assigned to follow and record Team Georgia. I worked with Spider, sorry, Jason Hayes, he was the Camera Operator. And Nicky Garcia, she was the Production Assistant and. Nicky was my best friend. We met at college. We were in the same sorority house. Team Georgia was a brother and sister team; Jim and Shanelle. I don't remember their last name, sorry. They were nice though. They were cave divers, explorers, or something I don't know. Nicky had all the information about them. I was just there to hold the boom mic and make sure everything came over nice and clear. I was looking forward to camping out for a couple of weeks. I loved camping. Growing up in Spokane, that was about all there was to do. Nicky too, I mean she was looking forward to it. She had broken up with some guy whose name I won't even try to remember. She told me, when we were getting prepped for it; A week of bossing some hicks around in the middle of no where would be just what she needed to get over the guy. Then we're there, and she's getting to know them, and they're just these sweet kids. I don't think they were that much younger than us actually. We talked at night, when we were done with work, or taking a break from it, since we were supposed to be "on call" at a moments notice. It was pretty miserable for them though. They could not get a fire going no matter how hard they worked at it.

Spider wanted to help them out at night, he looked all tough with his tattoos, but he was this people pleasing pothead. So yeah, I don't know when, the first few days all blend together into this long single memory, but he asked Nicky if he could just give them his lighter, let them get something going. But she was all little miss professional, and Miles, the producer, he was eating the drama up. He loved it. She was nice about it though you know? She really understood how difficult it was. I say that, and you think I'm being naïve. But she was genuine about it. I mean, she felt bad for calling them hicks before we got to know them. She just, she was good about separating the personal from the professional. She was there to make a show, and yeah, any good show needs some drama. And Jim and Shanelle bickering at each other for not getting the fire going was a good start. She'd get them each alone, then ask what was going on, how they felt about it. Reaction shots. And they would be annoyed that the other one wasn't doing what they wanted. I mean, they were nice, yes, but they had that sibling rivalry thing going. Each of them knew more than the other, how the other one was screwing up the fire making, how their shelter should be, how they should get food. They argued about everything. It seemed more like they were competing against each other than against the other teams. But when they laid down to sleep, covered up as much as they could, and snuggled up tight against each other. I heard them through the mic. "Love ya Jimmy." "Love you Channy."

Other problems, oh yes, there were loads of problems. Our food was raided at night, they took everything, bags included. That was before the radio went out, so they sent a guy with a box of these really bad army rations. And then those were taken too. And then the radio went out. Nicky was already in trouble for the food thing, she didn't feel like getting chewed out about the radio too, she convinced herself it was a problem on their end. If they wanted to have it fixed, then they had to come to us. I wish she had gone, I know the other assistants did, and that was the last they were seen of. The same thing would probably have happened to her too. I don't know. I just think, or wonder, sometimes even dream about, maybe it would have been better. Maybe like that it would have been faster. I'd like to stop now please. I'm sorry. *End of Second Interview*

October 26th 1896

I do not wish to besmirch the honor of my wife. I am aware, to some, she would be too knowing in the ways of the workings of the world. A witch to those with a fools sense of superstition. She has given me everything I have ever wanted for in my life, and has never demanded a single damn boon in return. But ofttimes I am worried to what lengths she may travel, to see her visions come to the fore. My time with her has shewn what little I know of the world outside of men. She has proffered doings to me, that should be impossible, and yet, by her hand they exist. I worry now that in knowing of the attack, she may have caused the event to unfold how she pleased. This morning, Bres presented at the door to her a folded blanket being of bearskin. Seeing this had reason to catch my heart by a hook, and I inquired as to the meaning of this. She innocently recounted how it was our wintering blanket, stored at the top of the wardrobe since the last snow. She had given it out to Bres to hang and beat any summer dirt out of. She then arranged it out over our bed and went about with her day.

I have inspected it, and surely it is the blanket we used before. There are no obvious marks of damage, and it is a small fraction compared to the size of the giant that attacked us. But there is a naggling that I cannot get the grasp of. I do not especially have the ken, to how the return of this blanket to our house is meaningful other than what has been explained. I believe myself to be learned of enough to know there is folly here, but the why of it escapes me. These thoughts are constantly at a twirl, and I fear madness encroaching if I do not solve this puzzle, or simply allow it to drift. We have now been together for over a year, we have produced a beautiful child. She has her mysterious ways, but this does not make her a stranger to me. I find myself at a personal impasse. I will not reach a conclusion of my own, and so I must trust in her, and will simply state my troubles. As I have said before, she is my rock to cling to. Nay, a rock is a cold uncaring thing. A danger for ships to beat themselves to death upon. She is the Lighthouse built above the crags. To keep the vessels afloat, away from certain doom. To be relied upon when land is needed and sight is mired by fog.

November 3rd 1896

Bres had assembled a large pyre near the top of the mountain. There is a clearing there Caitlin refers to as "ant gavel", as best as I can say. She was not appreciative of my jokes for this strange collection of words, and refuses to clarify the matter more for me. Privately I prefer to call it Devil's Fork. It features prominently three stony spires, rising vilely up near a cliff's edge. She first brought me to the area last year of this time to show me where she wishes to spend the night in a reflection to her ancestors and loved ones at the first of the month. I am not allowed to stay near it as my presence may cause an imbalance. It has spooked me greatly, and not being permitted to the same secrets to the inner workings of the world as she is, I did not mind waiting the time out. This year was to be different. On the 31st of October, she let it be known to me, that she intended to bring Louis. I was against this, as snow had fallen up there, and bonfire or not, I did not want both of them spending the night there as such. She was to reason that Bres would be near as well, and they would be protected from any harm. I found this risk to be still too much, and proffered to her an exchange. That for when she did not have need of our Lou, to have Bres return him to me, being set up a short distance away, so that we could make the trip back down the mountain and to the safety of our home. I kept my thoughts as still as I could for this moment, as I knew she had a way of spying them out and seeing their intentions. I am shamed to admit, my curiosity was up, and I wished to look upon her and our child. Surely it is only natural, when told you cannot attend to an event by your wife, also involving in your own flesh and blood, that you then only wish for one thing. To sight upon what is so secret concerning them.

I have done as such. I do not know to make of what I have seen, I believe I was given a tonic of some sort beforehand, and it has colored my recollection of events. As to the greater meaning, I cannot attest. As to what I saw, I will endeavor to put it to the paper as best as I am able.

The morning of, being the first day of November. I arose to Caitlin drying her hair by the fire, having strangely woken up before me and having bathed. She was in high spirits for the coming night. The day prior I had prepared a sack of traveling goods for us, and put together a carrier for Lou. After a nice breakfast we set out the back way, shortly joined by Bres, thankfully at respectful distance downwind of us. Hiking up the mountain was a peaceful event, Caitlin whispering to the child of the things we saw, pointing out to whatever caught her fancy and saying the word to him. I myself found it a fitting time to produce my pipe and spend the moment in quiet contemplation for the coming night. Frequently halting for rest, and a long stretch for lunch, saw us arriving to the tree line in the late hours of the day, the sun was beginning to cast its orange glow over us on its descent. Caitlin bade us stop, and for me create a fire. It was to be here, that I would await Bres with our child, and then be escorted back home by him, in the later hours of the night. She prepared a small supper of potato-hash, and a pot of tea, both of us preferring tea over coffee. I do not recall her drinking the tea, and I am sure it was such that was tampered with. It was shortly after finishing our meal, that she said it was time to go. I was overcome with a great sleepiness, and found myself on a blanket next to the fire. Caitlin wishing me a nice rest before my eyes could not stay open any further.

In sleep, I found myself standing in a great expanse of a field of wheat, golden and ready for harvest. It was a bright, cloudless day. However the Sun itself was not up in the sky where it should be, but was instead set onto the ground some distance away. I felt a pull from it, and so began to trek thither. Each step brought a greater radiance from it, and I was soon forced to hold both hands up in attempt to block its blinding light. Stronger and stronger it became, but I could not stop my march. It was so strong that closing my eyes changed nothing, so strong that I could see it through the skin of my hands, shewing through even the bones. When finally, I was sure that I would be reduced to a blinded, burnt out mass at the base of this Sun come to land, it resolved itself into the figure of a man, happily laughing at my confusion.

He had a bright mass of curly blond hair. A fair, if not pale, face of sharp contours. And appeared to be as the same age as I. He had brilliant sky-blue eyes, the likeness of which reminded me of my mother's. He wore a green mantle, pinned with a silvery brooch in the form of a spear. Under this, he had on a white tunic extending to his knees, wrapped with a belt of fine leather at the middle. Dangling from the belt was a sling. In his right hand was a spear, the same the brooch was fashioned after. I saw that the spear was of the similar kind that Caitlin's mountain men had created, though it was without the strange words, inlaid with gold. He pulled me to my feet, for I had fallen in front of him. He greeted me as a friend, but this was more of a feeling. He spoke what sounded like the same language Caitlin used with Bres, but rather than filling my head with a most uncomfortable ache, or sending a shiver down my spine, it instead lifted my spirits. Imparting a light and warmth spreading through my body as he spoke. I tried to explain that I did not understand him. This was met with a well humored smile, and a dismissive wave of the hand. He carried on, and I began to capture an understanding that I was meant to do something for him. This could be no small thing, for this being from the Sun, to need from me. It would take some time before my task were complete. He struck the butt-end of his spear into the ground, releasing it to stand on its own as he placed both hands on my shoulder. He said more confusing words in seriousness, before then changing his likeness to amusement and embraced me in much the same way my father had done when I was a youth, placing a kiss upon my brow and releasing me. I felt then that I was crying, but he shook a finger in my face, keeping the good-natured smile on his. He took a step back, and looked behind me, and signaled that something come forth, or be allowed to act. The act as such, was to pull at my shirtsleeve. I glanced down to find Sona being the one pulling at me, asking with her eyes for me to follow her. I looked back to the man, but he had turned and was away some distance from me. Sona's pulling became ever more insistent, and I awoke to her tugging at me trying to awaken me. My head spun, and I clung to her, the world appearing to twist and reshape wherever I looked. The colors around me were more vibrant than I had ever seen, and there was a gaiety to the plant life that I found amusing and sickening. Sona licked my face and helped restore me to my senses, the strangeness to the world persisted, and my limbs felt weighted, but I was able to capture my faculties a little better. I asked her how she had gotten out of the house, as we made sure to leave her within, but of course she could not answer. I was however grateful for her company. She whined to me with a greater urgency I felt then I understood. She would lead me through the dark to Caitlin and Lou.

She kept a slow pace for me. With my body not feeling as my own, and the moon being on the wane, it made walking difficult over the stony terrain. By and by, though how long I cannot say, we reached a ridge, and I finally began to see the glow of the fire. I was certain near on a hundred years had passed. That I had become like Rip Van Winkle, staggering over rocks, stooped with age, beard trailing between my legs. I constantly checked to be sure it was clear of my feet so that I would not trip. My consternation was not as silent as I thought, and Sona would stop to whine at me and bring me back into the moment and out of fantasy. She brought me near to the top of the ridge, pulling me down to the ground to crawl the rest of the way. I felt obscured enough peering between two large rocks to see the proceedings down below into the natural bowl with those awful stony spires reaching up, receiving the supplication of the fire. Again, I feel the need to state, to absolve myself of a challenge to whim and fancy. I do not know for certain, for what all I observed to be real, or a construct of what I took to be an opiate-induced state of mind.

I first saw the fire, in the center, blazing up into the sky, with opposite sides being stacked higher than the middle, thus the flame forked up like a serpent's tongue. Standing much closer to the bonfire than I know to be possible, was Caitlin, bare of all clothing, and holding an oddly phlegmatic Lou. Presenting him towards that fork in the fire. I bound to my feet in an instant, tearing down the slope with all the speed I could muster before she could offer him to the fire. It is an odd feeling, to know yourself to be making an action but to suffer yourself simultaneously not. For I found, I did not do this, and discovered myself pressed further into the ground where I lay, with Sona on my back. Struggling as I could, pleading with her to get off of me but not having the strength to force it. The fork in the fire cleared, and I saw through to the other side, a man stood there. Or at best, the semblance of what could be called a man, much in a similar way as Bres could have been. He was the night to the man of light in my dream. He was a giant made real, bald but having a dark curly mass of beard covering his lower face. An awful dark visage he had at that, shadows from the flame flickered over it constantly shifting his face into various grimaces. At one point I think that the left side from the eye on out was gone entirely, bloodlessly open to the sky. He looked down upon Caitlin and Lou, through that hellish gap in the blaze, and here I saw the truth in his presentation. With them standing such as they were, they should have been up in flames, and thus I told myself it was not real. Such a thing could not be so. I managed to tear my eyes from this horrible sight, and saw that Bres was prostrated on the ground next to Caitlin, his arms stretched out above his head and fingers going into the flames. In spite of this torture, he endured without sound or movement. Further out, forming a ring at the edge of the light, I first mistook them to be rocks, or part of the terrain, such was their form. Then I took those bulging distortions to be heads, small lithe bodies, and limbs. So many of them prostrate towards the fire, laying upon one another, their skin mottled greens and greys, like a toad's, arranged such that they appeared to be the ground itself. Had Sona not prevented my fantasy, I would have stumbled right onto them, how they blended so well. I suspect these are her Fir Glas Brecc. This leprous colony living somewhere in the mountain, excellent crafters, but I then saw why they would have need of privacy. Surely my tainted mind added so many awful details.

I looked back to the fire, and saw the giant's mouth moving, he then drew his hands together at his massive chest, and began walking backwards towards the rocky spires. With each step he lessened in sight until he was gone. As he vanished, the most awful ululation rose up in the night. Shared by all in attendance save myself, Lou, and Sona. If Caitlin's words to Bres were being injurious to my head when uttered, then this noise cut into me so deeply as to reach my soul. I do not believe anything could ever compare. With the ending of this hellish cacophony, so too lifted the weight from my back. Shakily, I made my way to my feet. I found that the angry din had helped ease the remnants of whatever Caitlin had slipped into the tea, and saw below that Lou was being handed off to Bres. I turned and hurriedly began making my way back to my fire, still shewing itself, lit as a small flicker down the mountain side. Almost to the tree line, I discovered myself alone and without Sona. I risked what I can describe as a loud whisper for her, but received nothing in sight or sound as reply. She had shewn herself to be highly capable this night, and while I missed her presence, I knew that I could trust her to be safe by her own. I arrived to the fire, and arranged myself to be languidly poking at the embers within. Bres came shortly and proffered Lou to me. I noticed then that his massive fingers were blackened, but not damaged. Doing my best to hide my disgust at the stink clinging to Lou, I accepted him greatly into my arms. Awash with a feeling of relief.

Meanwhile Bres made a torch from the fire, while stamping it out with his bare feet. I presumed it to be for my benefit, as I had not ever seen him with one. He made off towards the homestead, torch out to his side, and I followed. Where following Sona up the mountain in my state felt as if time passed so slowly, as to take a century of completion. The opposite trip back home was undertaken in a way that I do not simply comprehend. My mind was returned to its natural state, my faculties operated as I needed them, Bres kept his usual, wide sonorous pace, letting all in our path beware of his coming. And yet, when what felt like a mere twenty minutes had gone by, I spied a tree I knew well, a gnarled knot at its midsection, informing me that we were a passing short distance from home. Asking Bres anything would have been useless. And so, in less than thirty minutes time, we reached the back stoop of the house, in what should have taken two or more hours of slow going, picking our way through the dark. I further confirmed this, by checking my timepiece that I had left on the bed. When I had returned to my campfire, the moon and stars at their points in the sky, suggested the time to be sometime after midnight. My timepiece was to shew the hour being approximately one-forty. The mystery of Sona's presence had also been resolved as well. As I entered the cabin, she came bounding from her bed to greet us in the manner common to dogs. It's as if she never left, and how could she have? She cannot manage the door, nor could her pace have matched ours for her to return inside, and then lay in her bed to be as asleep and well rested as she seemed to be. I feel the deeper mysteries of this night will never be solved. I would need the wherewithal of Sherlock Holmes to make the leaps and bounds to ideas, then to the correct questions I do not know if I want the answers to. Who or what was this devil she communed with through the flames?

Lou, being sound asleep was delivered to his bed, and I went to mine. Light was beginning to make early morning known, through the window, when Caitlin returned to me under the blankets. A cold hand found its way under my bed-clothes, and I turned to greet her, smelling of smoke and as bare as when I espied her, her eyes were ablaze and the vixen's sly smile played upon her lips. I asked if her night had gone well, she told me it was as goodly as could be wanted. Her blood was up, and she wished for mine to be as well. This was easily accomplished with kisses about my neck. When she began to pull up my bed-clothes, the concerns I had from earlier were torn asunder. It is only now, these few days later and upon entry of them, they return to me. Maybe I am bewitched by her, to be so easily distracted. Maybe I want to be, so that I do not have to face a greater truth that I am ever clueless to.

XII. The Survivor

Third Interview:

Thanks for coming back. I wasn't sure if you actually would. Thanks for being so understanding. I suppose this will be it though right? I mean, sorry, no, I'm not trying to prolong this. I got distracted yesterday. Talking about Nicky like that. They tell me to focus on the good moments. Then I ask what I do with the bad? And I get these responses that are little better than an "him and a haw." The good moment lasted for the first day. After that it was just a decent into Hell. It's worse, because you don't even know you're going to Hell.

They stole our food, broke the radio, I mean, how else do you explain it not working? Then they destroyed our tent. We finally got the message at that point. They didn't want us there. At least, it seemed like that was what they were saying? I said as much to Nicky, it was escalating every night. We had to go. So, that's what we decided on. We would go back to the base camp, and tell them we had been harassed nonstop out there. Jim and Chan were upset of course, but this wasn't part of the contract they signed. And since stuff was happening to all of us, that said it wasn't related to the show. So we started off that morning to go back to base. It shouldn't have taken us very long, Jim said he was good with distance and stuff in a forest, and had a good idea where we were and where the camp was. A full day's worth of hiking should get us there shortly after nightfall. It was not a nice stroll through the woods that day. Getting there seemed easier actually, getting out was this awful slog of what felt like mostly going uphill, having to dodge either sharp pointy rocks, or roots to snag a foot in. It felt like we hadn't made any progress. We were exhausted, Spider and I had our gear, we weren't about to leave that behind for someone to steal too. Production would've had our assess for that, and said "screw your excuses" when it came to taking it out of our paychecks. We took turns carrying it that day. Useless junk that only slowed us down with every step. But we didn't see that. There wasn't a greater picture of danger. Why would there be? This happens to other people, it doesn't happen to you. By nightfall we had to stop. The going was too rough to continue. We found this space between two trees that made this natural alcove and settled in for the night. The crews were given these little single pot camping stoves, I think they may have come from the same place as the army food. But it worked, and Nicky had some hot cocoa packets, so we had that mixed into the hot water for "supper". We fell asleep that night jumbled together and with a nice warmth in our bellies.

And then we woke up in the morning, freezing like hell. We were so tired though, we slept through the entire night, and nothing bothered us about it. Spider got the little cooking stove going again, and the leftover cocoa stuff from the night before got more water added, and another packet. And that was breakfast. It was nice to have that warmth again, but the sleep we had, was much like what we had been getting, it just wasn't very restful. Tired, sore, a little cranky, we started off again with Jim leading the way. That was when we were fully in Hell. And even while being there, I never though "oh, this is wrong, I'm not supposed to be here." That's the other thing I decided about being in Hell. Once you're there, it's perfectly normal. You don't see the wrongness of it. You don't know you're supposed to be scared and looking for a way out. When the person in front of you starts swaying like a blade of grass in the wind. And you're trying to figure out why this piece of grass has legs, and clothes, and why does it look like their hair has turned to a great glob of paint? You might ask that, but you just accept it as being a part of your life.

I wish it had memory altering effects too, I wish I could have just woken up, days, weeks, months, whatever later and never known what had happened. I'd rather live with the mystery of that. No, I don't want to stop this time. Thank you, this is what you came for right? I don't know what you hope to get out of this. I guess if it helps pay for me to stay here, then I don't care anymore. It's yours to do with as you please after this. I've done drugs before, nothing hard. Had even smoked Spider's pot with him a few nights. This was something else. The world turned into a moving painting, still wet and overloaded with paint. It bled everywhere. It twisted and swirled. It was funny for a while. I remember Nicky and I holding each other up against a tree, laughing at the living bark. I could still talk, the others could still talk. We'd try to explain what we were seeing. I think Spider was handling it better than the rest of us. He was the only one who could walk more than a few steps without tripping. It didn't take long for any of us to forget what we were supposed to be doing though. When you can look at your hands, and see your finger's spiral into this fractal going down to the ground, how can you stay focused? Then Chan saw something in a tree. She said it was a witch. There was a witch in the tree, and she was going to take us away. And we looked, but there wasn't anything. Then Nicky said she saw it too, she said it was this old creepy hag with rat teeth, and she had feet like a bird, grasping on the branch. And both of them were freaking out saying how she wouldn't stop staring at them, she wouldn't blink. Just sat there like a gargoyle, watching.

I was scared, because I wasn't seeing it. Jim and Spider thought it was funny and were trying to make jokes about it. Nicky and Chan were clinging to each other, yelling at it to stop looking at them, to go away. And I was in front of them, looking at the trees, trying to see it. And I turned around to tell them I couldn't see it, why couldn't I see it? Was something wrong with me? Was I going blind? But I could see them, their faces. The fear in their faces deepening, getting stronger, bleeding and twisting with their mouths gaping wider and wider. That terrified me more than not being able to see their witch, and then I felt something go by overhead, that trail of wind, a whoosh, a swoop. They fell to the ground screaming, and I ran. I just left them. I couldn't help it. That was my "fight or flight" response, and I found out "flight" is what my body decided on that day. They tell me it's nothing to feel guilt over, it's a deep down thing that people don't usually have control over. Some people stand their ground and try to fight, some freeze up, some bolt and run. I ran so fast I thought maybe I was flying, everything was blurring by me. I guess that part deep down responsible for me running, was also able to keep me going like that on autopilot over the rocks and roots that had been giving us so much trouble.

When I stopped running, I had no idea where I was, nothing would stay the same anyway. I'd turn one way, then another, then turn back again, and each time I saw something different. I sat down against a tree then, I felt like my head was on a roller coaster, everything would swing and swirl and sway around, but I know I was sitting still. I tried calling out for them, but sometimes it felt like my mouth was still closed, and I was yelling with my thoughts, hoping they'd hear me that way. I felt much bigger than my body then, like my psyche was expanding outside my body, and if I could just get it to touch them, then we'd be linked and they'd know where I was, I'd know where they were. And then something stung my leg. It was small, like an ant, or a bee. Except I'm allergic to bees. And I jump up, and I look for what stung me. But I didn't see anything, and then it stung me again, this time on my back. Then again, and again, over and over. I was being stung everywhere. But I couldn't see them, I couldn't feel them. It had to be ants, tiny ants with big stingers. I dropped my pants first, and I had welts everywhere, tiny dots of blood at the center of them. Swirling around, then puckering like angry volcanoes. And I had to laugh a bit, you know? I had ants in my pants. And it just made so much sense, that if I took off my clothes, the stinging would stop.

The stinging stopped, like I thought it would. I tried so hard to look through my clothes to find the ants, bugs, animals, anything, but it was so hard to focus on one single point. It would swirl and melt and that became much more interesting than looking for some insect. Eventually I got distracted by something else, a noise, the call of a bird. And I was off, seeing myself as some nymph of the forest. Everything I touched swirled and bloomed a kaleidoscope of colors, I thought I was doing magic. It was so easy to leave the worries and fears behind. One minute running scared, the next, prancing around naked. I had entertained the thought of what would happen if I found one of the others, and I had decided that I would fuck them on the spot. Sorry, can I say that? It's too much isn't it? Most conversations in here kinda go full in, and sometimes I forget if what I say is as appropriate as it should be. I appreciate your understanding. Thanks. No, it wasn't that I felt like I wanted sex then, it was more of the role I thought I was in. Like I had stumbled into a Midsummer's Night Dream, and I was one of the fairies, a nymph. That's what nymphs do right? Find some person, seduce them, make a comedy out of it? I had really hoped it would be Nicky I'd find. It wasn't though.

I heard water, and came to this massive river. And yeah, I know, there aren't any huge rivers around there. And I knew this then too. But like everything else, I didn't question it, it was there before me, and so it existed. Out in the middle of this river was a boulder, and atop it sat a naked woman with a mass of very curly black hair. Her back was to me, and all I wanted to do was get out there and kiss it, her back, her shoulders, her neck. She didn't move, but I heard her voice, musical and lyrical, like some classy Irish or Scottish actor accent. "Then come and kiss me", she said. The water was rushing by, but I wasn't scared, I stepped off the bank into a sea of ferns, the rock rising up out of the middle. They were cold, and wet, brushing against me as I walked through them. I made it to the rock, it had an easy slope to climb up, and I made my way to where this woman was. I sat behind her, and pulled her into me, sweeping her mass of hair aside while I kissed her shoulders, her neck. It was amazing, I was in Heaven, this feeling of electricity was shooting through my whole body. I didn't know if she was real. I could have been making out with a tree stump for all I knew at that point. She felt real though, I felt her fingers on my arms. Her nails scratching at my skin. She turned her head to give me her mouth, I saw her face, and she looked older than me, even more so than I am now, then she looked young, younger, no more than a child, then back to an adult. It was dizzying to see. I had to shut my eyes, so I wouldn't fall over. She laughed and music came forth. When I opened my eyes, I saw her front teeth were larger with one overlapping the other a bit. I thought, who is this woman? I don't remember saying that out loud, but she answered me. She said she was everyone, she was no one. Then she kissed me. It was intense. I imagine it's like light getting sucked into a black hole. It felt like she was taking my entire being in, stretching me out. I felt it down to my toes. It was the best kiss I've ever had, the worst kiss I've ever had, it was the last kiss I have ever had.

I wasn't even aware that I had blacked out. I came to on my back. It was night then, and there were fires lit on these poles around us. She was sitting on me. I felt something on my stomach, and looked down, and saw that she had a penis, I gasped and blinked, and then it was a horn tied around her waist, like some crazy medieval strap-on. I looked at her then, I told her no I did not want that thing in me. But her face was twisted, contorted into this, I don't know, like, like, like a mask, like someone made a human face mask, but you know right away when you see it, it's wrong, it's what's it called? Yes, thank you, the uncanny valley. It was like that. Her face wasn't her face, there was something else under it. I said no to her. I struggled under her, but she was strong. She held me down, and I screamed and raged at her, but she was just so impossibly strong. She bent forward and bit my breast, hard. Don't take this the wrong way, but look, I still have the scar. That was real, I know that was real. You can even see the overlapping teeth. When she bit me, she took her hands off my wrists and put them onto my shoulders. Hitting her was like hitting a stone. And so I put my hands out, trying to find something, anything, and there it was, this smooth river stone that fit perfectly into my hand. I grabbed it and smashed it into the side of her head. She fell off me, out of me, onto her back, and I climbed on top of her, and started hitting her in the head with the rock. Over and over, until she stopped struggling back. I screamed at her broken face.

But something else was wrong, she didn't have the mass of black hair, it was just smooth brown hair, and in that bloody mess of her face I could see Nicky's eyebrow ring, a small gold one I bought her for her birthday one year. And the body I was sitting on wasn't naked, didn't have this torture device strapped on, it was Nicky's body. But she didn't rape me, she didn't bite me. Those were real, it happened in that moment too. "They" the always present "they who are them" tell me it was of course the drugs. That the whole thing might not have even happened. There was never a body, there was only my account of it. Maybe the bite came from someone else earlier, maybe it did come from her, it didn't match any dental records they had though. They know something awful happened, but that's it. It didn't help anything that when I began crying and screaming over Nicky, that these things started laughing all around me. These fucking nightmarish green monsters. The cops thought I meant aliens early on, like I was trying to make it into some fucked up alien abduction story. But these weren't aliens. They looked more like someone took a toad, and put it in a ten-year-old's body. They had large eyes, lots of sharp pointed teeth, a long nose, and big pointy ears. I know how it sounds. They pointed at me, and laughed. It was the most cruel laughter you can imagine. Malicious, that's the word, it was malice personified. At this point I was in shock? There were so many things going on around me, in me, even shock doesn't sound right, but I don't know if there's a better word. I ran again. I still had the rock, and when I went at this mass of monsters around me I hit one of them with it. I carried that rock with me for days after. It had this black spot on it that was the thing's blood. It smelled awful, fishy, moldy. That was my proof, that it was real, along with the bite.

Then the forest let me go. That part is blurry for me, I remember a guy asking if I was okay, then there were lights from the cops and ambulance, lots of people. Then I woke up in the hospital. My mom said a truck driver saw me stumbling out of the forest and falling on the road. I don't know how I survived up to then. I should have frozen to death at night. I don't remember sleeping. I remember clutching the stone. I remember always moving, always running away from what happened. I didn't eat, I didn't drink. I don't think I did at least. I should not have made it. I should have curled up and died somewhere. That's why I say the forest let me go. I ran so much I should have left it several times over. It went on forever, that mountain always at my back.

Then came the questions, constant infuriating questions. Had I been with anyone else, had I seen anyone else, where were they, what were we doing, why was I found naked? And I would tell one person everything I knew, everything that happened, and they would leave. Then the next day it was another person and the same routine over again. I wanted to help, I really did. But everything I said was picked apart, doubted. The doctors, nurses, they did what they could. My parents too. At first they didn't want to get a lawyer. I was the victim, why should there be a lawyer? They couldn't even say whether or not a crime had been committed. I came out covered in blood, mud, and anything else that could stick to you in a forest. It was all so jumbled up, that they couldn't even say the blood was mine, or anyone else's. And I get it now, I really do. I was a mess, everything I said was just beyond comprehension for everyone. Blood work couldn't even conclude that I had in fact been drugged. So all that got me was a "Huh, yup, sounds like you were under the influence of something".

Finally my parents gave in and got me a lawyer. After that it was sweet silence for a while. He handled everything, knew what to say to everyone. Somewhere during that whirlwind of hospital, interviews, and interrogations, the others were found. Their stories were more coherent, it was all just some fucked up cult. Fanatical college types trying to give their leader Miles the ultimate t.v. show. Oh yes, this is the exact same eye roll I had back then too.

My parents latched onto that narrative too. And then came the sleazy lawyer. He was going to get us all the money he could. He tried to "coach" me so much about what to say, I was drugged by the cult. Maybe I was a member? Maybe Nicky was? But oh, don't say anything about the little green men. No, no, no, we can't talk about aliens being there. I hated him so much. I would just smile and nod, be an idiot for this awful person, and he'll leave me alone. And then I was talking to another lawyer, this one worked for "the bad guys" as I remember thinking. And he was just as bad. Same questions as always. But he wanted to discredit me so much, throw a kink into the lawsuit to get it thrown out you know? I was the crazy one who saw aliens. Who claimed to have beaten her best friend to death with a rock. Who went against what the others claimed. That I was lying, that they were probably lying too. And just like everything else it just went on and on. Until it didn't. I never heard a reason why, I don't know if there even was a reason. But TKN folded, it's like they just said "fuck it, here you go." and paid out to all of us. And I thought, okay, it's done, it's over. My parents will be set for the rest of their lives. And then I swallowed a bottle of pills.

And back into a hospital I went, yet again, and then in-patient care at my first clinic. And it was nice, I could talk about everything that was bothering me, and I think for a time it did help. And then I was back home, with mom and dad. I didn't have much of a life going on, going anywhere was way too much for me. My parents were good about it though, told me it was okay, just focus on myself. Try to get better. And I went to my sessions, and life; it was looking up just the tiniest little bit. Then neighborhood animals started to go missing, flyers were beginning to pop up. I didn't think anything of it. Then knocking on the front door started one night. The next it was the front and back. They'd ring the doorbell too, until the day my dad disconnected it. He'd go barging out at night in his pajamas a bat at the ready to swing at anything that moved, but there was nothing there. I think it was about a week into this, they wanted to have a talk with me. That's when they asked why I was doing what I was doing to the animals. I didn't understand. I wasn't doing anything to any animals. My mom, ever the one to put a positive spin on denial, said to my dad that maybe I was sleep walking, I didn't know. I saw then, how upset my dad was, angry and disappointed, all with me. I told them to tell me what was going on.

In the morning, after the knocking had stopped, there would be one of the missing pets either at the front, or back door. Broken and mangled, splayed out on a cross of bundled sticks. Gutted, and with the eyes missing, my parents were horrified. Dad was for immediately calling the cops. Mom thought otherwise. What if this was me coping, what if I was sleep walking and didn't know it? What if, what if, what if? That's what it amounted to from them. I don't know why they didn't come to me straight away. I asked of course, there's no way it could have been me. I mean, I was even there at the door with some of the knocking, so how could that even work? But dad said that the night before, he stayed up, watching through the window in their bedroom, looking out into the backyard. The knocking had actually stopped early that night, a storm had come instead with its own noise. In the later hours of the night, he said there had been a flash of lightning, and in that flash, he had seen me out in the yard crouched over something big. More flashes followed, he said like someone taking pictures, a flash showed me standing, then the next saw me leaving. I asked why he didn't come to me right then, if he had caught me in the act, that's what he should have done. He said I was naked. As if that was meaning enough. But I understood it all then for him. He had had a puritanical upbringing. He could never have confronted me if I had been in the nude. Along with the sacrilege I was committing with the animals... They were scared, of me. I had gone out, their sweet college grad little girl, and come back some twisted version of that. Quiet, withdrawn, never leaving the house, let alone barely my room. Then these things at night. I didn't handle it well. I got angry at them. How could they believe that of me? I didn't know what my dad saw, but it most definitely was not me. What about after? Did I track mud and water into the house? Or better yet, blood? How was I gutting these poor animals? Where were their organs? They actually told me to settle down. Like they just hadn't put me in this position where I had to defend myself to them. After everything on that mountain, and then to have my parents scared of me. I said fine, I'll prove it to you. I had him nail the window shut. Then he changed the doorknob around, so the lock was out in the hall. The whole time my mother was nearby, making this I don't know, sad puppy dog face. I was just so mad. When he was finished, it was late afternoon, but I slammed the door and told them to lock it anyway. My mom brought me supper later, then I used the bathroom and went to bed. There was no knocking that night, no crucified, defiled animals, nothing. The next day, both of them, like sad puppies put this leaflet in front of me, there was a clinic nearby, a couple' hours to the west; it specialized in "problem cases" like me. People with severe trauma and poor coping mechanisms. With the payout from TKN, I would get the best possible care there. That was it for me, the straw that broke the camel's back. I was so emotionally drained, so tired. My thinking was that either I would try this, or try another way to kill myself. The thing of it is though, I loved them. Even through the anger towards them, and the apathy I felt for myself, I didn't want to disappoint them. So I decided I would try it for them.

The first night, I heard them, those little bastards, laughing outside my window. Taunting me. And it all finally clicked. I really did think I was going crazy. They're good at that. They know how to get under your skin, how to influence people, events, things, whatever they want. I wasn't smart about it. I told my doctor as soon as I was able. Hey doc, good news, I'm not crazy. It was the goblins that did it. Same as before. He had heard every excuse for every problem in here beforehand, so mentioning the creatures outright had zero effect on him. It was just another problem of a crazy person, so on he rolled with it. Every night they came, more taunts, more maliciousness spewing from them. Encouraging me to give up and die. They thought they had broken me, that I just needed some extra pushing. They were wrong, I was going to live to spite them. And I have. Sometimes I hear Nicky out there with them. Taunting, laughing, screaming, crying. Anything and everything you can imagine happening to her. I dread those nights, it's nightmarish. So yes, I am terrified of them, my bravery extends only as far as these walls do. They don't try to tell me kill myself so much anymore. The tactic they use now is to tell me what they'll do to me once they can get to me. I don't know why they don't come in here. I don't think they like man-made things. We had an old fairy tale book in the common room here, there was a story in it about a man warding off some magical creature with iron forged horseshoes. Maybe there's truth to that? I think the bars on the windows around here are wrought iron. I've been here for over 20 years now, you'd think if they could have gotten me by now, they would have right? I know I'm not living the life I wanted, but I'm okay here. And with your "donation", I can stay here even longer. But the others, you have to warn them. If they've talked about it, they're not safe. You probably aren't by now either you know? I don't think they were ever safe. No one is. *End of Interview.*

XIII. The Prospector

November 28th 1896

Edmond and his men have since returned to us and finished the work upon the house. It is truly most magnificent. Nearly doubled in size, the space is enough to host several families. The work being completed in finality without further delays, the workers appeared to be moping about at the demise of their job. For the hardships experienced, I granted them the bonus I had previously discussed with Edmond. Mr. Farkas himself will be staying on with us, in a bedroom made up for him on the other side of the house, originally designed to be parlor beside my office, it was easy enough to make a conversion. He of course proved himself masterful with a hammer, and having an excellent connection to the laboring class in Portland, I have put him in charge of all future carpentry and constructions. He was grateful to have returned to us, his time away seemed to cause him some sort of distress, though he could not explain the why of it. He had a great calling in his heart to be near to us. I am pleased to have someone else about the place. Caitlin abhors the pipe, and having another soul to sit with, especially under the expanse of the night sky in quiet contemplation while we puff away has been most agreeable to us.

Recently I have been hearing the howl of a seemingly lone wolf in the distance during the later hours, I believe it has established residence near us. I have asked him over it. Knowing he sometimes is taken to amble around in the night after our smokes, but he carries the appearance to be unconcerned. Wolves may like the easy prey of livestock at times, but they do not desire to be so close to people, I am told. They seem to have an uncanny understanding that man can be the more dangerous to them when provoked. He has not heard it, however, for when he is asleep lately, he sleeps as though dead. So far removed from the waking world he claims, not even the mountain exploding as a volcano could arouse him now. Still, it would not hurt to make better, the housing for the chickens and goats. The loss of which, while an inconvenience to us, are easily replaced. But setting a precedent to this wolf that it may lay claim to our stock is not something we wish to have upon us. Edmond does believe that the goddamned stink of Bres is probably enough to keep anything with a strong working nose miles away from us.

With assurances from Caitlin that we are to be soon snowed in to the point that travel will be nigh on impossible, I am sending Mr. Farkas out to Portland to buy up supplies for our wintering. I myself will set-out tomorrow to Seattle, having two more bars of gold I wish to make a deposit of. And to hopefully pick up an order placed the last time I visited.

December 10th 1896

There is a tragedy to life in this world, of which that gold has cause for men to become monsters most foul. I do not believe I will be returning to Seattle. I am expecting Edmond to come round any day now, having made use of the wagon, and the amount he should be carrying will of course set him to a slower pace. But on his return, and with the coming of spring, I shall send him in my stead to make an establishment in Portland for my needs. Dark tidings I bring once again to this.

I made it to Seattle making excellent time, Douglas was most invigorated by the cold weather, and the allowance to run full tilt did him much good. Gold exchanged, bank visited, I made my way to a specific store and found my order complete and waiting. An Edison Phonograph, along with a fine selection of what I'm told to be the best music from around the world to be presented to Caitlin for Yule. This practice of gift giving she is not fond of. But I find it hard to break with some traditions, and expect her to be most surprised by this. Happy and full of hope I was, I wish to stay only so long as to see my tasks finished, and allow Douglas a good rest in Mr. Johnson's stalls, having been asked to dinner and overnight with him and his wife, I was happy to oblige.

The next morning I set out on the return trip, taking the same path out of town as I have before. About an hour had passed, and along the road I came up to a riderless horse all by its lonesome, seeing it kitted for travel, I called out asking if anybody was near, rifle in hand to be sure. A youth appeared, coming forth from a copse of concealing pines. He was in great distress, claiming to have been riding with his pa when the horse reared on them, throwing them both. His father was in a frightful state, unable to get up. Wishing to administer aid, I dismounted from Douglas and bade the young man to lead the way. We came to his father, still and on his stomach and I feared the worst. I rushed to his side, placed my rifle to the ground, and commenced turning him. It was with that, that I was met with a heinous smile and the barrel of a pistol from him. I made for my rifle, but it was already up and in the hands of the youth, and pointed at me as well. I stayed on my knees, my arms up in the air. A call from the man brought forth three more men on horseback from hiding. A conversation went as follows.

'Told you it would work didn't I Art?'

'Sure did.'

'This the guy?'

'He was on that big black horse right?'

'Sure was.'

'This should be him. Hey, what's your name mister?'

Stupidly, I thought they were not there for me, and thus did I truthfully tell them my name. Imagining this to be a great misunderstanding since they were not trying to outright rob me.

'Yup, he's the guy.'

'Mister, we hear tell that you found yourself a claim out there, made you mighty rich. How about you take us to it, and maybe share some of that wealth with your fellow men here?'

I tried to reason with the man named Art, seeming to be the leader of this gang. I told him it was a small, decent find that set me up, but I had not found anything since then. As I see it now, he rightfully doubted me. I believe, those most often who are to traffic with thievery, tend to see their traits reflected in others. He had no reason to believe me. I received a hard cuff upon my ear for this, and was told to lead them on either way. To be miserly with it again would receive me a greater punishment than a slap upside the head. I was taken back to Douglas, happily chewing on grass where he was left with the other horse. Tied up with a line extending out to prevent my escape we set out.

The youth was revealed to being a young woman named Cora Lynn, wearing boys clothing as a disguise, she rode with Art, arms wrapped around him. No one paid any more heed to me except to tell me when to stop. I tried once again during the ride, to reason with Art, knowing that they would never get what they wanted. He did not understand that it was not for my family that I feared, but for him and his gang. When I brought this to his attention, it of course returned with a laugh in my face. They had heard plenty of threats before, but I was sure to give them the biggest haul of their life, and they were not about to back down. Ed, Henry, and Walt were the other names I discerned from the highwaymen. They talked often about what they wished to do with the wealth they were coming to. Miss Cora Lynn wanted to settle with Art, this being said, a look of sly knowledge would pass between the men. I presumed that she was not the first woman to be lured in by Art, and her naivety shewn as much as mine earlier on account of trying to bargain. Ed and Henry were brothers, planning on returning to their home state of Kentucky to reunite with another, older brother. Walt, being familiar with the legend of Wild Bill Hickok was planning on going to South Dakota to drink and dally in the brothels of Deadwood, I suspected this to be the same plan as Art, once Clara had filled her use to him.

We stopped for the final night in the same spot as when Sona came to me. With me taking up the position of the sad pathetic one in place of her on the other side of the fire. I had a passing thought, if perhaps she had belonged to them the year prior, and inquired thusly to them *losing a black lab, but was met with silence and a curious look. Miss Cora Lynn was given the duty of getting me settled for the night and provided me with a hard drink from a tin, and a piece of old bread, which I thanked her for. Her eyes did not meet mine, and I began to see in her a modest amount of regret. I awoke first, the next morning to a freezing wind and a dusting of snow over my blankets. The others woke up shortly after in a sour mood. Henry and Walt were in charge of building the morning fire back up, and providing us with something warm for our bellies. Their bellies I should say, there was not enough coffee to go around, and I was not proffered any. The snow kept falling, gaining in size, and it became clear to us that we were to be within a snowstorm. Again my naivety came to the fore, I saw this had to have been an act of providence, a blizzard to perhaps blow them off course, dissuade them from this doomed idea. It was not to be. Art said it would be a trip to Hell first before they turned around, I told him without intimation, following this path would lead him directly there. This was only met with a laugh. After they had the gold, maybe I would be allowed to have it out with Art, then we would see who the greater threat was. I told him he misunderstood once again. I was trying to save them, protect them from what would become a horrible fate. The only look of concern coming from Miss Cora Lynn, the rest of my words having fallen on deaf ears. I was put upon the horse for the final leg of the trip. Douglas knew the way home even better than I at this point, snow being such as it was by then. I only sat in contemplation of our imminent arrival while he led the way.*

The sudden coming of the blizzard slowed us considerably. We stopped for the others to tether themselves together as it became harder to see past our own noses. It came to the point for me to know I was not alone when I would feel the tug of the rope around me. I had a curious moment, when I became thankful to Miss Cora Lynn for bundling me up as well as she had, I was cold, but my extremities were protected enough I did not fear losing them. Unfortunately I was tied too well to my horse, and could not free myself as such, knowing they could not catch sight me ahead. Much longer was this ride to be than usual, for dusk had begun to quickly fall upon us, darkening our way even further. Art in his final bout of impatience rode up next to me. Surprising me with his appearance whilst Miss Cora Lynn hitched a lantern to the saddle, inquiring to how much longer it would be. I was able to give him a nod in the forward direction, for through the blinding snow were flickers of light from a cabin greatly lit. He let out a yell of excitement and told the others we were there. I wished to call out to Caitlin in this moment, but feared she would not hear me over the howling of the winds, and in truth, I feared too what retribution I would receive from Art. From making sight of the home, I dreaded every step that brought us closer. Then we were upon it, I directed them to the shed for the horses then was marched through the snow to the door, open and waiting our arrival.

I spoke of truth only a moment ago, another truth now is that I do not wish to write of what happens next. I hear a whisper from Caitlin even though she sleeps now. Sensing my hesitation, encouraging me to push further. They were thieves, they were to be our killers, us or them. Every good reason to justify their demise. Pain, suffering, heartbreak, loss, all these things they would have given to us had they had their way. Caitlin was not surprised to see them push their way in after me, Walt closing the door to the cold. She greeted them kindly, knowing how hard it must have been to get to us through the terrible storm outside, so grateful was she, that we had not lost our way. She bade us to come to the table, for a dinner was set for us. I knew for her, the game was on, and now any role I had in it, was finished. Their guns were out, but she said they were not needed, she was aware what they were there for, and she was happy to provide. A look of confusion was about them, and they followed her into our new and seldom used dining room. The table was set as she stated, and they lit upon it like starving dogs on meat, picking up the forks, knives, and plates, and marveling at the craftsmanship, the pure shine of the gold. Cora Lynn looked about in consternation, asking what they were playing at. There wasn't any gold there, just the iron implements. Art told her to fix her eyes, the forks alone would fetch a pretty penny. She looked to me, then to Caitlin, panic in her eyes, asking what was wrong with them. Caitlin spoke softly to say they had a touch of the gold fever. Art overhearing replied to say how could one not, when surrounded by such wealth. I was most surely lying when I told him my claim was a small one.

He demanded to know where the mine was, eyes wide with greed. Addressed as I was, it was again Caitlin who placed more bait under their noses. We had a small mine up the mountain, it in fact had a cart full of the precious ore just waiting to be carried off. Henry caught notice of her and breaking his eyes away from the cutlery, commenting how he was going to carry her off too, she blushed, giving to him a sly wink. From above us came the cries of Lou, woken from the noise. This seemed to break Art from his gold-lust, his short temper having cause to grow angry with a child for taking away from his enjoyment. Demanding someone to silence the baby, lest he bash it to the wall. Caitlin asked to be let to go fetch him, and Henry said he would attend with her, to make sure she would not be going for a gun. The fire in his eye proclaiming for more, I meant to fulfill a husband's duty, and speak against this, but a look from Caitlin prompted me to let it be. I bit my tongue, and watched them proceed through the door.

The men broke their reverie when she left the dining room, and set about scrounging away at the food and drink set therein. From above, there came a sudden thump to the floor, Cora let out a noise of fear and looked to Art for reassurance. He was this time lost in the food, his face buried in a chicken half, worrying at the meat like the dog he was, I saw that it was raw. With the departure of Caitlin, I suffered a loss of appetite. This seemed to lift a veil from my eyes, and the feast laid out on the table twisted to raw meat turned to green and black, fruit and vegetables rotted to the point where they should have been returned to the earth. Cora, I am sure noticed at the same moment as I, she turned from Art, mouth agape with such fear and confusion, I felt sympathy for her, much as I do now. I told her, in a fit of chivalry, that it would be most important for her to stay near to me, I would see her through the best I could. I was not sure if she understood my words.

Not much time later, Caitlin returned carrying Lou, Henry shuffled in behind her, silent and with the fire from before gone from his eyes. His countenance then resembled someone who had just been awoken in the middle of a good sleep. He slowly fumbled the way to the table, digging into the repugnant food such as his friends. Caitlin was not content to wait for them to finish, proclaiming them to be gentlemen, she asked if it were not time for them to collect their prize? Art, still managing to be the speaker of this febrile bunch, belched out a putrid agreement and rose from the table, slapping the heads of the others to stir them demanding for us all to get a move on. We filed out into the common room. It was here that Henry stated in a sluggish manner, that I should stay with the baby, and Caitlin could shew the way. The glint coming into Art's eye's was enough to tell me what he thought of the idea. Further setting it to stone when he told Cora to wait upon me with my rifle, to shoot me, and the child if I so much as tried to escape. Again I wanted to protest, and as before Caitlin gave me a look, this was her plan, she would see it to fruition, I was but a mere passenger to this horrible night. Cora however raised a voice of concern, couldn't they see that she was a witch? That she had put a spell over them, they should wait for the storm to blow through, then go out during the day. Art dismissed her concern as reading too many tall tales, they wanted to get there before the mine got buried, if not, they had to wait till spring to dig it out. It hadn't snowed so much this day that they couldn't get to it. His final nail came into his coffin when she asked what about her, to which he simply, cruelly retorted, what about you? A cold stoniness set upon her face, she told them to go on and get then, to freeze out there for all she cared. Caitlin in her day attire headed for the door, caught by the arm by Art, inquiring whether she was not going to dress for the blizzard. Her return of "I was born in a place much colder than this will ever be" was said so, that even I was surprised by it. With that she headed out, the men following, into the blustery dark.

The three of us left behind, left an emptiness to the room that I felt down into my bones. I knew there would be no way to save those men, that time had long since passed. But for Miss Cora Lynn I had hope. She set about to closing the door, fighting the wind trying to keep it open, getting it in place, she turned to me with tears streaming;

'What is this place? Why were they like that?'

'My wife certainly has a way about her. She always gets her way. I'm sorry you got into it. I do not believe your friends will be coming back.'

'What do you mean, of course they are, they won't leave me.'

'There is no mine Miss Cora, that was bait for them. There are others in the wilderness that are in her employ, they will be waiting. Put down my gun, when the time comes, get your self behind me, maybe I can save you.'

'When the time comes? What time would that be Mister?'

'When my wife returns. She will, and you do not want to be holding that there rifle when she does.'

'Shut up will you. They're coming back. Ain't nothing out there that scares Art, the Law's tried to get him several times, and he gave them the slip. You'll see. He's coming back for me.'

I sat then in silence, Lou sleeping in my arms as if no problem at all existed. Cora paced to and fro about the room, I tried once more to reason with her, but she would not have it. The wind ceased its incessant howling against the house, the resultant silence was as loud as it were without. I asked her to open the door, as I believed the storm had passed, she did so, shewing me to be correct, the outside ground covered in a thick coating of snow, the path carved through it was partially buried. I cannot say for certain how much time had passed in the interim, perhaps half of an hour. There was a silence to the outside air that only winter can bring. The type that allows one to hear a branch snap miles away as if it were next to you, this stillness held no indication that anyone was outside at all. We might as well have been the only people in the land. Cora waited at the door a moment more, watching for anything, a torch's light, listening for the men's raucous laughter coming back with their prize. She was given nothing but silence. I asked for her then to close it, to keep the heat in, and she did so. Resuming her pacing about the room.

A half hour more or so passed us by again with nothing, I managed to get Miss Cora to accompany me to return Lou to his bed. Her agitation was still high, but it was easy to see she had a soft way for him, and she did not begrudge me this. I was sure by then, Caitlin would be on her way back, having finished this sordid business. We both jumped with fright, when a panicked banging came to us from the door below. In her fear, and haste, Miss Cora left me by the wayside, so I yielded thus to quickly follow behind her. Knowing it not to be Caitlin. As Cora reached the door, I shouted to her to wait, but it was to no avail. She flung it open with Art's name crying from her mouth. In stumbled Ed, supporting Art with his arm flung over a shoulder. I saw that Art's body was littered with the same blackened quills as the bear. Ed seemed to fair no better. They fell to the floor, Art lay unmoving, but Ed was trying to stand back up, yelling in a drunken manner to close the door, that He was coming. I assumed this to be Bres, but was further surprised when Henry came limping in clutching my splitting axe in his hands. He had the look of a dullard about him, and had no care that the cause of his limp was his foot bent in a way that it was surely broken. He was bleeding profusely from bullet wounds to his chest, part of his scalp was hanging to the side of his head as well. I watched with a horrific fascination as Henry raised the axe, and brought it down on Ed's leg, biting deep into it, snapping the bone. Ed let forth a howl that I will soon not forget. Cora not understanding, cried for Henry to stop this. Art shewed himself to be coming slowly to, realization coming upon him, he bade Cora to shoot Henry, he had become touched and would kill all of them if she did not. Henry had extracted the axe from the howling Ed, and was preparing to bring it down towards Art. This set Cora into motion, being very close to Henry, she easily sighted on his head, and pulled the trigger. My rifle is sufficient to bring down an elk at a good distance, being so close to Henry caused the side of his head to explode out, leaving very little matter left inside. The gory mess was spread about the room, and a healthy amount of blow back to spray onto Cora. She, promptly dropped the gun, and ran to Art's side. Crying over him, she asked what had happened. His skin had gone to a sickly color, and sweat was beginning to come heavily upon him, in the same drunken manner as Henry, he began to explain. They were ambushed further up the mountain. A monster had come out of the snow, and crushed Walt's head between its massive hands absconding with him back into the night. He and Art began shooting at it, but Henry then grabbed him from behind, trying to choke him. He fought himself free, but still Henry came on. Art shot him some, and when Henry fell upon him, he pulled his knife and freed himself with it. He and Ed retreated some, and then the snow stopped giving them some more visibility. Not having an understanding of the quills, he explained whereupon, arrows came at them from the darkness, piercing them painfully. It was at that time that they decided on a full retreat backwards to the cabin, making the long trek back following their old path, being harried by the arrows, whoops, and calls from the attacking Indians. He tried to put out more words, but he started shaking tremendously, frothing red at the mouth, Cora yelled for me to do something. But it was too late. With a great arching of his back, and a sigh, he expired. Ed, being on his side, but out of his wits, appeared to begin the same process, he arched his back in such a way that the ensuing cracks, and the way his legs stopped functioning, told me he had broken it. It was shortly thereafter, he passed as well.

Caitlin, ever the one to make most of an appearance, chose the moment of Cora's wailing over the body of Art to come through the door.

Looking as though she had returned from an evening stroll. Cora seeing her, pulled at a quill from Art, fervently putting it between her, telling Caitlin to get back. Caitlin in turn began walking further in, talking to Cora, that I seemed to like her, there had been enough death this night, there need not be more. Cora being in a most awful state, demanded she stay back. That she was a witch. Caitlin answered Aye to that, and there was a great deal more she could do if she wanted. Cora had a choice to make, stay and serve, or she was welcome to leave and take her chances. It was then that Caitlin's forest men began their hideous knocking about the house. This prompted Cora to drop the quill, and herself to the floor. Caitlin came upon her, and brought her back up, with Cora standing only a hair's breadth the taller. Caitlin told her she had decided well, but that there was still a price to pay. She then placed her hand low on Cora's stomach, and leaned in to whisper in her ear. Cora's eye's went wider still, then she fell back to the floor, expelling the contents of her stomach. Turning then from the mess, she placed her hands about her waist, crying in pain. Caitlin pulled her yet again to her feet. Telling her to stand, she began leading her from the room and I saw that she was trailing blood. Lord, help us.

Ally: We cried when we first met, when they came into the camp. The stress was so high, and the relief of seeing other people, knowing we weren't alone in this, it was palpable. Just stood there babbling at each other, so thankful to see someone else. Ty, Dre, and Sam then collapsed at the fire. Acting as crutches for the big guy, had exhausted them.

Dre: I was pretty big then, wasn't I?

Ally: Big softy. I'm not calling you fat Teddy. You were so physically imposing back then. It's no wonder you got hurt the way you did. If you had been at full health, they would have had a much harder time getting us. But, as he was, shivering, feverish, he couldn't use the foot, let along the leg. Eric was in an even worse state. More of that poison had gotten into him. After we had shared what events transpired between us. It was easy to see that we needed to get the hell out of there, but with two people hurt, it wasn't going to be easy. Ty suggested we break down our shelter, and convert it into a litter to carry Eric on. From there it would be a group effort of moving him and Dre the best we could. Two people on each guy, and one person free to switch out so we could take a break that way. I didn't know how much help I would be. I'm barley five foot five, I would carry Eric as far as was needed, but I didn't think I'd be much support for Dre.

Dre: You've been the best support I have ever asked for.

Ally: You're so corny. He knows what I mean anyway. It was late when we wanted to get started. No one wanted to risk moving through the forest at night. We still didn't know what we were dealing with, or how many. It was very much a damned if you do, damned if you don't, scenario. So we decided to go as soon as we could the next day. Brandon had been keeping an eye on his camera the past few days, when the radio stopped working he saw he lost his connection as well for broadcasting. At some point that day, the light for it came back on showing we had a connection. This meant the people at camp could see us, and maybe learn something was wrong. We had both camera's going then, showing Eric and Dre wounded, the rest of us looking more miserable and tired than would probably have been expected. I talked to them, the cameras, pleaded for someone to see us, to send help. Told them to look for our smoke. That we were in danger and would be moving towards them the next day. We repeated the message several times over. We built the fire up as much as we could, turned it into a bonfire, then we built up our little wall and shelter as much as we could. Materials were so scarce, I'm sure I'm conflating it all in my head after all these years, but we worked with what we had. Ty and Dre shared the same thought I had before, that these things had anticipated us, had more or less gone through the forest clearing it of anything useful. After that there wasn't anything else to do except wait for the night.

We had gathered in the shelter makeshift spears in hand, Eric and Dre protected as best as could be, Ty staying in the back with them. The sun was down, and we were ready for them. Our adrenaline was up, and I thought for sure it would be "now or never". I was crouched there like a fool, ready to spring up and stab anything in the face. "Come on, come on, where are you" was the mantra for us. And then we waited, and waited, and waited. We had gotten into the mindset that these monsters were just mindless beasts. That somehow they would be waiting for dark, and once night came in, they would come rushing at us in one big final showdown. They had shown us already how clever they were, I don't know why we thought it would go down so straightforward. Because of course it didn't. Maybe I'm giving "them" a lot more than what they really had, but I think they knew that's what we were thinking. And so the longer it took, the more we lost our surge. By late night, possibly after midnight, one of the guys hoped that this meant they would leave us alone. None of us were going to sleep regardless, but the idea that we could relax was a very tempting one. After what felt like an eternity more of waiting, they finally came at us.

Dre: Well, they sent the bears in first.

I cannot impress upon you how clever I thought they were, because when four black bears came rushing at our fire, my reaction wasn't immediate fear. It was wonder. Rather than come in themselves and face whatever we might have done as a group, they threw a momma bear and her three mostly grown up cubs at us instead. They were more panicked than we were, the bears I mean. Rushing in with high- sounding cries; the biggest one, the mom crashed right into our fire, scattering most of it all around. The smaller ones, saw our shelter and came rushing right to us. When we greeted them with shouts, and waving sticks in their faces, they stood upright, posturing right back at us. When the mom recovered enough from the fire, she came barreling in to the rescue of her cubs. You could imagine that she came in snarling, making some sort of battle cry of her own, but she didn't. She just blasted between her cubs silently, seemingly unaware of our spears, and jumped right onto Nick. Biting into him and scratching with her claws. I stabbed her in the side, but the resilience of her skin, it felt like I was trying to stab a tire with a butter knife. I wasn't sure if I did any damage to her then, Brandon and Tim were stabbing at her face, and that made her stop. Luckily her cubs were confused and scared by Sam still waving his spear around at them, they stayed back. If they had come in to fight too, we would have been fucked. The momma bear backed off Nick, huffing at us, trying to scare us away from the shelter, but we stood firm then. It became too much trouble for her, she broke to the side and ran off, her cubs taking only a second to go after her. It was all so fast, and then over so quickly. Nick was hurt pretty bad though, he had a massive tear at his shoulder, and his shirt was in shreds. All of us were focused on patching him up, to stop the bleeding.

I think with the bears, we thought that was it. Brandon, Sam, and I were getting Nick fixed up. I heard Ty say something, and Tim replied. Then he was standing and going to build the fire back up. What remained was a little less than a normal sized one. We didn't say anything to him, no warnings, I wish I had been more aware of what was going on.

Dre: Hey, it's not your fault. You were doing what you needed to be doing. It all happened as it did. We can't change it any more now than we wanted to then.

They didn't wait for him to start picking up sticks. He made a noise, it got our attention and when we looked, he was falling to the ground, those quills sticking out of him from all angles. Brandon jumped up to get to him, Sam and I yelling to him to wait, but it was another moment where things just happened too fast. By the time we were telling him to stop, he was already halfway out. He was hit a few times, two quills in his stomach and one on his arm. He immediately came back to us, we pulled the quills out of him the best we could. They weren't stuck into his bones, so they came out mostly whole, tearing his skin open further though when they were extracted.

Dre: We didn't know it then of course. I found out, a few years back through some nature documentary, porcupine quills have these little hooks, ridges, to 'em that make them stick. Makes it real hard to get them out without doing more damage.

We don't think Tim suffered very much. The amount of quills in him, all that toxin. They didn't leave the body for us. We hid in the lean to, at some point they took him away. They left us alone, the damage had already been done. Before, with their crosses, I thought they were trying to scare us off. But it was just a fear tactic. And then with this attack. They knew were planning to leave, and this wasn't to encourage that, it was to prevent it. There was never a "message" intended for us. Not in the sense that I saw it in. They wanted us scared, and in killing Tim, they told us they didn't care if they kept us alive while doing it.

The toxin hadn't taken effect yet with Brandon, but he knew it would soon, what was in store for him. He was frightened, asking what he should do, what we could do. Eric was in a coma from the one that struck his back. Dre's foot was in a bad state. We didn't have anything to clean the wounds with anymore. We didn't bring water in with us when we retreated, so cleaning the wounds with that was out of the question. Our lean-to barely afforded any safety, they could have shot us through any of the gaps, turned the bears back to tear it down, came up and pulled it apart themselves. We were so terrified, in shock. Our primitive cave man brains came out and told us to stay huddled up inside this jumble of sticks, we were safe that way. After a while Brandon was feeling the toxin, throwing up, then dry heaving, said his joints felt like they were on fire. Then he started convulsing, thrashing about, We held him down, it felt like every muscle of his was tensed to the extreme. And we're just looking at each other, Sam, Ty and I. I was hoping one of them would just have the answer to what we were supposed to do, I think they expected the same of me. But there wasn't anything, then the seizure subsided, he was still alive, still breathing, but he was asleep, or in a coma, I don't know, he didn't wake up.

When the adrenaline wore off again, I was so exhausted, yet again. I remember wondering how many more shots of the stuff I still had in me. How much more could my body produce before it just said "nope, sorry, all out." When it left though, it took my concern for our safety. I curled up next to Eric and closed my eyes. At that moment they could have attacked us and I would not have mustered up a complaint. I was having a nightmare about them prancing around us laughing like maniacs, stabbing at us with spears from the dark, when Sam shook me awake. It was light, the sun wasn't up high enough yet to see through the trees. I wanted to lay there and not move anymore, what was the point. I looked over, and I saw Dre sitting up with Ty, their foreheads pressed together, Dre's hands on his shoulders, and I realized they were praying. I was religious when I was younger, but by my twenties I had flipped to being Agnostic.

. . . .

Dre: No, it doesn't affect us, just because I believe in God does not mean that she has to. I have my faith, and she has her understanding of the world. I go to church on Sunday, she gets to sleep in.

What this big goof is trying to say in response to your question, we don't let our beliefs get in the way of how we feel about each other. When I saw them like that, it gave me some of my drive back. They were a great example of how brothers should be right? If I couldn't get myself up, if I didn't have any more hope that Eric would come through, then at the very least, I could try to help these two guys. I got up and took stock. Sam, Ty and I were now the most capable, and we got started on making the litters we could put the others on and drag them behind us. Nick was able to stand, but he was in a lot of pain. He told me how to operate his camera, to see if there was a signal or not, I wanted to try to send the camp a message that we would be on the move. It was out again, so that idea was gone. We wouldn't be taking any of the equipment with us from that point.

And then we were ready to move. Ty would help Dre, Sam would pull Brandon, I would pull Eric, and Nick just had to move himself. It was not easy. We finished off what little water we had that morning, just a few sips to go around, and we had no food at all at that point. I felt like I had barely gone the length of a football field, and I was already worn out. Climbing gave me pretty strong hands, so I wasn't about to let go of my handles any time soon, but just dragging him behind me, on top of everything else, it just was not easy. It started snowing that day. I didn't think it had been cold enough, I'm not sure I was really aware of a temperature at all. But these tiny little spots of white started coming down. And I felt it then, just this chill breeze on my face. And I hoped it wouldn't get worse.

XV. The Prospector

1908

The Lord did not help us. He was never there. That mountain has been, and will ever be Caitlin's. Twelve years have passed now, in the blink of an eye. I did not have the heart to write more after that night. My accounting was finished, manifesting these truths to paper was more than I could bear. Edmond returned, vowing to never again leave our side, but I had use of him away from the accursed mountain. Into the world I sent him, my agent to do my bidding. Buying up companies, putting stakes in land, oil, industries of metal. He would return, time after time, always gaunt and haunted, visions of strange dreams, and an urge to make his way back until he could fight it no more. Arriving with deeds and papers, we lay secret claim with the fortune, expanding it further than I ever could have dreamed. Louis grew up quickly, seemingly at one with the nature around us. The beautiful child of the forest as Cora was fond of calling him. He would vanish into the woods with Sona, returning later, twigs and leaves in his long hair. Sticks collected to be his guns either on his shoulder or through his belt. During his eighth year, I began taking him on short hunting excursions around the land. He shewed tremendous aptitude for it, even bagging a Canada goose on our first outing from a distance I would not have thought possible.

Cora, she took well to being his maid, doting over him and making sure every need of his was met. Whilst the bodies of her friends were laid to rest, a short way from the home, she made lamentations to the high above, and there ended Caitlin's patience with the Christian faith, not that it were ever there to begin with. She told her to stop her noise. No one was listening. Days after, Cora ceased with her despair as if it had never started. I once brought it back to her attention some year or so later, to ask if she ever wanted for anything to lay on their graves, even a stone if she liked. Her confusion at this, I thought mayhap she

133

was playing at, to show she was now loyal to us. But now I understand it. One more trick to the long list of what Caitlin is capable of. Once we took Cora on, Caitlin's matronly nature with Lou evaporated. She was good to him, never raised a hand in anger to him, never turned her temper to him. But I never saw her dote over him further, never hold him, never even speak to him in her awful language. He became a character in a play to her, something to observe. I spoke much of this with her, of course I did. I was made to feel foolish over it, this was not a thing to be admitted by her, always claiming her love for him, for me, for us. In truth, this is what I wanted, that love. Is it what I wanted? Is it what she wanted? She had an exertion over all of us, a control that was not, is not easily shaken free from. I feared then to question it. She would tell me what I wanted to hear, and all was right as rain. To lay it down on paper, as I said, was more than I could bear. And so I stopped writing, I stuffed the journal away inside an old travel bag and set about to forget it. In the stead of this, I made the plans with Edmond, I devoted myself to Lou, and life continued.

May first of 1906 was to be a landmark day. Lou was to become ten years of age. Edmond and I were returning that day from a trip to Portland, a fine young horse following behind us, to be presented to Lou. Caitlin called a greeting to us, standing in the chicken pen, spreading feed. I was struck by her beauty, as I ever was when being away from home for a time. This surprise brought with it a clarity I have yet to understand, but a veil was pulled away momentarily, and I thought it strange, that while I had lines in my face, and grey in my hair and in my beard. Caitlin had not aged one day since our first meeting. Always youthful and beautiful. I had made my peace with all she had done, no, this is not true. I had forgotten all her deeds. Without the constant reminder of the journal, these memories had gone through a sieve, leaving behind only the good. I heard a tale from a mentalist once at a show, that nothing is truly ever forgotten, it is only set aside for later use. And there is the truth of it, I saw her then how I should have seen her from the very start. She was the serpent, and I was the rodent trapped by her gaze. All that was left was for her to eat me up. Eat all of us up. I did not understand my place with her anymore. Why had she continued to keep me on? What purpose did I serve? Edmond? Cora? Lord forbid, even Lou? Her countenance changed, and I was reminded of her ways again, I turned my mind to only seeing her and presenting the new horse. I am certain she became aware that I then thought of taking Lou and leaving. I do not know if this had cause for her to enact her own plan, or if the significance of the day was already the turning of the wheel towards that.

The horse was secreted away into the stable, Caitlin greeted us again and all seemed well. The rest of the day proceeded as normal. After a celebratory dinner of his favorite meal consisting of flapjacks, we presented Lou with his new horse. For reasons only he would know but claims to not remember, he named it Shiner. There ends the goodness. Nightfall brought a terror that forever mars this birthday. He claims to have no memory of the night, and for this I am grateful. But I have seen him jump with fear for certain noises that hearken back to that awful time. My recollection of events is much the same as the night in November when Lou was still just a babe, as to this, I am again certain to have been induced into a stupor by Caitlin. Not only myself I should say, for when I awoke in the evening to find her and Lou gone, I had the most difficult time rousing Cora.

My awakening was in itself difficult, I do not believe I dreamt this time, or if I did, I do not have the remembrance of it. However, as before, it was Sona who managed to bring me out of it. Only once before had she awoken me from my own bed, being just the very night before, large wolf tracks were discovered circling the house. Sona had tugged at my hand, whining to me. Now the next night she was doing the same once again. With the room swirling about me, colors bleeding into others I knew then what Caitlin had done. Stumbling to the night stand, I poured cold water from the pitcher over myself, trying to regain *my senses. This only offered a modicum of success. Sona, being impatient led me on. I looked into Lou's room, I was not surprised to see that he was not there, but my heart sunk all the same. Cora's quarters were on the ground floor. I stumbled my way to her door, and burst in unceremoniously. She lay twisting and writhing about, pulling at her night-dress, crying out for her mother to help her, it appeared to be some awful vision of a nightmare. I did for her as I had for me, I poured out her water into her face. She spluttered and shook about like a fish, and I resorted to sitting her up, calling to her loudly. She finally awoke and clung to me tightly, fretfully trying to explain the horrid dream and still feeling as if she were deep in it. I told her this was Caitlin's doing. She had left with Lou, I would rouse Edmond next, and we would set off for them. I needed her to go to the wardrobe, gather the travel sacks there, and set about filling them with clothing and supplies for a trip. Then get the horses ready. We would return as quick as we could, if we could, and flee straightaway. If we did not return, then I was sorry for leaving her behind, I kissed her forehead and thanked her for all she had done for Lou, taking him on like he was her own. Sona tried leading me out of the house then, I told her I had need of Edmond to help, she was persistent with trying to push me back, she knew he was not there, but I did not understand and needed to see for myself. His room was as a block of ice on account of his window being open. I hoped then that he, hearing Lou and Caitlin, had set off after them. I was worried however as his boots, and clothes from the day were on the floor near his bed. I could not give it much thought though, for Sona was pulling at me with frustrated insistence. I made to the door, dressing for the still winter-like weather outside. On my way out to the back threshold, I noticed the great bear slaying, gold inlaid, silver spear was not in its spot above the fireplace mantel.*

Being outside brought a new host of problems, I in my haste, had not considered. The moon was just a sliver in the sky, and without snow on the ground, darkness prevailed throughout all. I felt I could not waste any more time, and did not turn back to prepare a torch. Sona kept a slow pace for me, her dark fur blending well with the surrounding night. She led the way true. I could feel my hair freezing about my head, my ears turning numb, the very air felt as though filled with spears of ice, stabbing my lungs with each breath. My foot slipped upon a jutting stone, I put my hands out for better balance, but felt myself drive forward irrevocably towards the ground. I remember a flash of pain to my head, and my senses briefly leaving me. Coming to, with Sola's tongue at my face, encouraging me to get up. Her administrations giving the desired effect of reviving me to my senses and invigorating me. I felt my spirits lifted, my eyes cleared from the venom that previously caused the world to spin around me. I stood up, with a newfound strength, I couldn't help but to laugh and rub and Sola's face. Restored and renewed, I told her to lead on. We continued up the mountain at a much greater pace, I had the ken of every spot to place my feet, when to dodge larger outcroppings or spin around trees. Before I knew it, we had scaled an expanse of land in the blink of an eye. We soon reached the spot where I had spent the night, years before, and I saw that Sona was winded. Being the old dog she was, I removed my coat and placed it on the ground for her, asking her to lay on it. She had given me the strength to forge ahead, and had my deepest thanks. I knew the way from there, and could make it on my own, she would do no more except rest, and return to Cora. I feel she had an understanding, and so I gave her my love. Then I continued on to the final leg, hoping above all I was not too late for whatever it was, I was going into.

I believe I followed the same path as before with Sona leading the way. My lifted spirit carrying me over the stones in a way I would have claimed reckless even during daylight, guide or no. I soon reached the ridge I had hidden behind before, this time intending to use it as a launching point for an attack. One I was ill prepared for. I carried no weapon but my fists and determination. Peering down into that hellish bowl, I was met with a similar sight. The beastly Fir Glas Brecc circled the outer edge, filling the area several rings deep. Their number being many, I was not in fear of them but what lay further in. Bres lay again stretched before the fire, supplicating himself to it with his fingers grazing the flames. Caitlin bare to the world, stood strong and sure next to him, this time with the damnable spear in one hand. Speaking her angry language to the flames, gesticulating with her free hand from the flames, to my son, hanging limp and lifeless from a saltire. I feared then, he was dead, that I had come too late. Smoke from the fire drifted to him, and gave his body reason to let out a cough. My heart leapt at this revelation, there would still be time. At the center of the fire was the gap, through which before I laid eyes upon the horrid destroyed visage of the giant. During this moment, a murky ill-defined shape was slowly coming into view. This was the time for me to act.

I stood in full upon the ridge, then plunging myself onward and down with all the speed and strength I could muster. The wings of the god Hermes could not carry him faster than I. Meeting the outer ring of bent creatures, I launched myself to the first knobbly form I came to. Placing a foot squarely upon the surprisingly solid point low on its back, it released a startled cry. But so fast was I, so strong as with the might of Herakles himself, I thrust myself into the air with the greatest leap of my life before the foul thing could fully react. I soared over the groups, and landed full within the circle. Caitlin being disturbed by my entrance, turned to greet me. She had seen this one too she said, my appearance was expected, but I was too late. She would have satisfaction, with one more act, her lord would return. For all her visions of things to come, I do not believe them to be set to stone as the ancients did with their tablets. For as she turned, dismissing me, readying to plunge the spear into our child. I released a shout and brought myself to her, faster than she could ken. I ripped the spear from her hands, and hit her upside her face with the back of my hand with that awesome strength I still controlled. For a moment it was as if I had connected with granite and I heard more than felt a snapping within my hand. But the effect was considerable, sending her tumbling away towards her creatures. Wasting not the precious time I had, I set to removing the thick ropes around Lou's legs, the spear's blade cutting effortlessly the cordage. Caitlin yelled as from a distance, and then I was encompassed by a massive shadow between the fire and I. I was fast, but not fast enough to turn to meet Bres in full, instead receiving a glancing blow to my left shoulder. I felt it pull and drop with an awful pain, bringing me to my knees.

I looked up moving as if in water, to see this terrible form above me, a grimace of a smile exposing his tusk-like teeth as he pulled back his massive fist preparing for the next blow to my head, and most assuredly my end. A great furred form nearly equal to his came to my rescue, crashing into Bres taking him off his feet. I could tell then that my left arm was useless, separated from the joint. I pulled myself to my feet, using the spear as prop. What I saw confused me greatly, a massive beast, similar in body to Bres, covered with a pelt of long dark hair with what appeared to be the likeness of a wolf for a head sat astride him. Tearing at him with human-like hands tipped with great claws to put any other predatory beast to shame. Bres's arms fell limply to his side, and it seemed this new creature had won against the odds. It turned to me, breathing hard, it's scarred face revealed to me. Was that you in there Edmond? I believe it was. For in that moment, you told me in a strained voice not suited for speech, to go, to run. I stood stupefied, and you growled the words again. Then it was Bres's turn to retaliate. Great fists came up grabbing the werewolf's head tearing him to the side. Bres rose with the speed of a mountain cat, fists together as a battering ram driving them into Edmond's chest, taking him off his feet. With torn flesh and blood running about, he stood over the body and let loose a roar of his own, the first and last time I had ever heard him make a sound. He bent picking up the great werewolf with one hand about the neck, raising his limp form into the air. Turned from me just enough so that he did not see me rushing towards him with the spear, driving it in full to the guard, up and into his side, the tip shoving through his chest. Edmond, fell from his grasp. Bres turned slowly towards me, with what I can only presume to be pain and hatred clouding his ugly face. Then he collapsed.

I rushed back to Lou, finding the knots holding his hands easy to undo, I shouldered his small form and looked to an exit. Finding Caitlin with her mass of mountain men waiting to greet me. She was a woman of great spirit, easily showing her temperaments, more often than not these were of an enjoyment of life. What shewed now was a rage I knew not possible. Then it was gone, replaced by a softening. She bade me set him down, there was still time yet, I hadn't ruined it all. There would be a great reward for me after all this. The beating pain of my crippled arm saved me I believe, from the sway of her words. The gaze of a snake that I now see could hold me so easily when I began to doubt, to raise concern. Hers was the craft of subtlety. And it did not work. I saw the fear in the great eyes of her diminutive beasts, they had never seen anyone stand against her so. The softness left her voice then, an anger most foul returned. She said words to the creatures, and their faces changed to that of evil glee. They spread from behind her towards me, craggy smiles showing rows of savagely pointed teeth. Making sounds as of ravens fighting, slowly approaching me. I was saved once more, and suddenly by Edmond. He threw himself into the fray, hacking at the little creatures, tossing them into the air with each swipe, clearing a path. I rushed in behind and was soon out, climbing up the slope to the ridge. Coming to the top, I turned to see Edmond still battling the monsters, keeping them from ascending after me. But further into the bowl, I saw Caitlin removing the spear from Bres. She readied herself with it facing Edmond, I called in warning to him, but was too late. The spear was launched at him like a lightning bolt, driving through and cracking into the stony ground behind him. I spared a moment more for him, but he would not rise. The creatures danced a macabre victory around his still form, some taking note of me. I had to leave. I would mourn him in the days to come. Another victim of Caitlin's, I do not know how she did it to him. The why of it, I presume, was to make him yet another creature of hers, only he had given his life instead to save mine and Lou's. He will forever be my brother.

I veritably flew from whence I came, shortly reaching the spot where I left the tired Sona, as the years before, she was not to be seen. I was not worried for her, and suspected I would find her waiting back at the cabin. I swept up my coat, doing my best to place it over Lou's shivering body. I could hear the noise of the cackling mass from further up the mountain. I made haste, retreating in darkness, trusting in all that was good to carry us home quick and safe. Bounding over stone and limb, even with my arm as damaged as it were, my strength did not ebb. I saw then the darkness was not as replete throughout as going up, the world having taken a silver sheen of brightness to it. Like all else from the night, I did not understand it, but use it I did. I traveled swiftly, traversing in leaps and bounds to do an elk proud. The raucous monstrosities I left far behind, their swiftness could not equal mine. In a goodly time, I sighted upon the manor. I discovered the door bolted, I decided to not waste mere moments entreating to Cora to allow us in, I raised a boot to the center. The great oak door, claimed by a carpenter to keep bears from gaining entrance, blasted in twain. Cora let loose a frightened wail from the spot she had gathered our valises. Recovering just as suddenly when saw it was Lou and me. She had lowered her night dress to her waist, trapping it there by tying the sleeves together. She approached us, chest bared, arms up, a touched smile upon her face. She addressed me as the Lord Silver Stag, with eyes aglow, and how did I manage through the door with my great antlers? I shouted to her to see sense. They would be coming for us, it was time to go. She was confused for a moment, then saw me for who I am. Returning to a manageable sanity. Seeing Lou brought something of her back too, she took him from my shoulder, giving me a short reprieve. She had managed well on her own, still being under the influence of Caitlin's tonic, although some odd choices were in the mix such as feathers obtained from walks, a stack of books, and a stool with a pile of coal on top. With Lou being laid out in front of the fire, I opened a sack and saw my clothes within, I pulled out a shirt and told Cora to wear it. She took it with a curtsy, again calling me Lord. I asked her to stop this, and help me gather the wagon.

Douglas was no longer at my beck this night, Caitlin's voice carrying through the aether, broke whatever friendly connection he and I had had. Greeting him earned me swift kicks at his stall door, shying about. A fearful look took his eyes to rolling about. Fortune still favored us though, the other horses had no qualms with us, we hitched Cora's and Eric's to the wagon. Shiner we attached with a line along-side. I told him in passing to not slow us down, we had a fast pace to set. Delivering the wagon to the front of the house, we quickly loaded it with the sacks, and then Lou, fitting him snugly betwixt blankets, I had tried waking him, but received no response. Cora sat upon the seat, jaw agape at the stars twinkling above us. Seeing I had left my rifle behind, I re-entered the house to retrieve it. Coming through the back door as I returned through the front, we paused facing each other. The first of her men had arrived. I suppose I cannot call them men any further. Having the best sighting of the creature. Up on the mountain, with the light from the bonfire, I could excuse the strangeness with smoke and shadow-play. As such, in mine own well-lit home, I was given full view of these hellish beings. Diminutive they are, being of same height, if not shorter than Lou. With a bald pate, long pointed ears, a similarly long pointed nose, above which sat very large sickly yellowed orbs for eyes, and a jutting forward jaw filled with tiny sharp teeth. Its body was gnarled and knobbly, with mottled grey green skin like that of a toad. I suspect during the green months, these creatures would be very hard to see. It wore very little, only what I took to be a leather thong about its waist with a rough quiver full of those black venomous quills. It held what I first took to be a flute, but found to be the means by which the darts were propelled. We paused in our doorways, taken aback at each other. I remembered the fear I saw earlier in their eyes as I stood firm against Caitlin. And possibly suffering from madness of the night's events, I ran at the beast, arm waving, making noise as if to scare off a bear. Its large eyes widened further, raising the tube to its mouth, and with a spitting noise, launched a quill at me. Passing through my shirt at my side, but missing my skin. The creature let forth a squeal, and turned about face preparing to run out the cabin, it was tumbled backwards with a black snarling mass atop it. Sona had arrived. I will admit, in my haste I had not thought of her. I believe deep down, that I had trusted in her, and thought her to return when she could. I grabbed my rifle, saw it was at the ready and yelled to Sona to move. She leapt from the creature. As it rose, I planted a bullet between its hate filled eyes. It dropped to the floor with no further noise, a brackish blood issuing forth. I knew then these things could be killed.

We left along the only path we could, every noise of the night reaching my ears over the clopping and squeaking of our travel menagerie. I do not know if any more lone goblins, for goblins they are, I am sure of it, followed us, but there was no more accompanying noise from the greater mass of them. No ambushes. I pushed the horses as hard as I dared. Shiner being young and full of vigor was happy to run alongside, still wanting more even as we stopped for a short rest with the raising of the sun. After what felt an eternity of fearful travel, we finally reached Portland. A doctor saw to Lou, but proclaimed him to be fine. After sheltering there a few days more, he awoke. Fearful at first, but then returning to himself, he did not ask for his mother, seemingly content with Cora's administrations of motherly duty over him. After making preparations we boarded a vessel traveling south to San Francisco. From there, we traveled East by train. Eventually coming to New York City. I had assumed this journal to be one of the many things left behind in our escape, but Cora discovered it at the bottom of one of the sacks, right where I had secreted it away years ago.

A year after our arrival in New York City, Cora and I married. She has shown a care for both Lou and I, that I see now Caitlin never had. She is the true lighthouse I have ever needed in my life. Caitlin was the cold craggy rock after all. I intend now, to carry on with my life, to see Lou into his, and try as best as I might to leave this previous life behind me. For two years we have been here, with nary a word of Caitlin or her awful ilk. I do not believe she will travel far from her mountain, nor will her beasts. From what research I could find not being in a children's section, I believe her kind to have an aversion to man-made metals.

After the food had gone missing, I tried bringing it up with Miles. There was someone else out there. Ryan was with me on that, he had a certain stiffness to him, but he was a pretty good guy. But when we told Miles, he didn't care. Just threw his hands up, and was like "so we feed some forest animals so what?" He hadn't even understood us. Ryan said "No, someone else is out here and is messing with us." And then all the other problems we had, the wiring was "rats" but these rats were cutting the wires pretty smoothly. The generators cutting out was because something inside must have gone bad and we had been scammed on them. Miles had an excuse for everything. And then, as long as it didn't mess with the production too much, he just didn't give a shit.

It was in the coffee that we had constantly been brewing in a pot. That's what got us. We were all drinking it. I mean, okay, I'm not a hundred percent sure it was that. But we didn't share those shitty army bags, and when could those have been spiked anyway? No, it was the coffee. It affected us each differently. Ryan was massively sick from it. Miles became paranoid and hid out in the trailer. Ash and Tyler went chasing glowing butterflies or something, and I had a conversation with a ball of fire. I mean, it didn't speak English, and I didn't understand what it was saying to me. But it wasn't scary, it was comforting. I laughed a lot with it. I think it laughed with me, a kind of bobbing up and down in the air. And then it seemed tired. The flames dimmed, and showed this glowing ember inside it, it looked almost like a heart. And when I saw that, I told it that it must be mine, and that it needed to come back into me, so it wouldn't go out. And that's what it did. It floated right to my chest, and then sunk into my skin. It was relaxing, a big wave of peace came surging out from my chest, spreading itself across my body. I knew I was falling backwards, but it felt like I was falling slowly, through water. I gently landed on my back in between these tufts of grass, snugly fitting in a space I thought was made just for me. It was so nice I couldn't have left my eyes open if I wanted to.

I woke up sober, freezing my ass off, and buried under a layer of snow. But I felt good, like I had just had a great night's worth of sleep. It worried me a little, I still remembered everything, but I didn't know how long I had been asleep for. The snow wasn't in the forecast for at least a few more weeks, and it had gone on long enough to cover me completely. Somehow I hadn't frozen. I knew I hadn't slept for those weeks though, because, come on, who would think that? I thought that at most it was overnight, and the snow came in the morning. The sky dumped a nice amount, and then I woke up. I wasn't too far from the camp, but I didn't see anyone moving around. Either they were in the tent working, and I was in trouble, or they were just getting over the effects too. Whoever had done it though was most likely going to catch hell from Miles. I got closer and saw the state of the camp, and just thought "oh fuck." I ran the rest of the short way. The main tent was big enough to block my view of the trailer, and coming around from behind, I saw that it was on its side. I shouted asking if anybody was there. No one answered. It looked like the camp had been abandoned for days, with the layer of snow covering everything I couldn't tell for sure what had happened. The tents themselves were slashed up, and if I had been told to take a guess, I would have said a bull and a bear had been on a rampage, our things were strewn about the site. I went around to any bigger lumps in the ground, making sure they weren't people. The four-wheeler was gone, the ambulance that was supposed to be there in case of emergencies was nowhere to be seen. But they all wouldn't have left in it. Especially not Miles. I had gotten the space heater inside the tech tent up and running. There hadn't been any damage to it, it was just knocked over. And I heard a clicking noise come from behind me. Like the sound t.v.'s used to make when you turn them on. I turned around, and a couple of the monitors that hadn't been scattered about were showing a black and white image. It was Ally, from team Arizona, standing in front of the camera, she did not look okay, she looked like a strong breeze would have knocked her over. She was saying something, then it would pause for a second, and start again. I found the dial to turn up the volume, and in this monotone, dead-spirited voice she said "we have gone to the Mountain." Then it would repeat, and she'd say it again. Yeah, it was pretty creepy.

When I left the tent, warmed by the space heater, the temperature outside felt like it had dropped about fifty degrees. It hurt to breath as the warm air was chased out of my lungs by the cold. The sky had also become a lot more overcast, you could tell that a mother of a storm was building up. I had already decided in the tent what I was going to do next, and with that storm brewing I had to do it quick. I salvaged what I could from the sleeping tents; a thicker pair of gloves, and my sleeping bag that I draped over my shoulders. I found a pair of pink rimmed skiing goggles that I could only assume belonged to Ash, and decided to put them on too. And then I left headed for the road. The main camp really wasn't that far off from it, I think a few miles? Definitely walkable. As I passed by the tipped over trailer, which, I still did not have a feasible good idea as to how it became that way, I saw the first big flake of snow fall in front of me. Twenty more steps, and it was as if someone had dumped a container of cotton balls over. I've never seen anything like it. I still don't know if it's actually possible. Maybe it was some holdover from the drug? They weren't heavy, they still slowly fell like you'd expect. It was just the size, I caught one and could see it was several massive flakes grouped together. In any other circumstance it would have been beautiful, like palm sized cutouts made real. But like this, I was confused, and worried. The further I went, the thicker it came, it became harder to see. Then the wind picked up, right into my face. I was glad for the goggles, but the lower part of my face was getting beat up. It became bearable when I pulled the sleeping bag up higher and wrapped it around me tighter. I turned back and couldn't see the camp anymore, and my footsteps only went so far behind me before they had been covered up completely too. I turned back in the direction I had been going, and hoped I was still going in a straight enough line to reach the road. From there it would just be a matter of getting someone to see me, then stop for me.

For almost two hours I walked in this blinding storm, trudged through snow getting deeper by the second. My toes were nonexistent, my legs felt like I had been on my stair-master at the hardest setting. I should be hitting the fence or opening any minute, and yeah, I was worried. I was regretting my choice and wishing I had stayed at the camp, the space heater becoming a reoccurring thought. Then wham, I had been driving on autopilot not really seeing anything in front of me, lulled by the snow just coming at me nonstop. I hadn't seen this thing looming in front of me, and it put me on my ass. I got up, and saw it was a white wall, so of course I didn't notice, it blended in nicely. I walked alongside it, and came to a corner, turned that, and my heart dropped. I could still very easily see a door, positioned sideways. I was back at the camp. Fuck.

That damn storm, it turned me around so easily. I could've been circling the camp the entire time and not even known. I was probably lucky just to hit the roof of it like I did then, another twenty, thirty yards to the right and I would have passed on by without the slightest awareness. I made my way around, and got back to the tech tent, still warmer than outside. I turned the space heater on and sat right in front of it, feet first, shoes off. I wasn't thinking of a new plan aside from "get warm". In the back of my mind was the idea to wait for morning and hope the storm had moved on by then. I drifted off after eating a packet of dried chili and crackers the size of my hand. I woke up to chaos. The whole tent was on fire, acrid smoke burned my nose. I had enough forethought to grab my boots and scrambled out to safety. I saw that everything was ablaze then. This wasn't a malfunction from the space heater, someone had set fire to the whole camp. I tried throwing snow onto the smaller tents, but as shredded as they were to begin with, my efforts were pretty ineffectual. Have you ever seen a blaze in a blizzard? These two opposing forces beating back at each other. Fire rising up and twisting with the wind. The snow swirling around the flames. It was mesmerizing, otherworldly, and frightening. Then of course becoming aware of the danger I was in set in. The fires provided light, and heat, but what if the person, or people, that did this were still around? To run off into the night in deep snow would have been a death sentence. The choice was made for me. As I stood there, weighing my options, a smell of rotting sewage carried on the wind hit me. The trailer didn't have a toilet on it, so I knew it wasn't that. The tech tent in front of me collapsed on itself with a whumpf of flames. Standing on the other side with their back to me was a massive, and very hairy man wearing little in the way of clothing. If I had believed in it, I would say it was Big Foot. He looked enough like what you'd expect him to look like I suppose. Except he was holding a torch. I wasn't about to ask him for help, or why he burnt our camp down. As far as I knew he was most likely responsible for why everyone was missing too. His head cocked to the side like he was listening to something, then he slowly began turning around. I dropped into the snow and scrambled back towards the remains of the tent, concealing myself in the drifted up snow, and the little bit of the structure that was still standing. It was just enough to hide me, but if he walked around to my side there wasn't anywhere else for me to go. I sat there holding my breath, straining hard to listen for him. The blizzard was still on going, and hearing anything over the sound of the wind was next to impossible. So I sat, and waited. I finally heard the faint sound of something snapping, I risked a look over the edge of the remains and saw a faint outline of him through the snow and flames. He was tearing apart the remains of another tent flinging pieces away. I was sure by then he was looking for me, and was becoming frustrated he couldn't find me. After stomping around he stopped and stared off in the direction of the mountain, cocking his head again to some noise only he could hear. Then he ran away in the direction he was looking, vanishing very quickly into the snow. I watched the spot he disappeared into. Watched the snow fill the ditches he had carved on his exit. Watched it fall and put out the remnants of fires still burning.

As the morning light came on, the blizzard stopped, the campsite had been reduced to a series of snow covered lumps, the former trailer being the largest with a house sized drift built up around it. I was so tired, but to sleep then and there would be to freeze and die. But with the recession of the storm, I thought I had a chance now. I still didn't want to turn my back from the mountain, I was scared that the man I had been thinking of as Big Foot, would still be out there, watching and waiting for me like I had been for him. As I slowly stood, expanding my field of view, I was left in awe of what I was seeing around me. It was the storm, still on going, surrounding the mountain and land like we were in the eye of a hurricane. It was another magnificent contrasting view, like the fire and storm dancing together the night before. This was, well, it gives me goosebumps to think of it now. This immense power in the distance, creating a wall around the land. I was never a believer of "supernatural" forces you know? I'm sure there's some logical reason for it, but I just couldn't figure it out. It was some magical thing happening right in front of me. And it dawned on me, that I wasn't getting through it, it became a living thing to me then. Not just a collection of ice, water, and wind. It was this massive creature of chaos, and it did not want me to leave. The creepy video that played by itself, getting turned around in the storm, the giant man, now this.

I knew then I would do what this thing, this force, wanted me to do. I was going to the mountain.

1917

L has left to join the war in Europe. I said to him, I could make him stay, he does not have to go. He is young, twenty-one, Cora is stronger, she says for him to go, says he is strong too. I was lucky to not go to war. I do not want him to go to war. Cora says he will come back to us.

Did I write of goblins, of a wolf-man fighting a beast of a man? It is hard to remember. There is much fog, this story I wrote. Was I writing it for L? A grand adventure of monsters? Of this Caitlin, I remember Kate. I think Kate? I ask Cora, and she says it was not a good marriage for me. She says we left because Kate was bad. I do not remember. It was not a good story. It did not bring joy to read. Why can I not remember? What is wrong with me?

Sometimes, when a sound, or smell touches just the right spot in my brain, I'm back there again, and I can't help but to see myself, us, having a different outcome. I am able to drag Eric miles to our destination. Our progress didn't come to a complete standstill when the freak blizzard came. Nothing happened the way it did, and instead we make it out earlier. A therapist asked me once; how would I have wanted my life to go then, if that were the case. And I said still the same, just with different variations. The biggest one being that Eric and Ty survived. That Eric had a chance to really discover who he was, had the chance to have what he wanted out of life. I get so angry about how he was cheated out of that. Dre and I coming together, I fantasized that it would still happen from some sort of survivor's group thing, the whole shared experience. Then those moments pass, and I'm accepting what happened all over again. I've had to discover that, that trauma never goes away. Sorry, where were we?

Dre: Biggest snowflakes I've ever seen in that storm.

And they were sharp. When the wind kicked up, and they started coming at our faces, you could feel the sting from each one. You can't see it very well anymore, but I have a little dot of a scar, here next to my eye. One of those flakes hit just right, poked hard enough to break the skin. We had to stop and take shelter. The litters we made had an unintended use of making walls for us that we were able to wedge between a tree and a boulder. Sam, Ty, and I arranged the others as best we could. Then Sam and Ty went to see what they could find to make a fire. Of course it was the same as before, there wasn't anything. A stick here, a twig there, we scraped bark off the tree next to us, but it was wet underneath. We couldn't get anything started. The snow was drifting up fast. We still had some tent material to use as a roof, and it wasn't long till it was sagging down, forcing us to lay down. So that's what we did, huddled together, watching the opening to our little self-made burrow fill up by the minute. Sam passed out little packets of pocket warmers he had been hanging on to, "for a moment just like this". I activated some and put them around Eric, then a few more for Brandon too. It had a sort of finality to it, when the opening was filled up completely. I thought "okay, that's it, this is where we stay now." The pocket warmers could only do so much, the ground was the biggest culprit of leaching away our warmth, it would be a matter of time before we froze in our little cave. Ty was having doubts too, voicing them to Dre. Dre had hope though. Told him he knew how hard this was, how scary. But they didn't have a choice about stopping. They couldn't leave their mom all alone not knowing what ever happened to them. They were going to get out of there no matter what, even if he had to crawl out missing both legs and everybody tied to his back.

Dre: This the part where she makes me sound heroic.

You were. You are. You have the biggest heart of anybody I've ever known. I had given up, was ready to go to sleep and let the cold take me. And you had this boundless hope, coming out with inspiration. A simple "we can't die because our mom needs us." Sam had been listening too. Asked 'em what they would have done if they had won. And in perfect unison said "give it to momma" and cracked up laughing at some in joke of it. But it was nice, it made me smile. And Sam asked me. And I told them the truth, of Eric and I. That we'd split it, and then go our separate ways. I didn't have a plan for the money aside from that. I guess just put it in the bank. Dre with his words of wisdom said that it was okay not to have a plan, sometimes stuff happens, and it's good to have a bit of extra cash set aside anyway. I've always been on the more pessimistic side of life, and couldn't help myself saying that it didn't matter anyway, because here we were. Dre took the bait, but instead of letting it get to him, he challenged it. He asked "So what are we gonna do about it?"

Dre: And Miss Spitfire here, punched our saggy roof and said "I don't fucking know." She and Ty were a bit similar in that they could see the big picture, and have a rough understanding of how to go from A to B. But throw in a ton of little things, and it'd trip 'em up a bit. That's how I saw it, what we had right there was a stumble. Just like all the others before it. I told her we just had to take it one thing at a time. Break it all down. So what about the end of our trip? We weren't there yet. We were here. We knew what we had to do. Wait out the storm. If that snow packed as tight as it felt on the canvas above us, we wouldn't have to drag our people through it, just set 'em on top and slide them along. This snow wasn't going to make our life more difficult, it was going to make things easier.

While what he was saying was nice, he was neglecting at the moment to tell us about his leg. It was worse, dark lines were moving up under the skin, the puncture wound looked more like an untreated rattlesnake bite, there was no way he would or could get through the snow with it. Even with Ty's help, it would be a struggle. Nick spoke up then, he said he didn't think he had it in him to be able to trudge through snow like that. That he was "pretty messed up."

Dre: I faltered a bit at that, and then another plan started forming. I told Ty he wouldn't like it, the others probably wouldn't either. But we had to do what we had to do. The three that weren't hurt had the best chances of getting out if they went on their own. Nick and I would stay behind with Eric and Brandon. Then when they got help, they could lead it back to us. Day saved.

I hated that plan, I didn't want to leave Eric, I didn't want any of us to have to separate. Ty agreed with me on that one. Sam and Nick were with Dre. I told them that this wasn't really a time for a vote because we weren't splitting up. But Dre talked it over again, more directly to Ty. We couldn't all stay, and we couldn't all go. With three of us going, we'd be there to support each other, increase those odds of getting out. Ty finally agreed to it, I don't think he really had much of a chance trying to hold out against his big brother as it was. I told them I couldn't do it, I wasn't going to leave Eric like that. We quieted down again after that. I could hear whispers of conversations, but I was tired and didn't feel like listening anymore. Then I closed my eyes.

Dre: I can take it from here if you want me to.

No, it's okay, I've gone through this before, it happened, I accept it, there's no changing it. I woke up and it was pitch black. And so, so cold. I found Eric's forehead with my hand, and noticed it felt cold too, his fever had finally broken. I curled up tighter against him, my hand on his chest, and something felt off. His chest wasn't moving, I held my hand up to his nose but couldn't feel anything. So then I started patting his face, saying his name, asking if he could hear me. But there wasn't a reaction to that. I told the others to wake up, to give me a light, I needed to see him. Sam still had an electric lantern, and he turned it on. And there he was, his eyes were open, staring up into nothing, the color gone from his cheeks entirely. He had probably been gone for a while then. I know there wasn't anything I could have done, I mean, I know that now. Then, I see it in pieces, Snapshots of sadness and misery. I coined that in therapy. That's all I really want to give you, say to you about it. The other's expressed their sympathy, I remember hearing it, but I didn't feel it. I stayed awake till morning. Sam and Ty worked together to dig us out from the snow, it had piled up into a huge mound around us and on us. How that canvas held it all up is a minor miracle. When they were getting ready to go, I told them I would come too. My reason for staying behind was gone.

I had been trudging my way through the snow for what felt like the better part of the day. Keeping mostly to a straight path through the now covered wetlands, and then into the forest. All the dips and crags were filled in, and I damn near broke my ankles on them multiple times. The mountain did not feel like it was getting any closer. If anything it's size rose up before me, looming even larger than it had before. I had come over a rise, and laying ahead was a valley with a smooth river of snow marking a path leading right up to an expansive log cabin. I stopped and looked around, especially behind me, to check where I had come from, and I could follow my trail through the trees until it went out of sight. This valley and house ahead of me should not have been there. As visible as it was, at least one or two of the teams should have stumbled upon it. Even the scout probably would have seen it, and he had hiked further in. I've always been an open-minded type of person, but the weirdness of everything was not normalized at all for me. But looking at the house, and seeing a trail of smoke from a chimney, made me realize how cold I had become. The coat and sleeping bag shawl had only carried my warmth so far. My toes and fingers had a numb ache to them. My body made up my mind for me, and I began following the path of the snow, the ground underneath was flat and even, much easier to walk on. Humor was, maybe still is, a coping mechanism for me, and I had the thought that at least the house wasn't made out of gingerbread. I made myself laugh at that, and the sound carried easily across the snow and was echoed back at me. A minute later and the door opened, a small old woman appeared, a long twin barreled rifle in her hands. To add to the surrealism, she looked like a character from a period piece about settling the West.

I approached cautiously, her gaze gave me no indication on if she was planning on using the gun or not. It looked like it would just as likely knock her on her butt if she fired it. When she felt I was close enough she raised it smoothly to her shoulder, and in a thick accent said to me *"that'll be as good a place as you need be for now."* I put my hands up and told her "I come in peace" about as calmly as I could. Her stony gaze broke into something of a toothy smile, and she said "*Aye, brave enough cub you are, you'll do for a bit o' coffee won't you?*" And she lowered the rifle and waved me in, going in herself. I thanked her for her niceness, but the warning bells were ringing like crazy. It's such a cliché, but this whole setting had the makings of a horror movie to it. And here I was, invited into the witch's house, never to be seen again. But still, I found myself walking the path, then on the first steps of the porch, then at the door. I could see her in the entry-way waiting for me. This frail looking old woman, a fraction of my height. She spoke "*You have came to my home in peace, by the geass of hospitality, no harm will come to you within*". For some reason I got goosebumps when she said that. Getting them now just remembering it even, look at that. Should I have trusted it? Hell no. Did I? Yes, those warning bells stopped when she said that. Something in my subconscious just went "oh, well okay then". So in I went.

It was nice inside, dated, and reminded me of those old places turned into museums, left as they were from another time period. Furs hung from the walls, the furniture was velveted and patterned like it was shipped directly from the Victorian era. She told me to remove my boots and coats. She took a strange delight in my using the sleeping bag as a shawl. She took my boots over to a big fireplace, and hung them on those old-fashioned racks meant just for that use. She then had me sit next to the fire as well, while she vanished through a door. I heard the usual kitchen sounds coming from the room she had gone to. After a minute she came back with two tin mugs, a large kettle, and a thick packet wrapped in wax paper. "*I 'spect you'll be having some hunger so I brought this as well*", removing the wrapping she revealed wide strips of jerky. *"Dried hind, from the best of the Silvers that run through here from time to time."* I told her I did not know what "silvers" were and she gave me a disappointed look, like I had missed a vital part of a quiz. *"The Silvers, boy, the oldest family descendent from the great Sylvan-Hart Lord himself, when the great bridges existed before the cold came and swept them away"* I nodded along with her, as if what she were saying made sense. I don't think she noticed or cared. It was delicious meat though, and very rich coffee. She sipped at the coffee, ate none of the meat, and watched me in silence. She asked if I was "wanting for more" as I finished the piece of food and last of the drink. I thanked her profusely for what she had given me, very likely saving my life. Or at least my fingers, toes, and nose from frostbite. She scoffed at that, saying it *"t'weren't nothing yourself wouldn't have done as so"* in her strange lilting accent. I kept expecting her to ask me questions, who I was, where I'd come from, what was I doing there. But nothing came, she would just watch me. It felt like she was waiting for me to ask something. It was probably my imagination at this point, but I swear there was a fire in her eyes that had only been growing brighter since I arrived. I asked if she had a phone, and she cackled, like a straight up witch's cackle. In any other situation it would have been hilarious, I've never heard one for real, but it was just another thing added to the list of oddities. She quieted down and apologized, she had one, but the storm had knocked it out, it would be days before it would be up and running again. Then I asked the question I think she was waiting for, if I could stay for a while, that fire in her eyes lit up further at that. *"Of course you can, young cub, I would never to dare send you out without properly regaining your strength. I have just the room for you to stay in, tomorrow you may finish your journey up the mountain."* While I was thanking her, she swept the mugs and kettle away, leaving the meat saying the whole of it was now mine. I took another piece and sat staring at the fire. The fullness in my stomach, the heat radiating out from the fireplace, the comfort of the place, all worked together in such a way that I didn't even try to fight it when my eyelids closed.

I woke up in a dark room, dimly lit by a nearly full moon through a large window. I was warm and comfortable, in a bed, under a layer of blankets, entirely without clothes. I was embarrassed at the fact this ancient old woman somehow managed to get me here on her own, then proceeded to undress me. The warning bells that something was very wrong began to ring again. A floorboard creaked in the darkness at the foot of the bed, beyond the rays of the moonlight streaming in, drawing my attention. Feeling every bit like Scrooge, I was fully expecting Marley's ghost to come flying at me, chains rattling. I said "hello?", and a naked pale-white leg stepped into the moonlight, followed by more nakedness as a beautiful young woman appeared, coming up to the foot of the bed. In the same accent as the old woman, she asked if I had slept well. A million questions were racing through my mind, I didn't know which to settle on first. Who was she, where did she come from, what was she doing here, why was I naked, why was she naked? She raised a thick eyebrow and laughed in amusement at me. Slowly she began to draw back the blankets covering me. *"Oh, if only you could see your face now young cub, truly a delight. Food, drink, and shelter I have given ye, and by the rights I come to make the final exchange. When you next wake, the geass will have been met, and you must leave."* Blankets pulled to her at the foot of the bed, she climbed over them, her pale body gliding up over mine until she sat atop me, straddling my hips. She leaned down to my face, a mass of dark curls falling about my head, tickling my cheeks, shrouding us in darkness. My heart felt like it was going to explode out of my chest. She had the strangest scent, a mixture of ice and sea spray, but it was far from unpleasant. She put her mouth over mine in a kiss, and thrust her tongue into my mouth. It sent a jolt of, I don't even know, something like electricity, but also that feeling when you take a bite of rich cake and the first bit of sugar hits the back of your mouth. I don't know, and frankly the look you're giving me says you've experienced that too, and I do not want to think about that. Sorry, getting through this part, and trying to pretend you're not across from me. Yes, it sent a jolt of excitement, adrenaline, heat, electricity, anything and everything that can go through you and make you feel like you're going to die if you don't let it out when it reaches its final destination. That's what it was, and I could not do anything against it. I didn't want to do anything against it, against her. Nothing else mattered except the act that came next.

After, she stayed on top of me, her face buried in the crook of my neck, her hands balled up on my chest. She bit me then, on my neck, and that same energizing jolt shot down through my body, I grabbed her by her hips and guided her back down. She went slower that time. Where the first was a frantic rush, the second was comforting, it felt more intimate. Afterwards was an atmosphere of luxurious languidity, my life was complete then and there, like I had done all I could with it, there was nothing more to give, to take. All that was left was to close my eyes and drift away into oblivion. Her delicate, porcelain-like fingers lightly swept my face, she told me to sleep. The next time I was awoken with my nipple in between her teeth, biting at me to just over the point of pain, sending pulses down through me the same as before. Her hand was tightly grasped onto me. I tried to taker her on top me again, but she said no, that she was *"well satisfied, I only wish to bring more out of you one last time."*

I woke up later well rested. And alone. I found my clothes folded neatly on a chair not far from the bed. Afterwards I took time to look around the room, it was sparsely decorated, but the window the moon had shone through earlier was massive in size, easily 6 feet across, it must have cost a fortune at the time it was built. The framework around each pane of glass set into the window looked freshly painted. I ran my finger over a piece of trim, and it came back clean. Then across a nightstand and had the same result. Even the floor was spotless. I don't think it meant anything other than she liked to keep a clean house, I was just surprised by it is all. Sorry, lost in the moment there. No, I heard you. I was weirded out, of course I was, come on. It's not like midnight sex with strangers is a normal thing for me. Sometimes I wish I had challenged it more. That feeling of want and need that came over me when she appeared, that wasn't normal, not like that. But, I mean, what do you want me to say? It happened and I can't change anything. Just like what happened to everyone else. Sex aside, it's not even the main thing I'd change. You know that.

Transcribed from a pause in the re-telling

"I'm sorry, I know it's not your fault. I wrote some really stupid questions for you to ask me, didn't I?"

"Look, Ron, you know how I feel about this, I wouldn't even ask you these things anyway, let alone for an entire accounting of it all. You know how dangerous this is, writing it all down, putting it out there."

"And that's exactly why this needs to be done. We can't challenge them on the mountain, there's too much there for them to draw from. But if I can draw them out, maybe we have a chance to put a stop to whatever it is they're trying to do."

"I think they're trying to live. Just like you. Just like me. Putting this to them will draw their ire and bring destruction to us. Nothing good will come from this Ronan."

"You'll still help won't you?"

"Of course, I gave my word on it. But I'm still going to tell you if I think you're being foolish. And this is foolish work."

"Your opinion has been noted, and also disregarded. Lets get back into it."

The door to my room opened into a hall with stairs leading down right in front of me. I was tempted to check the other rooms, to snoop around, maybe find something useful or of note. But a small voice at the back of my head piped up saying that, that would be a bad idea. So I stifled the urge and took the stairs down. Another door at the bottom lead me back to the main room I had been in the day before. There was no fire burning this time, and it was cold enough I could see my breath. There was a silence to the house, no hum or buzz of electrical appliances, just the inert quiet, and feeling of being cut-off from the modern world. I called out, in case the old woman, or the younger, might make an appearance. No one came, no creaks in the floorboards or distant steps sounding out to let me know there was anybody else in the house. On a long dining table offset to the left of the room sat a tin cup, a pitcher of water with a skin of ice already formed on top, and the packet of deer jerky.

Seeing the food and water made me realize just how hungry and thirsty I was in that moment. I had no idea what time it was, or how long I had slept for. I assumed it was early morning, but I didn't really have any way to be sure of it. The water was cool and delicious, the meat was as perfectly seasoned as I remembered it. I sat in the same chair as before, savoring this small bit of breakfast. That last bit of comfort before I went back out into the wild to face whatever it may be. And then I thought I heard something, or rather felt, more than heard. Like a soft vibration in the floor. I stood up, cocking my head to catch it again. Very faintly there was a thump, thump, thump. I loudly called out a "hello?" Again came the thumping, faster that time in response. I looked around, trying to figure out where it was coming from, which direction to start in. The noise stopped, I didn't know how well they, it, whatever, could hear me, but I shouted to them to keep making noise if they needed help. I stood still waiting for the noise to start again, after a minute it happened again. I still had the sense that I was feeling it just as much as hearing it, so I knelt down and put a hand to the floor, sure enough with each thump there was a thrum of vibration. I tried to see if I could follow that vibration to the source, but it quickly faded away when I stepped away from the spot it was strongest.

That's when I realized it was coming from directly below me. The first door I checked lead to a darkened formal dining room with no windows, mirrors running the full height of the room at either end. Seeing my reflection at the other end of the room scared me before I realized what it was. Two other doors were locked, hitting against them with my shoulder only told me they were sturdily built. The last door was the one the old woman had gone off into, what I figured to be the kitchen. Which it was. Various pots, pans, dried herbs, and other things you'd expect to find in a witch's kitchen from the Victorian era filled the room. It looked like it would have been the model room for every 'still life' style of painting ever created. A thick woven rug decorated the floor, moving it to the side proved a guess of mine about the place having a cold cellar; the trap door had a well-worn ring and had a solid heft to it as I raised it up.

As soon as I opened the door, the thumping turned into a dull banging sound. The noise no longer diffused by the sound-proofing of the thick floor. I called out first, wanting to make sure I wasn't disturbing some basement dwelling beast that would grab my legs out from beneath me as I walked down the steps. There was a pause to the banging, that then very quickly came back sounding like a series of slaps. I told the noise I was coming down. I knew what a cold storage was, just a space under the house to store perishables, before the invention of the refrigerator. This, wasn't a cold storage, at least not a conventional one. It was a damn dungeon. The steps went down part ways, stopped at a smooth stone landing, then turned left and continued on into near darkness. I went back up into the kitchen, out into the main room, then to the formal dining room. I took a candelabra from the table and was just about to go back to the kitchen to look for something to light it with, when a glint of light caught my eye from the other end of the table. That end of the room sat in darkness, the open door, with me standing in it, was reflected back to me from the mirrored wall. But it wasn't enough to illuminate everything. I couldn't even tell what the light had reflected off of for sure, but again, I had a small idea. More childhood fears of things with long arms reaching out from under the table for me came with me walking further into the room. It sounds so immature admitting to that, here, now. It didn't stop it from being any more creepy than it already was though.

The shape of the padding on the chair backs from the corner of my eye, made it look like they were occupied. My brain had gone into overtime with playing tricks on me. The occupants, dimly lit, sitting in the chairs like withered old corpses, bald headed and stationary. Trying not to see them only made them appear more real. I reached the end of the table. I moved plates and silverware aside, feeling, more than seeing, for whatever it was that caught my attention. I was about to give up when the shape in the chair in front of me moved forward and grabbed my hand, I swung the candelabra at it like crazy, meeting no resistance except the back of the chair. I tried to pull my hand free, but it had me locked in a hard firm grasp. It was cold and felt like bones were wrapped around me. I tried hitting it at my wrist, but again, there was nothing there, all I did was hit myself. It began to turn my hand over, I resisted, I fought, I cursed, I didn't know what was going to happen, but I had to get out of there. Another skeletal hand wrapped around my fist, prying my fingers open and placing what felt like a piece of ice into my hand, closing my fingers over it. Then it let me go. I fell back against the wall, gracefully sliding to the floor in about the same way as a thrown egg would. I scrambled up and ran to the door practically throwing myself through it. The dining room behind me released a great sigh of air and the door slammed shut. I looked into my hand, it was the object that had glinted at me earlier, a thousand years ago. An old butane lighter, an intricate carving of a man holding a spear, ready to throw, on the front. On the back, an inscription in a small cursive script; *"L– To always find your way back to me.–T"* I opened it, the wick was fresh like it had never been used, but lit strongly on the second flick of the wheel. I looked at the room, not sure what to do exactly. So I said thank you.

Back at the hatch I lit two of the candles, the third I had broken off in my frantic thrashing. The noise had stopped, I don't know when, and I went down the stairs slowly. The, ghost? Spirit? Whatever it was, had restored in me an even greater sense of caution that I was not aware I needed. I reached the bottom without anything grabbing at me from between the steps, and found myself in a large room, dimly lit because of the candles, to my left were several casks stacked on each other to the ceiling. To the right a shelf with various jars and containers with what looked like food. Hanging from rafters were multiple thin chains ending with large chunks of meat hooked through. The cold larder? I'll take your word for it, I guess your knowledge of these things is much better than mine. The candles weren't strong enough to show me the whole room. I sidestepped the hanging meat and made my way to the back. A large wine rack appeared in front of me, mostly full, but showing some gaps, the majority of the bottles were caked in a layer of dust, but there were a couple with handwritten labels that looked used even recently. I went left first, and soon discovered the corner where the rack met the wall. I turned back to go the other way, and discovered a smaller doorway framed into the opposite corner of the rack and wall. There was some damage to the wine-rack next to the doorway, and bits and pieces of wood lay scattered around the floor. The doorway continued into a narrow passage. I stood for a second, not knowing how deep it would go and already feeling claustrophobic about being hunched over in the space. But standing there, I heard a rustling noise, the kind that's made from fabric being pulled off a drying line you know? I hunched over and made my way into the small tunnel.

Okay, for this next part, I need to back track a little, and tell you about Steven and Carl. Just bear with me and it'll make sense. It's the least I can do for them. Steven Sorensen, and Carl Goodkind were the team Kansas guys. Best friends since day one of kindergarten. While playing during recess, Carl on a swing goaded on by another friend to get "really high" and then jump, launched himself off at what he felt was a very dangerous height. Steven, who was merely running by ended up being the cushion to Carl's fall. Carl was never by any means out of shape, but he came from very hearty corn fed stock and was just naturally bigger than his classmates. All that weight came down on a very scrawny Steven, causing him to piss his pants. Steven ran off in pain, and embarrassment. Carl, feeling the first bout of guilt and responsibility in his young life followed after, wanting to make sure this smaller kid would be okay. Those feelings would endure for the rest of their lives. Steven growing up with a penchant for causing trouble, Carl following after to reap the consequences for Steven's actions. One time getting caught stealing from the local IGA grocery store, or another time, setting off fireworks during a fire-ban drawing the ire of the local fire station. Or a favorite story of Steven's dad, told to me over a few beers in his workshop.

"When they were in high school, somewhere around sixteen, maybe seventeen years old. They got it into their heads, that they were going to prank a teacher of theirs who'd been coming down a bit hard on them for not taking the class so seriously. And boy howdy, when those two put their heads together, they could cause some right trouble. Now, behind their school were a few dumpsters on wheels, this was also where the faculty parking was. So, they happened to get a hold of a long, thick rope, and don't even get me started on where they managed to lift that from. But, they took this long rope, fucker was probably about a hundred feet,

and they got it tied off to one dumpster, looped it through the teacher's car, and then finished tying it off to the other dumpster. Then they paid a friend of mine, can you believe it? Let me say it again they paid a friend of mine twenty bucks, to call the teacher at the school, tell him his house was on fire, then hang up! So you know what he does then? That teacher goes tearing out of the building, gets to his car, and floors it out of the lot, and just yanks those dumpsters right along with 'em. Guy had a couple wrecking balls tied to his car and was too worked up about his house to even notice! Well, one got wrapped around a tree just as he was leaving the school grounds and that put a quick stop to his car. But then the other one just went right on by him, jumped the curb, snapped the rope, and flew right into the fence around the tennis courts. School needed to replace the old fence anyway. Scared him so bad another buddy of mine said the car smelled like shit when he went to tow it away, damn kids tied it around his rear axle! Broke it all to hell, tore up the whole undercarriage. Afterwards, they denied it. 'Course they did. His mom and I backed him up, Carl's parents backed him up. It was just stupid kids doing stupid things, didn't need to bring anything bigger out of it. But the balls on them. My old man would have skinned me alive for pulling a stunt like that. We worked out a deal with the teacher, any jobs needed doing, those two were the ones for it. Mowing lawns, picking up trash from the side of the highway, maybe they're the only two throwing bales for a day or two on Carl's family farm, running errands on their own dime for the teacher. Stuff like that, he liked the idea of working 'em to the bone. But you know what. There was a secret to Steven and Carl. They were the hardest working boys I'd ever known. Steven was like a machine, skinny as a twig before the army bulked him up, but once he got going he wouldn't even take a break, and if Carl started lagging behind a bit, Steven would be there telling him to come on, just a little bit more. Those two, I was proud of them." We drank in silence for a while then. Afterwards I thanked him for his time.

After high school, Steven enlisted in the army, following in his father's footsteps, and his father's before him. Carrying on the family tradition. Carl went to college, but after his father suffered a mild heart attack, dropped out to move back home to start taking over the family farm duties. In a reversed bit of story telling clichés, his parents were actually against this, with Carl being the one to insist it's what needed to be done. They were ultimately proud of him, and just a little bit relieved that Steven wasn't around to get him into trouble. Steven did eventually come home from basic training. For about three weeks, before being informed his unit was shipping out for Desert Storm. He was part of an engineering division set for a twelve-month tour. He came back from the war, as those who do, a different man. His mother and younger sister saw someone who was more stoic and less boisterous. His father saw a man that had had responsibilities thrust upon him, and rose to the challenge, much like he did years before. Carl saw someone who had grown up, matured greatly, more so than he, working on the farm. A man who was content with just sitting quietly over a camp-fire with a case of beer between them. It was a strange adjustment for everyone, but one they accepted, and life went on.

Steven, always having a strong aptitude towards math, had been encouraged by his commander early on towards getting a business degree. Which he easily obtained. Eventually coming to work at Carl's Farm, running numbers and increasing profits. They never drifted apart, their friendship remained strong through the years. One night during the evening news broadcast out of Topeka, a short segment listed the casting call for Peak Challenge. Steven, seeing this, felt a rare burst of excitement spring up from his inner wild child. Being avid sleep-under-the-stars campers for the majority of their lives, he decided that this was going to be something he and Carl would try out for. Carl was a little reluctant, as he always was to

Steven's plans, but he gave in, just as he always did. They made their submission, and were accepted.

Events for them proceeded similarly as they did for the other groups. Things were fine at first, then the little things started happening, then the radio difficulties, leading to the eventual attacks. The difference comes up in that the crew assigned to Team Kansas, in a very small granting of serendipity from the universe, happened to be comprised of three men who had also been enlisted men. Steven was senior in ranking among them, holding Major. Camera Operator David Bailey was a recently promoted Specialist. Boom Operator Zach Hill a Staff Sergeant, and Production Assistant Matthew Cooper also a Specialist. When shit hit the fan, there was no better prepared troop than them. They banded together, and did what they had been trained to do. They held their own much better than the other groups, suffering no casualties, no life-threatening wounds. The attacks stopped, and the snow came, it was rough, but again, it wasn't enough to finish them off. There was no doubt in any one of their minds that they would get out of that forest and get help, summon the might of the whole damn army, come back and lay waste to whatever it was that had been tormenting them. Then "the monster" came.

The attack, same as the others, was at night. The Specialists had taken the first watch duty. The others, having been asleep for maybe a couple of hours, when they were woken by shouts from David. Rushing out from their shelter, torches and spears in hand, they encountered a scene that neither Carl nor Steven could make sense of at first. A very large man,

"Like Bigfoot" coming from Carl

"It wasn't fucking Bigfoot" from Steven

...had David up in the air at arm's length, holding him with its massive hand wrapped around his head. Matthew's body was being held by the other arm of the creature, his head hanging limply to his back, being nearly torn off. Zach had been the first one out, and had already thrown his spear at the monster, striking it in the chest, but ineffectually bouncing off. He approached through the deep snow, torch held in front of him, waving it towards the creature trying to get it to drop his friend. He got close enough to hit it once with the torch. The monster was unfazed and only looked down at the man in front of him, then swung a struggling David up and around like a club, smashing Zach into the ground. Again, and again, and again. Steven turned to Carl and told him to drop the torch and run. There was, what felt like three or four feet of snow on the ground, and Carl cut a path through it as easily as a hot knife through butter. Steven followed, ready to spin around with his spear to give his friend a chance to escape, although he wasn't sure if it would've been possible. They ran until Carl's adrenaline ran out and exhaustion set in. Steven watched their trail, sure that any minute, if not second, a large dark form would appear barreling towards them. But nothing did. He didn't know why it wasn't following them, but he was happy it wasn't.

There is however, another problem he's becoming aware of. They left all their gear, what little of it they had, behind. They had been slightly cocky coming into the production, wanting to show off how easily they could "rough it" in the wild. Thankfully they have winter coats, heavy-duty khakis, and hiking boots. They've left what little food they had behind, but more importantly in Steven's mind, is that they have no water. Somewhere in the run Carl had lost his spear. After a short break they decide to keep moving through the night, looping back at times to make false trails in the snow. The sun rises, they trudge on.

Hours later, they come to the valley at the base of the mountain. And stumble upon the large cabin. No one answers their calls, or the banging on doors and windows. They can see inside and can tell that someone is definitely using the place as a home. There's even a fire burning. They end up forcing a door open. They find the kitchen with bread, dried meats, and a fresh brewed pot of coffee. They practically can't help themselves fast enough. Justifying breaking in and eating this food on their life or death scenario, surely whoever lives there won't begrudge them that. Afterwards, they sit in front of this roaring fire, comfortable and safe. Not being able to help it, they doze off. Steven wakes up later and of course knows something is immediately wrong because he's hanging upside down in a cold, stony room, lit by a lone candle. Carl is hanging next to him. Boots and outerwear are piled off to the side, thankfully they were left still wearing pants and long-sleeved shirts. After a while of Steven making enough noise, Carl comes to. They're trying to figure out what happened, when they hear noise above them. It's quiet, but it's there, people talking. They shout and yell as best they can, but hanging upside down, and having been in that state for who knows how long, weakens them quickly.

They surface to consciousness together some time later. Steven can hear his heart pounding in his ears, his head hurts more than the worst hangover of his life a year before did. It's hard to think, it's hard to breathe. He slowly turns his head, to see Carl looking about the same as he feels, he has a plan that he has to get working on before they pass out again. It takes a few tries, talking to Carl, getting him to focus is hard work. Carl is having a hard time hearing, and then is slow about understanding what is said. His whole world has devolved into a miserable slow motion. He doesn't understand why Steven wants his shirt. He feels like someone lit a fire inside his head, and it's spreading up through his body, getting rid of the shirt that's uncomfortably gathered around his chest isn't a great loss to him.

The candle has almost gone out, there's still just enough light for Steven to see where the support beam is to his right. He's managed to get the shirts tied together, a simple act that leaves him seeing black spots popping in and out of existence before him. Now comes the hard part. He lashes the shirts out in a makeshift whip, but misses, tries again, and gets it to wrap around the beam a little, when he yanks, it just slides right off. He's already breathing hard and decides to try a different approach. 'Carl, hey, focus buddy, I'm going to throw this to you, I need you to catch it and give it a pull for me okay? I need to start swingin.' Carl's confused, why does Steven want to swing? This isn't kindergarten, this isn't any sort of fun. His mind must be going. 'Carl! Come on man, focus!' The fog in Carl's mind clears just a little, he catches the shirt end and pulls on his end. He's got about fifty more pounds on him over Steven, physics does the rest.

Swinging makes Steven feel even worse, he doesn't know how much longer he can keep up, but he's so close, just a little bit more. He tells Carl to let go of the shirt. He lashes out again, there's more than enough left now to wrap around the post and itself. He pulls it tightly at the same time and his movement stops. He's hanging at an angle, but the shirt snagged in just the way he was hoping for. Inches away from the other end of it, he needs to carefully pull himself to it. Luck is still on his side, and he's able to painstakingly climb his way up the sleeve and grab a hold of the other end. Grip and position secure, he can't help but smile at this small victory. 'Hang in there man, we're getting out of here' he says to Carl. He pulls himself up the shirts, twisting the ends around his fist as he finally reaches the beam. He starts hitting it with the Morse code of SOS. The post is solid, he's settled into a beat, it doesn't sound like Morse code anymore, but he doesn't care, he just hopes to be heard.

He wakes up from a nightmare of that giant *thing* slowly pulling his left arm from the socket. Simian-like smile growing on the monster's face as his arm stretches further from his body. He panics, thinking the massive hand is still gripped around his wrist, then he realizes it's just the shirt, he passed out again. It's pitch black, the candle having finally given up the ghost. He whispers Carl's name, but doesn't get an answer. Says it louder, but silence is the only thing returned. The arm tangled up in the shirt hurts bad, hanging from it like he was, it's tightened around his wrist like a boa constrictor. It hurts like a bitch, but he's able to slowly turn himself towards the post, gripping the bad arm with the slightly less bad one. He rests for a moment then, relishing in the small relief he gets from having some of the weight and strain taken off his arm. Then it's back to the painful work of getting himself to the beam. When he hits it, he knows he's not going to be able to keep it up for long, he can barely make a fist, he's sure that something in his hand is broken. He steadies his breathing as best he can. Thump, thump, thump. He thrust his fist against the post, his mind insisting to give his most. Thump, thump, thump. And then he hears it, faint and far away, a small "hello?" The excitement of a response sends the adrenaline flowing, and he slaps at the beam in reply. The adrenaline is burnt up just as quickly as it was released into him, and he clings to the beam, his head pounding in pain, waves of nausea flowing over him. He hears some muffled words, louder than the hello, but with his head going critical, he can't sort out anything specific. He's able to rest his head on his arm, gets his breathing under control, and then hits the post three more times as hard as he can, waits, relaxes, breathes, hits it again.

You know the rest from there. I show up through the small tunnel, the light from my candles is enough to fill this tiny room, there's not much to it. Steven and Carl are hanging from ropes tied around their ankles, secured to the wall. There's a table to one side, the remains of a candle in an old brass holder, several types of knives on the table. Their coats are in a small pile on the floor next to the table. The room smells bad, I'm very certain Steven and Carl were not the first to wake up in there. I was surprised that I didn't end up in there too. I manage to get them down from the ceiling. Steven is awake, he can barely talk, barely move. Carl is out, but he's breathing. I tell them to hang on, and I go for the water. When I come back with it, Steven has managed to get his back against a wall, Carl is on his side, trying to get up, but he's in a pretty feeble state. I help him get to the wall where Steven is, and then give them the water. In the light of the candles, they look ghoulish, more dead than alive. Their eyes are dark, bloodshot to hell. They're bloodied, bruised, and looking like they were driven well past their breaking points. The water helps a bit. Steven finds his voice, Carl just sits and stares into space. I tell him who I am, he tells me who they are. I help them get the shirts back on, then their coats, and then we just sit there for a while. Letting them gather their strength. Steven tells me about the events that lead to them ending up hanging from the ceiling in a dungeon under a cabin that shouldn't be there at all.

They're shaky on their legs, but use the wall as support, we make our way upstairs. Getting back up into the main part of the cabin is a relief. They still look worn out, their skin sallow now. I get them seated in front of the fire place, a cup of water in one hand, a stick of jerky in the other. There are split logs in a holder next to the hearth, and it doesn't take me long to get a new fire going, pushing the cold away. We sit there for some time, not talking, I know they've been through a lot. I don't want to push them, but it feels like it's the middle of the day now, and I don't want to lose any more of the light. I tell them about what I had been through, that I didn't have any idea of what to do, except to go up further on the mountain, and hopefully find the others. From there, I guess we'd just have to see. Looking through the windows, I could still see the freakish storm swirling around us, I think it may have closed in more, but I could've imagined that. Carl is in shock, he'll take a sip of the water, but he hasn't touched the meat, hasn't said anything aside from small noises of acknowledgment. I notice Steven hasn't touched his meat either, but he's had more of the water at least. His voice is raspy, but he's using it. He says we should find weapons. He had a wooden spear when they first got there, but doesn't know what happened to it. I get up and go to the kitchen, then come back with two butcher knives, and a filet knife. They feel so useless in my hands, like toys. I keep the filet knife and stick it into the front pocket of my coat. I hand the butcher knives to the guys. I can't help but say that it feels like they won't be much use, but Steven says it's better than nothing, and I leave it at that. A door creaks open above us, and heavy footsteps cross above us, stop, turn back, and cross again. The door slams shut. Steven stands up, knife at the ready. The hairs on my neck stands up, I can feel the goosebumps on my arms. I tell them I think it's time we go. I've had enough in this fucked up place.

XXI. The Prospector's Son

July 5 1927

Mother has given me this journal, a keepsake of my Father's. I remember seeing him writing away in it when I was younger, but not as much as I grew up. We laid him to rest this past Sunday, under the oak tree he was fond of, next to Sona. These last years of his life were difficult for him. I hope he has found the peace he sought before the disease of the brain set in. I like to think he is in a better place, with a similar oak tree, Sona resting by his side, smoking that pipe of his and just enjoying the quiet. He used to say mother talked enough for the two of them anyway.

Now, to his, this, journal. Some of these things I can confirm, Caitlin, she is my mother in that she is the one who birthed me. But Cora, she is the mother that raised me. They never spoke of how it came to be that she joined us, I never thought to ask when I was younger, after reading this, I never will. She has given so much, I will not ask her to remember something so awful. Was my first mother a witch? That, I cannot say. I am inclined to say the latter parts were of a pure fantasy of my father. He was adept at telling long weaving fantastical stories. It could be that this disease that took him, had been already at work even then. It would explain the oddities I suppose. But, there are other things that hold no explanation.

Before I left to the front in Seventeen, I was twenty-one, and my father had only just started a noticeable decline, but we were still given many conversations. One morning at breakfast, I was in the habit of presenting myself fresh from bed, part of my wilderness upbringing mother says, I sat at the table, shirtless, hair unfashionably long and not even tied behind my head. Father stared at me from across the table, his usual jovial self looking lost in thought, I asked him what was the matter. He looked at me with confusion, and asked how I came to be in front of him, what message did I bring with me now? I was confused myself, not understanding it was one of his "attacks" happening. He asked how it could be that the son had come down to him once more. After reading his journal, I finally understand that he wasn't meaning me, his son, but that he meant The Sun, the one he dreamt when I was just a baby. I'll admit, I do fit the description. As to that breakfast, I was younger, and fearful then of what was happening to him. Mother swept in quickly, shooing me away and taking care of him.

Later, he had no memory of this moment. Then it was back to our discussions about why he thought I shouldn't go to war, and why I thought I should. I know he worried about me, but there was this, and it sounds crazy to write it down now, but there was this burning in me, like I was the arrow pulled back on the string, and I could feel all that energy behind me. Ready for it to let loose and direct me to a target. And then I was off and away. Hair cut, rifle in hand, and joining an infantry company in France. How stupid I was, how young. War suited me well, it was like the hunting trips when I was a child. With weapon in hand I was unstoppable, driving forward and into enemy positions thinking I was some invincible warrior. Even when a stray bullet planted itself into my arm, I still fought on, not even aware of it until, I think it was Benny, that crazy little Italian, noticed and said "Holy shit, Lou's bleeding out!"

Then it was over like it had hardly begun. I wasn't happy then, coming back home, my father beginning to haunt the house as this faded copy of himself. Moments of clarity shining through less and less. I threw myself into university, but I couldn't help myself against getting into row after row at the local places. Some guy would start running his mouth about where the country was heading, why the war was a bad idea for us in the first place, and there I'd be swinging on them. Then I met Thea, and she helped me, I think much the way mother helps father. There's a calming that a wife can bring the husband. And then a couple of years ago, Orwin came along. And now, that war, the fighting, it's as if it were all a dream. Mother has asked if we'd like to move back into the manor house with her, Thea has agreed to it, and I don't see anything wrong with it either. Father saw fit to place me on several of his company's boards, it's purely a figurehead gesture, but I think I'll start researching into them a bit more. It was always his dream that I'd be there right next to him, making whatever decisions needed to be made. These places practically run themselves, but I'll see what I can do.

I thought I saw Uncle Edmond downtown the other day. That handsome ruggedness was there, as were some dark scars on the man's face. He looked just as I remembered him, and the last time I saw him was my tenth birthday, before we ran away. He'd be an old man now just the same as my father. Father's insane story not withstanding, I do think I saw another veteran who just triggered the memory of Edmond. I don't know what happened to him, hell, to any of us that night. Mother doesn't remember much either, it does seem my first mother had a habit of drugging us. So whatever my father saw Edmond as, he did see him killed by that spear we had hanging above the fireplace. After his library and university visits, he would come home excited, crazy claims swirling in his head. "Lou! I talked to so-and-so today, they have a theory that the wolfman can heal from any injury! Don't you see, there's a chance he survived!" As a child this always thrilled me. My Uncle, the werewolf. And after reading through the story, it was also my mother the witch, and me, the forest sprite. It was not always so amazing as that as a child, I remember long moments of boredom, mother before she became mother reading to me from our collection, or playing with the phonograph making the voices warble, slow, or speed up. I don't remember this giant of a man named Bres either. I did ask mother about him, she shivered at the question, and said he was someone close to Caitlin, but that he lived further up the mountain. Father hated him, and he was not allowed at the house. But if he was really some giant ape-like man she would not say. Only that he smelled terrible, she would hide us away in my room if she knew he would be by.

Lately I have been having more dreams about the old homestead. It seems to be the same one recurring. There is a gravel road leading up to the house, I'm walking with a pack over my shoulder, like I'm coming home from war. It's cold, there's a voice in my head telling me to get there before dark. They'll get me if I'm out after the sun sets. But I don't know who "they" are. Probably father's goblins. But I'm still trying to rush, but it's as if I'm walking through molasses, every step is just a slow, struggle to the next one. Mother, Caitlin, is on the porch, arms crossed in front of her, looking how I remember her, dark and broody, with this awful smile on her face, like she knew, that you knew, she would pinch you the moment you relaxed. Like she's playing with me, teasing me like a schoolyard bully. She's the one to have told me I need to get in before the sun sets, and yet it's she who is also putting this "slowness" to my stride. Taunting me that I'm not fast enough, strong enough. Then from all around comes the cackling laughter. Angry ravens like father said, but these ravens sound like the people in an asylum. Then the sun sets, and I'm left stranded in the dark, and the evil laughter gets closer. I pull my lighter from my bag, and flick it several times. Finally it takes, and I have the smallest of flames, just barely enough. But still enough to reflect the light off of the large eyes surrounding me. Then I wake up, breathing hard. Thea, sleeping with the fragility of parenthood wakes with me, first asking about Orwin.

I wonder if they can be more than dreams. If that mother is, was, what father said she was, what if it's a challenge. What if she's telling me to come back and find out? All I've had are father's words, words even he was careful to never really share outside our home. All his studies were only for the sake of academia, of course he never believed it. Behind closed doors was another matter, filling my head with all this. That I was set to be a sacrifice for something? And yet, much like the war ten years ago, there's this burning in me, pointed across the country to my childhood home. I know I should be fine and happy with all that I have here. And I am. But what if she wasn't really that bad? What if there's a chance to reconcile? I think I will try for it. I can arrange for a trip, make my way out there, get answers straight from the source. She was my mother, how dangerous for me can it be?

make my way out there, get answers straight from the source. She was my mother, how dangerous for me can it be?

Once we were out in the snow, Sam and Ty turned to me. I asked "what?" And Ty said that he just thought I'd have a plan. I was the shortest one there, and they were looking for me to lead them through the snow? I told them to just pick a direction leading away from the mountain. If we kept it at our backs, we'd find out way out. I had Sam go first, then Ty, they pushed through the snow enough to give me a bit of a path to follow. And that was it, that was our day. It was hard, we slipped and fell about a dozen times, but we kept going with the mountain looming behind us. The path we carved made it easy to tell we were going in one direction, weaving around trees, boulders, finding our way around ledges and whatever other obstacle presented itself to us. The forest seemed larger, like at some point it had expanded out to twice as far. But it was just the snow slowing our progress that made it feel that way is what I told myself. We had to put in about double the work just getting through it. By the end of the day though, it wasn't enough.

We had crested a rise and the trees had left a bare space for us to see further. I couldn't believe my eyes. Ahead of us lay miles and miles of forest, and then at the edge of that was the wall of the storm, following that wall showed it was circling us, surrounding us. Sam gasped, and Ty asked 'what the fuck is going on?' Grabbing at his head and pacing. I put a hand out and touched him, scared him, he looked like he was going to jump out of his skin. I held my hands up to him, and told him we'd be okay. He turned and pointed to the storm, to the forest that went right up to it, asking how were we going to be okay, how did I know? I told him it was because that's what his brother thought. He asked what do we do now? And I didn't know. I was thinking just the same as him, but I didn't want to share that, what would it help? I think, after losing Eric, I was numb and developed a bit of a death-wish. I wished I could have set out on my own, we had counted on being out of the forest by that point. From there it wouldn't have been a stretch to have gotten to a road. Or, on my own I could've just gotten too cold, sat down for a break, and then just have closed my eyes. It's not that I wanted to die, it just would have been an easy way out. And here I was with these two men, and I didn't want them to die. In the face of what was laying ahead of us though, what were we to do? So I said the same as that morning, lets just keep the mountain to our back and keep going, we needed to find somewhere to shelter for the night soon, so we needed to keep our eyes open for that.

By nightfall though, we hadn't found anything that would work for us. We hadn't said a word to each other for some time. I don't think we needed to by then, we were all thinking the same thing. We were fucked. It was like we had been walking on a treadmill all day, the mountain didn't get smaller as the distance from it increased, there was no end to the forest, there was a storm raging around us, but we hadn't even gotten closer to it. Ty had taken the lead, camping light held out in front of him. He was scared, and angry, or letting the fear turn to anger I suppose.

Dre: Anger leads to hate. Hate leads to suffering.

Ally: Shush it Dre. Sixty-two years old and somehow he's able to maintain the man-child attitude. Also deflecting I think.

Dre: A little bit of both. Ty would come down and revoke my nerd card if I didn't take the chance.

He'd be proud of you for everything Teddy. And that night when he was mad, he was cussing at everything. Fucking trees, fucking rocks, fucking sky, and then he stopped. Like entirely. Then said 'no way' and went off again. Sam and I both said 'what' but it didn't take long to see for ourselves. We had intersected with our path, somehow, but the real kicker, was that Ty was following it to our left, and heading right to the shelter we had left behind that morning. He vanished inside, with us coming up right behind him. Dre was happy to see us come crawling in, Nick was surprised, then disappointed. Not that we had come back, but that we hadn't been able to get help. Dre told us that Brandon had passed away during the day.

Dre: Was a damn shame, he started convulsing, Nick got to him first, and I dragged myself over, but there just wasn't a thing we could do. The convulsions stopped about thirty seconds later and his breath went out with it, and that was that.

Ally: Brandon and Eric lay on one side of the shelter, their coats covering them. The five of us lay huddled together on the opposite side. I listened while Ty and Sam reasoned with Nick and Dre about why it was impossible for us to have made it back to the shelter how we had. Keeping the mountain at our back during the day all but guaranteed that. And yet, there we were. Dre, ever the believer, wanted to say that God had saved us, had led us back to relative safety. And I being the cynical pragmatist that I was back then, spoke up to say he was wrong, his "God" should have led us to the road and to help. Something else brought us back there, to the shelter. Something didn't want us to leave.

Dre: And you know what, that shut me up then. When Ty came back that night, I was over-joyed to see him. I was singing praise be, from my heart. I was happy they all made it back alive, when they left that morning, I had doubts about seeing any of them again. That my leg would take care of me long before they were able to make it back. Because of that wound, that infection spreading through me, it was making it more difficult to distinguish between the reality of our situation, and my personal feelings of faith. So Ally introducing this "Other", it helped me make sense of things a bit better. I asked what could be doing this to us, not in challenge to Ally's words, but because I had no answer for it myself. The things from before, with their blow guns, and noise making, this wasn't them, I was sure of it. What the hell was this place?

Ally: Nick spoke up then with a cliché, he said "yeah, exactly, this is Hell." We didn't really have anything to disagree with him on that. But Dre said that it was all the more reason to fight. The optimism was nice, but I don't think we expressed it much then. It ended up being the conversation killer, with us going into our own thoughts after that. I was wedged between Dre and Nick, and was actually feeling some semblance of warmth. Combined with the exhaustion from hiking all day it did not take me long to fall asleep.

It was a weird sleep though, I know I was dreaming at some point during it. And then I stopped dreaming, and slowly became aware of things around me. Like sleep paralysis yes, but I couldn't open my eyes. I couldn't even feel my body, I was just in this black space with bits and pieces of noise filtering through. It sounded like *them*, those things that had been harassing us, killing us, their nasal whine of a voice. I was scared, and confused. I don't think I've ever experienced such a complete and utter sense of helplessness in my life. It was awful. Sometimes I wonder if that's what it's like for people in a coma. That they're awake somewhere in there, but so locked away they can't do anything but *be*.

Dre: Yeah, I was going through the same thing too. After I had "killed the conversation" as she put it, I lay there looking at the ceiling of our shelter. Wondering what would come next. We hadn't been attacked since before the snow. My body felt like it was still on fire. Something was going to have to be done about my leg if we stayed longer. I was terrified of that. Ty had fallen asleep, I wanted to give myself just this one more night, before talking to him about it. I felt relaxed then, and decided that would be a good time to try to sleep. No sense worrying about what I couldn't change in that moment, and cross that bridge in the morning.

And then same as Ally, I was asleep for a bit, then I was awake, but stuck in Limbo. I thought maybe I had died, and this was the last bit before the next big thing happened. I was sad, for Ty to have to deal with it when he woke up, then later for Momma. But I told myself that I was just going home, and after a while they'd be there too. Except I didn't go anywhere. And I could hear those things too. I was aware of breathing too. I had a down right horrified moment of thinking that maybe death meant being trapped inside your head for eternity. Can you imagine that? Well hell, I sure was then and there. I kept circling back to that feeling of breathing though. How was that supposed to work anyway? Nothing made sense, and the more I went around and around with it, the less it kept making. So I did what I do it times of hardship, I prayed.

Ally: I didn't have that luxury. Oh no, no, no. I do not begrudge him anything. I'm glad for him to have had something that gave him comfort. I never once thought I was dead, I just felt trapped. I wanted out. I wanted to open my eyes, I wanted to feel my body. I'm glad I could still hear, even if it were in bits and pieces. And even if it was just to hear those things. It was something, it was grounding. It was already the worst thing ever, I can't even conceive of it without sound. Maybe I could have died then? In fact, I believe that, that is why we could hear, I think without that, it would have disconnected us entirely, and then we would have just died. So we were "allowed" a sense or two. Time was there too, we were aware of time passing. That internal clock was still ticking. But without many points of reference to go on, it could have been any length of time. I've said it felt like maybe two or three hours? Dre said for him, it felt like sitting at a desk for eight hours. So who knows? It of course came to an end. My head came back first, and I was aware of something pressing hard on my forehead, I was finally able to open my eyes. And wished that I still couldn't. There was this ancient, naked woman in front of me, her middle finger was what was against the center of my forehead. When I say ancient, I mean it, she had gone beyond old, she shouldn't have been able to stand, her legs were just bony sticks. Her skin was pulled tight against her skull, she barely had lips to cover her mouth. Brown crooked teeth were exposed in a permanent grimace. She stood back, just staring at me, what hair she had left on top of her head was black and wiry, sticking out in all directions. I was so shocked at seeing this living skeleton that I hadn't even been aware of coming back in control of the rest of my body. I was sitting and tied with my hands behind me to a pole. Dre was to my right, and tied up the same as I. His head was slumped forward, his chin on his chest. I couldn't tell if he was breathing or not. The woman-thing went to him next, and placed her middle finger on the center of his forehead, raising it up and bringing her face close to him.

Dre: When I opened my eyes, I didn't see some old hag. I saw a small girl, she might have been about ten, maybe even younger, I'm not sure. She had a lion's mane of black hair. When I saw that she didn't have any clothes on, I looked away. She took my head in her hands, and brought it back around attracting my eyes onto hers. "You, bear witness." is what she said to me, plain as day.

Ally: I saw her grab him, but I didn't see her mouth move, only that then he seemed locked in place with her eyes. She backed away slowly from him, holding his gaze, she straightened up and threw her arms open wide, gesturing to me, to look around. She had captivated me so well, I wasn't aware of our surroundings until then. I saw the chaos that was around us, what she, they, had done to everyone. Saw Eric hanging, mutilated. I screamed.

XXIII The Prospector's Son

From a letter folded into the same page as the last entry.

My Dearest Thea,

July 27

It has been a long arduous journey, but I have arrived in Seattle. I find myself missing you and Orwin more each day. Much is changed from my childhood, and I fear I find myself a stranger in this fast growing city. Upon arriving I realized that I am close to the same age Father was when he first came to the area. I was able to confirm through the ledgers of Saeweras Holdings, that Firmara Lumber does, and still, exists! The work-up that I had accounting pull for me showed that we own fifteen percent, and pay out a marginal sum for upkeep. Father never mentioned this to me before. I believe he was still supporting Caitlin all these years. I have hired a lawyer here who helped me discover the original registrar form Father filed. He paid for it in perpetuity. Firmara Lumber will outlast the very office its registered to! Unfortunately that is where the trail has stopped. There is no one around from his time here to remember him. The locals are aware of Tenas Tilikum, but they claim no one has ever lived there. I could not find anyone willing to lead me to such a place either. The lawyer has found that my father had the majority of his holdings transferred to an office in Portland at the time we fled from our home. I am set to travel there tomorrow and will continue from there if, no, sorry, when I learn more.

July 30

And learn so much more I have! My dearest, my darling Thea. I have met a man who worked for father. Or at least claims to have. For my dealings with him, he has been soused to the eyeballs. He says he was one of the carpenters brought on to make additions to the cabin. To his credit he remembered Uncle Edmond quite fondly as his foreman. He was also able to describe the area of my childhood home, rather well.

AND most of all, you will not believe this, he claims the bear attack did happen, he described it much the way Father did. He calls himself "Charlie White-Feather" and I believe him to be the "Charles" Father briefly mentioned. I have offered to buy him a lunch and dinner if he will meet with me tomorrow in a much more sober state. He agreed, and explained he had been waiting to speak with me for 20 years.

• • • •

July 31

My Love, I have learned that Charlie White-Feather is never sober, he seems to operate in levels of drunkenness the most devout drunkard would kneel before to learn from. However he is a jovial chap, and not given to the drunken antics of rowdy behavior as I was before you saved me. Unfortunately, I do not know how much more useful this information he has held on to for twenty years is. However, it does solve one of Father's mysteries. Tenas Tilikum is the native's name here for the mountain I was born on. "Little Friend or Little People" is the English translation. Charlie further explained, that after the events that took place during the work there, he was hit with an awful curiosity to delve into the history of that particular land. Their stories are passed down through the ages by word of mouth. So each collection of peoples has their own stories. Some persist, and in others, the elders may pass early and those stories are lost. Or illness strikes and a whole tribe will vanish. Here Charlie smiles very proudly, as he was able to track down the remaining elder who just so happened to have the story of the Mountain. She passed the story to him, and he passed it to me. And now, I shall record it here for you, and the sake of posterity.

'Long ago, shortly after the birth of The People from the eggs of Thunderbird, there flew another bird from the east. She did not have the Thunder, nor could she block out the sun like Him. She was as black as the space between stars and knew many secrets. She called herself Feeakna. She named Thunderbird cousin, and asked for safety. She had

come from a great battle carrying the body of her husband, a powerful leader, and needed the appropriate mound for him. Thunderbird had pity for his little cousin and granted her a mountain. Feeakna carved out a great piece of the mountain and buried her husband within the rock, as was the way of her people. After he was interred, a great many small people sprang forth from the rock he was buried in. These people of Feeakna were great crafters, and The People traded with them for many years. Earning the mountain the name of "Little Friend Mountain". Then the white-man came, calling them monsters, they would clash with these little people whenever they would meet. This made them very angry, and they stopped their trade with everyone, choosing to hide, and kill any trespassers. The name of the mountain may still be Tenas Tilikum, but there are no friends there anymore.'

Charlie helped me record this. He was fairly well into a few bottles near the end, so I am not sure just how accurate it is, but I believe it comes across well. I wish Father were around for this. He would have loved to hear it. As it is, Charlie seems to recall the way into my home, and for a hefty sum, has agreed to act as my guide.

Of course I do not believe there is any truth to this story, I will not give in to old superstitions. I am going to visit my mother, not a pitch black bird and her minions sprung from stone. While it does lend credence to a race of people living there, at least per Father's journal. He met Caitlin when she was all but seventeen. In a few days time I will have the truth from her, if she even still resides there. After twenty years it is just as likely I'm going to stumble upon the ruins of my childhood home. I will post this to you, and write again when I am returned to civilization. Wish me luck.

All of my love to you and Orwin,
Yours Forever
Louis
-Author's note: There are no further entries.

All things considered, the hike from the cabin up the mountain was about the easiest part of the past few days. Steven walked with me for most of it, Carl lagged not far behind. He was talkative at first, giving me the cliff notes story of his, and subsequently Carl's life growing up in Kansas. But the further we moved up the mountain, the quieter he became. I don't think Carl spoke at all during the hike. I assumed it was exhaustion setting in from their ordeal. Steven wasn't sure how long they had been hanging there, under the house, but seemed to believe it was possibly for about a day, maybe a little longer. It was hard to tell. I told him I understood and we moved on. We were making a surprisingly good pace, I would ask every now and then if we needed to slow down, or to take a break. Steven would shake his head, or answer with a "nah I'm good" in that Midwestern easy going way as if nothing bad at all had been happening during the entire week out there. I thought it was a little odd that he was answering for both himself and Carl, if I turned back to ask Carl personally, Steven would still be the one to give an answer. I just figured that was the dynamics of their friendship.

Even with the surprising speed we were moving at, it was clear that we probably would not be reaching any destination until after nightfall. The sun was already in the process of sinking down behind the raging storm clouds, casting a dark twilight shadow over us. That same storm, by the way, that I wondered about growing closer earlier, had definitely tightened up around us more. Yet another thing sending us up to whatever was in store for us. By the time we reached the tree line, the sun had fully set, what little light we had to work with was gone. Through the eye of the storm above us, a peaceful starry night was visible, the silver light from the moon was just breaking over the edge of the clouds. We passed through the snow and trees into the great wide open space of the body of the mountain. I stumbled as we came out, my legs had grown used to the resistance of the snow that was suddenly not there, and caught myself on hard rocky terrain. It had stopped at the tree line. A waist high line of snow behind me stretching out following the trees in either direction. Another wall in that fucked up place. I voiced my concern to Steven about how we were being led, and that I didn't like it. He shrugged, resigned to whatever it was that had happened and carried on beyond me. Carl didn't try to pass me however, and was just waiting for me to follow on behind Steven. I told him I just needed a breather for a minute, and to go on ahead, I'd be right there. He didn't move, didn't make a grunt meaning "okay", just stood there silently waiting. I asked him what the fuck his problem was, started walking down the gentle slope to confront him better, but Steven yelled down to us that he could see a light. I apologized to Carl, snapping out of my frustrated state and saw that my anger being directed at him was undeserved. He still stood there, waiting silently. It was weird, but again, he had been through a lot too. So I let it go. I turned around, making my way up to Steven, hearing Carl's feet crunching on the ground behind me. I got up to him and asked what he saw, he pointed up the mountain and said he saw a flicker of light. I stared intently into the distance, waiting to see if it would make a return, but nothing reappeared. I told him to lead on then, maybe another would show to guide us better. He led on.

The moon had finally made an appearance from behind the clouds, a massive looking one, it's light illuminating the land inside the eye for us. Everything had taken a bluish tinge to it, the colors of our coats washed away, the landscape looked more like we were walking on the surface of the moon rather than being under it. I had been looking beyond Steven for some time, trying to catch an indication of anything ahead of us. But for all it felt like, we could have been the only ones on the mountain. I asked him for the umpteenth time where he had seen it, he replied "Just a bit further, we're almost there." And on we hiked. With the help from the moon, no snow, and no more trees, it was an easy climb. The air had a fresh crispness to it, I was aware of altitude sickness back then, how people coming from the lower-lands in the States aren't used to the lower oxygen levels the higher up they go. But I felt good. We all should have been dead on our feet, barely even making it out of the trees. Yet here we were, still steadily climbing. I could take a lung full of air, and it brought the same sense of satisfaction as drinking a perfectly chilled glass of water had. I should have been worried about that too, but when my frustration from earlier was broken by Steven's mention of light, it took all the "wrongness" with it. I wouldn't say I was relaxed, or unaware of the situation. I knew I wasn't out on some late night hike just for fun. But my guard was down, these things, I should have been questioning, I wasn't.

I could smell smoke from a fire before seeing it. We had just come to a steeper inclination when the strong acrid smell came sweeping down the slope to us. We were close, the intensity and freshness of the scent gave me the impression it was just on the other side of the hill we had come to. Steven had the same idea and cautioned me with his hand to go low, and be quiet. Aside from the crunching of rocks underneath our feet, there was a silence around us that did not feel normal. Like we were in a sound proofed bubble of air. As we got closer to the top, I could finally see faint glimmers of firelight reflecting off the slopes above us, how Steven caught a glimpse of that from the edge of the trees was beyond me. The last bit of distance to the top we covered at a near crawl. I saw two jagged boulders with a v-like space between them and made my way to it. I felt fairly well hidden as I stared down into hell.

Where do I even begin to describe what I saw? My first initial impression was looking down onto this red jumbled mess. There was a fire sweeping around, forming half of a ring around the opposite edge to me. Behind that were three tall spires of stone, they looked like claws. In front of the fire was this, it was awful, it was a great pool of blood. Gore surrounded the pool, led into the pool, led back to people. My people, friends, co-workers, the cast. It's funny you know, I see it so perfectly in my head, I mean, how could I forget that. But when I try to describe it to you, at first, there are no words. How could anything I say describe the depravity, the horror of the situation. I saw Miles first, recognized him first. It was his glasses and dark eyebrows that stood out. His face looked relatively clean, but oh fuck, it was twisted, the agony he must have felt was frozen there. He was missing one arm entirely, and the other was mangled from the elbow down. His chest and stomach were split open, and he was hollow inside. Scooped out. His organs were most likely in the pool, around the pool, scattered every which way, I couldn't tell. He was crucified, they all were, naked and tied to logs shaped like an X. Next to him was a woman, I couldn't tell who at the time, but from Megan's interview, I think it was Nicole Garcia. Her face was smashed in, even with her head slumped forward on her chest, I could see the inward curve of it. Outwardly, her body wasn't in much better condition than Miles' was. Internally, it was the same, gutted. All of the ones I could see were like that. Some sort of extreme damage to their bodies, chest and stomachs cut open, spread apart, and all their organs gone. And see, once I get going, it's easy to pick out those details. There are words for it, but they feel weak you know? Nineteen people were tied to those X's. The line of them curved towards me, and ended with their backs to me. And there at the end, tied to stakes were Ally and Dre, in front of them stood the beautiful woman from the night before. Caitlin. She looked the same as when she came to me. The wild mane of black hair, the smile, those dimples you could see from a million miles away. Her pale skin. Her arms were slicked red. Her body covered in red splatters, her legs were the same. She looked like she could have been having a normal conversation with a neighbor, so calm and relaxed, and this smile on her face. Bewitching is an excellent word for her, yes. Safely hidden behind rocks far up the slope from her, I could feel this pull to her, the same feeling as the night before. Even now, thinking about her like that its there. Surrounded by everything else. It's enough to make me feel like I'm the crazy one, and I can recognize that it's her doing.

She stopped talking to them, stood back, and that giant ugly fucker was next to her, I don't even know where he came from, he was just there, a tall spear in his hands, offering it to her. She took it from him, walked casually up to one of the crucified people and with a quick downward slash at them, opened them up. Dre was screaming at her to stop, crying it out. She stepped back from the body, holding the spear out for the big guy to take it, and then a shape from the outer edges sprang forward. It was small, about as big as a ten-year-old, lanky and lumpy. In the red light cast over everything, it looked dark, and had still even darker patches on its skin, like camouflage. It had a big head, no hair, long pointy ears, and a long pointed nose. And as I was seeing it, it dawned on me that it was an actual fucking goblin. I mean, sure, maybe it's something else, but that's what it became to me, and so that is what it continues to be. It reached the body, and with their back to me, I couldn't see what the goblin was doing, but I could hear it. The rending, the cracking of bones. He, the person, it was Ty, he had been screaming since Caitlin cut him open, but then he stopped, and his head fell backwards. The goblin went away from him, and I saw him throw Ty's organs into the pool, making a splash of blood. Then it ran back to the edge of the light and sat down, and I saw all these other lumps around it, it was hard to get a count on them, hundreds maybe? They were bowed forward, their bodies were so contorted, distorted, along with the lighting, not to mention the lack of it where they were, they looked like boulders, rocks. Maybe some of the shapes actually were rocks? They had this natural way of being hidden, I could've walked by one and been none the wiser. Maybe I had, maybe any one of the people down below had.

I wasn't thinking then, nothing specific, a strong urge to get the hell out of there. In the face of it all, what was I supposed to do? I turned to ask Steven if he was seeing what I was seeing, what we could do against it. I didn't get the chance. Carl's large fist came like a club, smashing into the side of my head. The snow-cap I was wearing gave me zero protection, I fell down hard. I don't remember fully how the next few minutes went, he got me pretty good. I think one of them kicked me. I was on my back, and had slid down, head first, on the wrong side of the ridge. I was looking at Steven and Carl, standing higher up, lit from the red light. They had undergone a change. The skin was sagging, the muscles had stopped trying to hold anything up, cheek bones protruding out further than before. Deep sunken areas surrounded their eyes, eyes that had turned cloudy and lifeless. There were dark splotches on their faces, I think where blood had pooled, congealed while they were hanging upside down. It didn't even seem like they were looking at me while they were walking down to me, roughly grabbing at me. I struggled against them, but it felt like I was fighting slabs of iron. Up close they smelled bad. Any semblance of life they had before was gone. They began dragging me, practically kicking and screaming, down the slope. I remembered the knife I had stored away in the front of my coat, Carl had my left arm locked in his grip, but Steven had ahold of my right shoulder, leaving that arm more or less free. I got the knife out and slashed and stabbed at Carl with it, there was no reaction from him. Thinking on it now, the worse part was going down backwards, not seeing what I knew was coming. And seeing the safety of the slope getting further and further away. They weren't fast about it either, slow shambling steps drug me along towards the inevitable. We got to a point where we were crossing between Dre and Ally, and they stopped. I twisted my head around as much as I could, and saw that Caitlin was facing away from us, hands up in the air, yelling something towards the fire. I knew it was just a matter of time before it was my turn to be gutted. I thought that at least if anything, I could go out fighting against them as much as I could, and give Dre and Ally a chance. So I threw the knife towards Dre's hands, landing it cleanly between them. His head shot up in surprise and confusion, not understanding what had come into his hands. Steven and Carl began dragging me again, I shouted at Dre to get free, save her.

They spun me around and dropped me right at the edge of the pool of blood. It smelled so bad. I thought they had smelled bad when they got close to me, this was worse. Caitlin was standing in it, knee-deep, wading her way to me. I tried to get up, but Steven and Carl took hold of my arms and forced me back to my knees. She came right up to me, smiling so happily. She said some words in her language, discordant music that pierced through to the center of my head. My arms were released, but I was frozen to the spot. She knelt down in front of me, placed a bloody hand on my cheek, this look of compassion on her face. It wasn't mocking, or evil. She looked, I don't know, thankful? I get it now, with what you've told me about her, but the utter confusion and despair I had at the time, it was maddening. Then she took my left hand into both of hers, my arm and wrist easily bending and moving along with her motions. She held my hand up, in between our faces, straightening my fingers out, one by one. She kissed my palm. She kissed my fingers. Then, she bit off my index finger. As clean and smooth as the Vorpal blade did to the head of the Jabberwocky. The insanity of it, the situation, one second it was there, then the next, it wasn't. I couldn't do anything about it, I couldn't move to cover it, I couldn't scream, the pain was there, the blood was flowing freely. All I could do, was sit there and endure. I didn't see what she did with my severed finger, but I believe it was added to the pool. She then straightened my arm out, and I bled out into the pool, mixing my blood into it. Then to make things even worse, she turned my palm up, leaned over it, and vomited my semen into it. She tilted my hand so it would flow into the blood as well. She left me like that, having taken what she needed from me, she turned around walking out towards the middle of the bowl, sinking down further into it until it was up to her waist. She began shouting towards a space in the middle of the fire, hands held high into the air. Then walking counterclockwise in the pool, moving in a spiral until she was standing in front of me. She knelt down in front of my hand, placing hers over it. I was still in immense pain, no amount of adrenaline was going to cover that up, but I began to feel a coldness spreading through my hand. Like I had dipped it in an icy river. It became more intense, and painful, and then she took her hand away. She had frozen the stump, stopping the blood. "T'would be no good for you to bleed out any further" she said to me. Then she dipped her hand down into the blood, scooping it up.

She walked away from me along the edge, and seemingly found the appropriate spot to stop at, she flung the blood out, sending a much larger spray than what she had collected, out into the air. It flew out across the pool, hitting a point in the air where the fire had the opening, splattering as if it had struck a wall. I could see behind it, into the space, through the smoke and waves of heat I saw a giant of a man appear. He was extraordinarily tall, heavily muscled, and missing a large portion of the right side of his face. A quarter of his head looked like it was just blasted away, the eye and everything above it was gone. He was bald, and had a large beard. He stood there, breathing heavily. Looking every bit like a deranged barbarian. Psyching himself up is what comes to mind for it now. He was so damn big, easily ten feet tall. Caitlin yelled, called out, and he bent forward, stepping into the smoke and flames. It looked like he was fighting his way through, something was holding him back, holding onto him. He would reach out with his massive arms, shoving them into the flames, and then drag himself forward. He was moving slow, every inch a fight. He had just made it to the hanging blood, his body stretched out horizontally over the fire, and I noticed that the flames were going through him. He bunched his legs up under him and pushed forward. His hand reached the blood and began to come through, it stretched with him, a thick film holding his hand behind it, like he was pushing outward on a sheet. His other arm came through, along with his head, and finally the center tore. There was a noise, a massive shrieking, tearing sound. It was like nothing I had heard before. Like thunder and metal rending, like a ship being torn apart by an iceberg, and even those sounds don't do it any true justice. It was horrible, and painful, and absolutely frightening. There was a wrongness to it. A mind breaking noise that blots out all others. A noise that is never, ever, supposed to happen.

With that tearing, the resistance that was holding him back had vanished and he came sliding out, falling into the pool of blood below, vanishing beneath a great splash. Then he stood up, slowly. He towered over everything. The blood, running off him, clung to him at the hips, a venous membrane forming a skirt around him. The level of the blood and gore in the pool was rapidly going down. He was absorbing it, filling himself up with it, the missing section of his head was knitting itself back together, healing. When it finished, he threw his arms out wide, and roared upwards to the night, to the full moon hanging overhead, filling the entirety of the eye of the storm. Caitlin came rushing up to him, tiny and small in comparison. She yelled up to him, and he looked down at her and smiled. He leaned down to her, and in the process his shape changed, became smaller, more human in size. He was still large, it just looked normal now. He picked her up in his massive arms and swung her around in a circle. Both of them laughing. He put her down, and she placed a hand over his still missing eye. They exchanged words. And then they turned their attention to me.

Whatever she had done to me before, paralyzing me, still held. Again, there was nothing I could do. No trick to counter it, no ruby slippers to clack together. The complete and total helplessness I felt is something I wouldn't wish on anybody. It was maddening. They walked to me, Caitlin circling around behind me, gently placing her hands on my head, taking off my cap, pulling my head backwards to look up at the man leaning over me. He did not have a smile for me, no compassion, no thanks in his face. He took hold of my face with one hand, at first I thought he was coming to kiss me. Then he placed his mouth over my eye, his tongue slid about over my eyelids. I shut my eyes tight, not knowing, or even understanding what he was doing. But his tongue. It was so strong, it didn't wriggle, or squirm, or try to pry. It just thrust its way into my eye, forcing my eyelids apart, following the curve of the socket. Pushing, tearing, scooping and then pulling. He stood back up, I watched him chew, and swallow. I watched as a new eye grew in the empty cavity. I heard him say to Caitlin "Again, I am whole." Caitlin put her hand over my ruined eye and the same painful icy current added itself to my misery. She replied to him "Welcome back, Balor my love." She released my head, and the hold she had over my body. I fell to the side. It wasn't until a few days later that I realized they had been speaking their language.

XXV. The Testimony of Edmond Farkas

I hate this, you know I hate this, I told you what happened. Why do I need to put pen to paper and record it? You say it is to heal. I say time has healed you. No good will come of this, I can assure you. Yet, this is what you want, is it not? To bring them forth, to challenge them with testimony. So, here it is. My addition to the pain. To the misery. To the anger and rage we need to proceed.

My name, is Edmond Farkas. I was born, on an overfilled boat of immigrants crossing the ocean in 1866. My mother died during childbirth, the responsibility of raising me fell to the eldest of my siblings, fourteen-year old Ester. The captain of the ship, my sister told me, was a nice man who christened me with my name. Our father was a man of short stature with a penchant for alcohol, who lamented the loss of his wife, but did not much care for another mouth to feed. We made landfall, then went westward. My earliest memories are of a dry, arid homestead surrounded by browns and gold. I do not know where we lived, what state it was, but I believe it might have been Texas or Oklahoma. My father had accepted a proposal from some distant relation of ours in California, to marry my sister. Ester, not wanting to be separated from me, brought me with her. I understood it from her at the time, that she, through little effort on our father's part, had plied him with drink the day of her departure by train. When he was good and drunk, she walked out of the house with me, leaving 3 other siblings behind. Went onward to the neighbors some miles down the road, who had agreed to give us a ride in their buggy to the train station. Then we were off. Some months later, she had received a letter from her father (through a correspondent), stating that since she had a greater fondness to me, than what he had, then she was more than welcome to keeping me, and good riddance. Afterwards I grew up with her and her husband, going to work with him as a carpenter, and learning the trade.

Years later I would be a foreman for a team of good hard workers, and we would be approached by your ancestor, Dylan Merglen. He was a good man. A sly sense of humor about him, but he was direct and straight forward with his dealings. Some of the men on the team felt some animosity towards this man, who being the same age as us, had apparently struck it rich. I sorted that out rather quickly, as jealousy never helps anyone to anything good. But that is neither here, nor there. We were hired to build up a cabin on his land into a mansion. He and his wife had drawn up specifications for it. A deal was struck, and we were hired. And therein my doom was settled, as the saying was. By this time, I was, I believe somewhere around the age of thirty. Dylan recorded it all in his journal, but as I have not seen it in some time, I do not remember fully the date. When you get to live for as long as I have, you tend to find those dates that were earliest, are harder to keep track of. I am only sure of my birth-year being eighteen-sixty-six from finding the ships manifest some years later. Until that point, even that I was not entirely certain of.

As it were, we arrived to a beautiful valley that any one man would have given an arm for to claim as his own. And then Caitlin made her appearance, and I was lost. Please do not think less of me, as I admit to this, as I was married going into this, my wife, was a beautiful woman from the Chinese immigrants, Xiao Mei. I had met her at job three years prior, she was working as a housemaid for a family in Portland. She took a liking to me, and would bring me coffee in her free time. I took an equal liking to her too. Her parents were not thrilled with the arrangement, but I agreed to look after them as well, and we were quietly wed. We were happy, she did not always like me being away for some jobs, as my team and I travelled where we were needed, and would stay on location.

Meeting Caitlin though, ruined me to that, I knew as soon as I saw her come out of the cabin that I was smitten. Would do anything to please her. She made eye contact with me, and where there should have been a spark, there was a lightning bolt. I know it now, that this is just what Caitlin does, she casts a spell over you, and there is nothing to be done for it. It is so subtle, so insidious, to this day I am still ashamed at myself and my actions. Hell at whatever thoughts I might have had. And yet, I was under a spell from that witch. I think what it does, is that it works like a drug, or alcohol, it takes something that is already there, and increases it. As much as I want to say it was all her, there was something in me as well that went with it. I did not fight it.

The job, proceeded to plan. My infatuation with her caused no trouble for my team or I. I thought at the time I was doing well to hide it. Dylan had taken an interest in our work, and was more than happy to help out alongside me. In spite of the feelings I had for his wife, I found that I quite liked the man. While I may have struck down the attitude of the men in regards to their jealousy, I was not so optimistic either. In my experience up to that time, the rich people had their side, and we the laborers had ours. That Dylan crossed it so easily spoke greatly of his character. It wasn't until the time I lived there fully that I learned he had not been born into the money, but only recently come into it. Being away from the "high society" types had helped prevent a corruption that was only too common, and still is these days. But I digress. Bres had been spotted early on, but none of us believed the man who spotted him, so the matter was looked over. With the coming of the bear attack, and the events following, there were whispers amongst the crew, strange things being afoot and all. Discovering Bald Jake's body upset them greatly, and they were ready to high-tail it out of there. I convinced them otherwise, and Dylan was generous with handing out pay and allowing time off for recuperation. With the gift of the belt and arm bracers, I felt well and truly among a family, the type I was not even aware I needed or wanted. I named him my brother, the blood of the bear and our wounds was enough to join us in mutual respect. A benefit of it was that it broke the spell Caitlin had over me, or so I thought. I could say the moment when I put on the gear is when I was well and truly damned. But I do not believe there was any avoiding it. The moment I was born I was already lost. Everything to my life had just been a waiting game to that point.

I have never put to paper, hell, into words, what I am now. But it needs to be said. I've carried it with me all these years, and she deserved better. But for what we must do next, I do not think I can manage and hold onto it at the same time. Not without it being used against me. Once the belt was buckled, and the laces tightened, I felt something right away. Not anything I could have put into words then, I had confused it as an uplifting of spirits, of pride at this gift, and at finding a family such as this. I felt, as the people of today would say, fucking amazing. On our way back to Portland, I had a plan all worked out in my head. I would pack up Mei, our meager belongings, see to it that her family would be well taken care of, and then she would travel with the men and I on our return to Tenas Tilikum. I had not mentioned her one bit to Dylan, but I knew that after a bit of surprise, he and Caitlin would greet her with open arms. I was, as the saying goes, riding high.

We made camp, and settled up for the night. I made myself comfy next to the fire, preferring to sleep under the stars. As soon as I laid my head back, her laughter had me sitting upright, staring at her across the flames. I asked what she was doing there, how she got there, was everything alright? Her answer was to gracefully stand and swirl away, running into the night. I was up and after her, yelling for the men to follow along, to bring lights. She ran swiftly, trees, rocks, dips, and rises were nothing to her as she made great strides over the land. On after her I ran, surprised at how well I could see her, how readily I could see everything. Most of all, it was becoming easier for me to keep up with her. When I put my hands on the ground, pulling at the dirt with my fingers, running on all fours, I went even faster.

Soon, she wasn't running away from me, but with me, playing with me. Brushing near me, her scent filling my nose. Letting me take the lead as we ran and leapt over the ground. Finally, she took the lead once more, sending us out onto a grassy knoll, the scent of the ocean nearby, the sound of waves crashing onto a shore filled my ears. I stopped, standing up, confused as to how we could be anywhere near an ocean. I raised my nose to the smell, the scent told me it wasn't the Pacific. Spinning in a circle, inhaling more air, images came into my mind of being in a wholly different place, practically another world. I looked to Caitlin, I tried speaking, but all I could produce was a whine. She laughed at me, amused at the confusion. She opened her arms to me, the front of her night clothes untied, showed me a glowing pale line of skin. She called me Bear Slayer, told me to come to her, she would keep me safe. And so I did.

I woke up before dawn, stiff, cramped, freezing, and; but for the belt and bracers, naked. I was covered with mud, dirt, and other debris from the forest. My head throbbed and I had a great thirst, not my first time for that feeling. I stood, calling out for Caitlin, freezing as I was, her waif-like frame would have had it worse. Instead, one of the men yelled back with surprise. I don't remember who, but as I found my way back to camp, I took much flak for my disappearance, and the rather uncouth reappearance. Much was made about where I had hidden the hooch, and then as to how much of it I drank. It was all in good nature from them. No one had seen or heard me leave the night before, or knew when for that matter. As the day wore on, it became a joke among them. One I took directly on the chin like a champ. I was certain it was just a dream then, but it was like no other I had before. The next night had me curious before sleep if I would experience it's like again, but as far as I know, nothing of the sort happened. The rest of the trip was made without incident. As we came into Portland, I squared away the debt with the men for their work. With the excess pay from Dylan, they had fairly hefty funds weighing them down. I made it clear there would be no hard feelings if any of them did not wish to return to finish the work, but that I would certainly be doing so. I had need of them to tell me there and then, so I could make the proper arrangements. Being spurred on by the idea of more good pay from a generous employer, one and all agreed to meet again on that spot in a few weeks time.

I made my way home to Mei. She fussed over my wounds, and I was surprised at myself for almost forgetting about them, they did not hurt and were healing much better than I thought they would. She was not thrilled about my idea to uproot our life to one of solitude on a mountain with people she did not know. Especially when that person was my current employer. I tried to explain to her, it was more than that. That these were good people. What Dylan and I had done, in taking on this bear, we had struck a bond that would not be so easily broken. She was very strong-willed, but she knew how to pick and fight a battle. She gave me words of placation, there was time to spare, I had only just gotten home, there's no need to rush back immediately. I remember feeling disappointment then, I thought for sure she would see the joy I had and share in it. And then there was a resentment, it felt natural, it is natural I suppose, to resent people for the things they do, the way they do something that goes against your wishes. Barring childhood grievances, to that point in my life, I had never felt resentment towards anyone. Ester had instilled in me an appreciation for what I am given out of life. If God wanted me to have more, He'd give it, she'd say. Her voice, was gone. It was replaced by "I want this, why shouldn't I have this, how can she take this away?" Was this something deep from within me, brought to the forefront by this curse? Or was I always like this, blind to the fact I felt this way towards people, secretly being led by my biases? Do you see what I am getting at here? To this day, I take accountability, and at the same time wrestle with the idea that all this was put in me by someone, something. The thing you need to understand about Caitlin, her influence is far and wide, there is no escaping it. She had a plan for me, had it all along. She only had to wait for the time I was to appear, then play it all out exactly as she had seen it.

My time at home was not pleasant. Each day I had a desire to return, a need that was growing stronger. I argued with Mei constantly. She had finally made it clear to me, that this plan was not in her interest, nor should it be mine. She was fighting for me, I did not see it, anger clouded my vision. It is strange, to look back on a situation, to remember being present for it, but seeing it through the eyes of clarity. To hear the words that were said, to yell at myself to see the love in her, the care, that she saw something was wrong with me. To know there is nothing to be done. This is where I must be careful. I watch it happen. I see this fool of a man eventually raising a hand to her, putting her to the floor. The anger and fear on her face, the disgust. I have viewed this scene on a loop for years. Now, with committing it to paper I must shift my perspective. It is not something to be seen in a theater, an act to watch between actors. I did this. My beautiful Xiao Mei, not knowing what was causing this change in me, the anger radiating off of me that had never been there before. She was trying to help. And I struck her for it. Ran her out of the house. I had purchased a home for her parents and brother a block away, she stayed there.

Good riddance I thought. The irony slipping by me at the time. She was holding me back, there was a dream of a vibrant living future out there, of having the forest, the mountain, ready and waiting for me to run wild and free. Of Caitlin, leading me to strange new lands, beckoning me with arms wide open. Of Dylan giving me kinship, a brotherhood I now desperately wanted. I was still troubled by Mei's rejection. I would go out, I would drink, I would come home to an empty and cold house. The wrongness of it. I would rage against the walls at their audacity for making me feel so unwelcome. The next day would be the same, the day after that, and the day after that. What had once been a warm inviting home, cared for so much by my wife, I had trashed. Turned into a den to match my thoughts. I had had plans of selling it before my departure, but now no respectable agent would agree to take it on.

Near to my last days there, when my excitement to return was at it's most palpable, Mei knocked for the final time to the door of her own home. She had brought her brother for safety. He was a fine and able young man, I had offered him a place among my crew, but his parents had need for him in their own shop. Sadly I cannot remember his name, his face is blurred, or replaced by one or other current actor I feel reminds me of him. It is a disservice to his memory, but I do not believe it can be changed. I suspect that without the help of notes, or journals, much of my past will eventually become forgotten. I can imagine myself some day in the future, finding this, having those "ah ha" moments when a specific memory is dredged up from the depths. It is unfortunate how little of this there is that is good. I trailed off. Mei. Her brother waited outside. Taking stock of the current state of the household, her face and voice took on much pain. I asked if she had come to reconsider. She had not, she came to make a final plea to me. To not return. To stay with her, to rebuild the house, or to move away, far away if that is what I wanted, to rebuild a home of our own somewhere else. Not to return to the job. Something there had changed me. Why could I not see that? I gave her clichés, idiotic lame excuses that were justified in my head. That surely put her in her place. It was a challenge for me to win, to come out on top. The hurt in her eyes was from the loss of her selfish desire to back me down into subjugation. I can hate Caitlin for this. I do. But the hate I feel for myself is paramount to what I have for her.

They left, I went out to celebrate. My singular affair was too much for the people of Erickson's and after many warnings I was finally put out onto my ass. It was raining, had been for a while. I began a losing battle against the ground to keep my feet planted to it. A tinkling of familiar musical laughter came to me from the end of the street, her wild mane of black hair vanished around a corner. My heart lurched to her before the rest of me could, practically throwing me to my feet like some cartoon character. But I was up, yelling for her to wait, to come back. Stumbling after her the best I could. The damn boots wouldn't find any purchase on the ground, so I took them off. It became easier to run. By the time I reached the corner she had vanished behind, my trousers had grown tight and restrictive around my legs, it was astonishingly easy to pull them apart. Her scent lingered, mixed with the rain. I was locked into it, rushing through the streets eager to get to her. I would hear her, calling to me, catch a glimpse of her vanishing yet again. No matter how quickly I moved, she was consistently ahead of me. I didn't enjoy this game. Weeks I had gone without her, the urge to return driving me mad, but still having the forbearance to wait. Now here she was, making me pursue her through the streets. Chase her. Catch her. Less in words and more an image of blurring scenery as I sped by to my singular objective. Her scent led down a street, into a home with a door made of paper.

I woke up to a man kicking me in the ribs. Covered in mud, pants missing, shirt torn to shreds but still on me, and of course the ever present belt and bracers. I was huddled up next to a building. The man kicking me awake was a policeman. My face was bloodied, to him, it had been evident I had been in quite the row. My confused sluggishness and general state gave him good reason to believe I was still inebriated from the night before. He was not rude or rough with me, but did say he would have to take me to cool my heels in a cell until I was in a better state to walk home. He was kind enough remove his coat and allow me to wrap it around myself to hide my nudity. At his station, I was led into a cell, and sat my sorry ass on a foul smelling cot. To say I didn't care would be an overstatement of my thoughts. I was not yet to the point of comprehending where I was. I was still hung upon the night before. Had Caitlin been there? Was this a dream like the other? I remembered the door, it looked familiar, it had been so easy to tear through it, like it wasn't there at all. And then nothing. And then I'm being woken up, and here I was in a jail. Embarrassingly enough, without any pants. I came to quickly, begged for some water and clothing. As I was finishing up, a man rushed in, another policeman. I remember my jailer proclaiming loudly "Bill, you look like shit." He did, pale and sickly, like coming off the worst boat ride of his life. I couldn't hear what passed between them, but I was released immediately. Something had come up my jailer said, his morning was soon to be ruined, no sense in having me hang about to hear of it. Please return the pants later, and we'd consider the matter no further. I went home and promptly fell asleep again.

I was awoken to banging at my door, I had missed the meeting time, and two men who knew where I lived had come to retrieve me. I had been asleep for three days. They were concerned as to my state, I was not much cleaner than the perfunctory washing I had given myself in the cell. I told them I was fine, my bag was ready to go just as it was shortly after I arrived. I did not look back, or give any thought to Mei. Nothing else mattered. We met with the others, and hit the road, I took the lead setting a fast pace. I overheard one of the men ask another if he had heard about the family that had been attacked by an animal inside their home. The man had. He had wanted to join the posse that was on the hunt for whatever it was, but his wife convinced him to stay home. This set a bee buzzing about in my skull, but it was a reality I was not ready to face at the time, and it was easy to squash it.

We made good time, after several days of an easy ride, we came upon the valley. Sighting it sent a shiver through my body, every hair stood up with such an intensity I thought my very skin would burst. It took all I had to keep myself contained, from lighting off the seat of the wagon and running ahead on my own. Dylan came down to the camp and greeted us warmly, happy to see us back. Grasping me firmly by the arm, he led me back to the house alone, eager to talk of society. Caitlin greeted me inside the home, a cup of coffee at the ready. Her sky blue eyes, deep pools pulling me in with raised brows, telling me she knew of our time together in dreams, promising me more. I choked on my coffee. I heard her in my head, clear as day, but outwardly, she only gave me her gorgeous smile, and was speaking with Dylan, something about Louis. Giving poor excuses to depart quickly, I went back to the men. Time passed, we finished our work. Dylan asked what Caitlin whispered. Stay with them, be his brother, work with him in the world as a partner. Right hand to his left. What a team we made. What a home I had.

The first times I changed, they had been triggered by Caitlin. Something she became fond of doing often. As I recall those times, I still cannot see how I was not aware of it. It is easy of course to write it off as something else attributed to her. But giving her so much credit for everything rubs me the wrong way. Am I being willfully ignorant with this? Possibly. But I think this gets down to how natural it felt, how easy it took over. I do not believe animals question their existence. A dog doesn't look up from the food bowl one day and say "why am I a dog?" They just are. Why question a fundamental fact of what you are? It serves no purpose. And this is what it was like when caused by her. When the first full moon rose, I was treated to another form of the change. The one that came from me, from within. The one the stories are about. The one that hurts. It is a remaking of your body into something else. It's being the larvae inside the cocoon, breaking down with all your nerve endings staying intact. Then bursting through your own skin, everything gilded with a haze of pain. There is only pain. And then it vanishes. And then you're okay again. Reborn anew and capable of taking on the world. A vast feeling of freedom running over the land. Each time is like that. My memories of changing back are far and few between. It hurts as well, and there's a reduction, a loss of mass and of self. By that point, I've run my body so ragged that when the reverse change comes, my waking self more or less shuts down. At the start, I was not my own person. Caitlin could sway me however she wanted. The wolf was a baby, a mere pup. As Dylan would send me out into the world, I found that distance from Caitlin, from the mountain, helped me to overcome my base self more. I could change, and be in control. I could handle my emotions. For a time, the urge to return would abate. The longer I was away, the less intense my feelings for Caitlin would be. She understood this as well. With a timely fashion, she would "send" for me, as it were. I could be doing any such thing, and it would be like falling into an ocean of "need". The need for her, the urge to be with her. The pull to her. And rushing back I would go. I never intended to stay gone forever in that time. I believed I loved her, I told her I didn't need those urges to come back. She caught my heart, saying those weren't for me, not a reminder, but for her, it was what she was feeling, her need for me. A common term I hear frequently now, which explains this wonderfully, is gaslighting. And how, you ask, could I claim Dylan as my brother, and yet do this to him? It was painfully simple. I believed I didn't have a choice. She said I was hers, Dylan was hers as well. But she was not mine, not his. We could love her as we did, but never, ever, own her. For a time, it was true, I had given myself to her fully. With the coming of the Bandits, while I was away, a chance to change into something better came for me.

Part of what I think I understand about how Caitlin works, is that she deals in possibilities, not absolutes. She kept her ways to herself mostly, Dylan was aware of them, but feared questioning too much, he was content with where he was. I would try to get more out of her, I wrongly assumed that because of what I had become, I carried a deal of equal footing with her. But she was something else, she was never human, even though she looked like us, acted like us. She wouldn't speak much of where she was from, she told me I had a glimpse of it, the first time we laid together. She missed it, but she had everything she needed right where she was. She claimed to have the "rusk of the weald" at her fingers. She would not say more. I think these are the possibilities that she encounters, causes them to come into being. Dylan had explained that she had a way of knowing of things forthcoming, but was very careful with what she would outright say about them. Only giving sly smiles, as they come to pass. When I was away, and the bandits came, she was aware, of course she was, an event like this. How could she miss seeing it coming? What I don't think she saw coming, or that she chose to ignore, was that it pulled her attention off of me.

What I learned to be the day they made it to our home, becoming caught in the storm, and then falling under Caitlin's sway, had for me, been the day the "need" made its appearance. It lasted for only an hour. This was in itself an oddity for me. When it came upon me, it didn't stop, not until I made it back home. It would ride my back like the demon would the backs of opium addicts. By the time I got home, before the sweet relief of its release would come, it was all I could think of. And this time, it had stopped. I didn't know what it meant, did she not want me anymore, did I not want her anymore? It was a freedom that scared me. And then it released me. It freed me in a way that made me realize it had an even stronger, deeper, grasp on me. For the first time since before I put on those damned gifts, I felt like myself. I still couldn't bring myself to remove them, they had become so much a part of me, to remove them would have meant skinning myself. But the obsession I felt over Caitlin, the so-called "love", had dissipated. I had staggered to a stop on a sidewalk somewhere, I don't recall the city, but I remember I was in

California. The jubilation I felt at this freedom caused me to "woop" loudly in the face of passersby, earning me concerned looks. And I thought of Mei. Sweet, beautiful Mei. How I treated her. How awful I had been. I couldn't imagine she would have me back. But I thought perhaps she would have my apology. I made plans to return to Portland first, I had to see her, to speak with her. Caitlin got to me first.

It was much like the first time. I was camped out, laid out on my bedroll next to the fire. The horse made a noise over my shoulder, I turned my head and said a word or two to him. When I turned back, she was there, on the other side of the fire. There was no smile this turn, no warmth save what the flames could spare through her gaze. I stood up in Portland, facing the white door I had been keeping as deeply buried as I could. My body ceasing to be my own, I became an unwilling passenger to this vision. I approached the door at an incredible speed, tearing through it as if it were not there. The parlor to the right is dark and empty, the family sitting room to the left as well. A narrow anteroom runs through the center of the house, stairs going up are to the right. At the end of the hall is a room lit for the evening. Voices are already raised in surprise, a small silhouetted figure appears in the door, shouting at me with angry words I do not understand. I spring towards it, on them in a second, biting, clawing, tearing away at anything that gives my mouth or hands resistance. There is more noise from further in the room. I hear "Ma" yelled, feel something crashing into, splintering over my back. It draws my attention. I stand, my ears brush the ceiling. I look down into the horrified face of Mei's brother, remnants of a broken chair slip out of his hands, its falling so slowly. He barely has time to react as I reach out, digging claws into his shoulder, pulling him in to me, biting his face away.

I'm screaming. I don't want to see this. I want it to stop. But it continues, she wants me to see it all. To remember. Something stings me, Mei's father has driven a knife into my side. There is no fear in his face, only sadness, resolve. He pulls the blade out, readies to stab it in again, yells to Mei. Hide. I lash out with my hand before he can stab again, his head explodes. I drop her brother, look around the bloodied kitchen. Sniff the air. I turn back to the hall. I hear something crashing in the rooms above me. I'm to the stairs in an instant, going up on all fours. Doors are closed, the upstairs hall is unlit. I follow the scent right to the room. This form is so strong. It feels like I barely exert myself as I push on the door, breaking through, splitting it in half, sending it flying into the room. There was a dresser shoved in front of it, it was sent tumbling away, crashing onto the bed. She's smart, the window is open, a fresh scent trail leads to it. I'm thrilled at this, she's gotten away. Amends will be paid for her family. I will pay, Caitlin will be held to account. In short, I'm going to fuck her up when I see her next. The window isn't big enough for me to leap through, I turn to leave, my nose latches onto another scent trail, stronger than the other. No. No. No.

I pull the bed up to its side, and she scurries away, tries to make it out the room. I catch her. My hand around her neck, I pull her in, I make a noise like a laugh. A word comes out of my throat, garbled and malformed from the different anatomy. Caitlin. I pull her in close. I see her face, I see that she's not Caitlin. That it's Mei. This angers me. She's kicking at me, scratching at my arm. This angers me. But I know it's Mei, and it's hard to think. I was chasing Caitlin, she wasn't letting me catch her. And then I finally caught her but it's not her. Around and around I go, the wolf's mind can't comprehend. With the casualness of a child bored with a toy, I toss Mei aside. But she is small, and I am only just aware of my strength to revel in it, not control it. She careens head first into the wall, then through it, into the other room. I follow, sniff at her, her body is bent awkwardly, her neck and shoulders at angles not meant for people. The wolf-mind finally knows it has committed a great injustice. I cry, howl. I tear out of the room, head to the stairs. At the bottom, standing in the door, there is a short, portly man with a shotgun. He has a sweet cherubic face, like the one of Santa that will be famous in years to come. He fires well over my head, I had long left the spot he saw me in. As I run by him, I reach into his stomach, pulling out entrails and organs with my passing.

I get outside the house, and I'm falling. I hit the ground, and I'm back at the campfire. Caitlin is there. There is sadness reflected on her face, watching me grovel and cry, asking why, begging her to bring them back. This of course is not something she can do for me. But it is in her power to make me do as she pleases. There is nothing for me to go back to there. If I did try to leave her, she would send me after others. My friends, my sister and her family, Dylan if it came down to it. And then she's gone. No discussion, no argument, just the threat. She knew a fight would come bubbling up from me, and so she took it away.

I returned an obedient dog. When Dylan began to enact his grand empiric plan, asking me to go out into the world for him, I was thrilled, anything to get me away from her. She would eventually call me back, the need would arise, but it was greatly diminished, could be resisted easily, and for longer each time. Dylan worried about me, once he asked me if I had become an opium smoker. I confided in him only so far as to say dreams had been disturbing me, travelling was rough, we were nearing our forties, and I was feeling it. He offered to pull back on his scheme, to give me a chance to rest and relax at home. I wouldn't have it. When I was away, I trained myself, the wolf-mind. I understood it to be a near separate entity from me, something I still saw as myself, but not to be under my control. With the mental training, I was eventually able to understand, it was me. The base me, a dangerous version of want and need. Without Caitlin's will exacerbating the situation, it became a matter of building my own up to counter my mind's simplicity and retaining who I was, not what I had become. It was finally put to the test on the night of Louis' tenth birthday.

Caitlin had something planned for the night, but would not tell me what. She had need of me to be up the mountain, at the place she called the "An tGavul", The Tines, Dylan referred to it as the Devil's Fork. When the others were asleep, I was to make my way there, meet Bres, and wait. I do not understand how, but I think I was able to trick her. I made myself believe that I would do just that. What else could I do otherwise? Whatever she saw in her possibilities did not give her any concern, to look at me in any other way except to see me follow her command. When the time came, I slipped out the window, then out of my skin. Reaching near the point I was assailed by the stench of Bres, and the more earthen-snake-like scent of the diminutive forest people and of a great fire. I knew whatever came, whatever she was planning, I would be there to counter it. To stay hidden from Bres would be my safest bet in taking him on. As fast and as strong as I was, he was more so. In all my years there, in the few confrontations I had with him, he had never spoken. He was a mere extension of Caitlin, her slave in a way I never came close to. But I understood his deadliness, his devotion to her. He would allow for nothing to come in the way of whatever she wanted. I suspected that if I were in his presence, I would be his prisoner, able to do nothing but observe. He couldn't contain me if I wasn't there. I circled, I waited.

She appeared first, stepping out of a shadow that followed her, carrying Louis in her arms. Several of the fir glas brecc ran forward, taking him from her, removing his bed-clothes, tying him to a cross. I wanted to rush in then, but contained myself. She exchanged harsh words with Bres, I assumed about me. I waited more. A ceremony began. Bres produced the spear, presenting it to her, and then laying himself down towards the fire. She spoke, waved the spear around, waved her hands around, stomped the blunt end of the spear on the rock, producing a clear chiming noise. There was a primal fury to her, I want to belittle the ceremony, make a joke of her. But it was mesmerizing, captivating. I had never seen the like, and I never wanted to see it again.

When Dylan appeared, roaring over a ridge, racing down to them, I expected him to die. I could see the fir glas brecc rising up, swarming over him like piranhas, leaving nothing behind. I had seen them do it enough to the wildlife, they could be voracious. I could not have been more wrong, he was glorious. He leapt off one of them, launching himself into the inner ring. I was distracted by him, I did not see what Caitlin was intending to do. Bres was beginning to move, and I knew Dylan would soon have need of me. He tore the spear away from her, and when he hit her, the force produced a loud thunderous crack, sending her flying. I couldn't have been more proud, more surprised by him. He began to untie Louis, unaware of how close Bres was to him. At the last moment Dylan became aware, barely dodging a full blow. Bres had clipped him well enough, and had time to prepare for a more deadly attack. Before he had a chance, I reached him. I hit him with every ounce of momentum and might I had, taking him off his feet. I beat at him, I clawed at him, I thought I had the better of him and my pride swelled. I turned to Dylan, forcing words out of my throat, telling him to go, to run. I saw the recognition on his face, the fear of seeing me that way, and my pride faltered. He knew me, but he still saw a monster. I had my attention off of Bres for too long, and it was his turn to show me how little I knew of strength. A flury of blows brought me down, I blacked out, I felt myself being raised up high, and then falling suddenly. My head swam and there was little I could do as my senses slowly came back. When I did, I saw Bres on the ground, the spear impaled into and through him. I staggered to my feet, and saw Dylan and Louis being surrounded by the evil little shits. The wolf-mind reacted well enough for me, throwing me into the mass. Clearing the tiny monsters away, making a path of freedom for the father and son. Close enough to him, I could see he had a fine glow permeating off his body, it wasn't until I discovered his journal that the pieces fell together for me on how he had been able to do what he did that night. He flew up the slope, I stayed behind to keep the horde busy. I heard him yell my name and then all went black.

I awoke human, in small cave, lying on a cold hard slab of stone, I couldn't move my legs. Inspecting my body, I saw I had a large wound just below my navel. The belt was missing. I heard a small nasal voice, full of anger and fear "Spear go through, split back, Mother says you die in sky. No more use." I had heard them speak their own foul language, but I was not aware they could do more. A small form approached from the shadows, as ugly as the others, but smaller in size, apparently a runt. His large eyes roamed over my body, an outlier of curiosity showing as he examined me. I asked for a drink, and he seemed pleased to be able to give me a drink. He called me by Krall Slack, quietly saying the name. "Waylos more good to heal, you make waylos come, leg work." I asked who Waylos was, and he jabbed me in the chest. "You, you waylos." then he made a poor rendition of a wolf howl. I understood, but I didn't think I could change then, I was so tired from it all. I asked him if Dylan had escaped, he cocked his head quizzically, reminding me of a dog. The Man and boy, I asked, did they run away? His eyes lit up, happy to be able to answer me now. He said they left, two moons coming and going since. Mother was angry about this and all the fir glas brecc were hiding until she cooled off. At least, that is my take as to what he said.

A handfull of days I lay there, slowly regaining my strength until I could force a change. The goblin would sometimes grow irritated at me, trying to yell at me in it's simple English before devolving to its own discordant language. The gist of it was that it was tired of feeding me, tired of seeing me weak. The Krall Slack was his hero, and seeing his hero defeated was something he was not adjusting to. I gained some favor with him, when I asked where the belt was, it had been damaged by the spear, finally falling away as the small creature was laying me on his sleeping slab. He had it wrapped around his own waist, whatever magic or means of it's working no longer in effect. He reluctantly handed it back to me, I inspected it, and told him that it was his to keep, for allowing me the use of his home, and for taking care of me. Wholesome joy is not an emotion I believe these things are capable of having, much less expressing, but the evil glee he brought forth was enough. On the next night I was able to change, able to feebly move my legs for the first time. When I changed back, I was restored further. After another round of building up my strength for a week I initiated another change and felt whole again. I had taken to calling the creature Speck, with no reason to wait any longer I decided to leave. I turned to him at the entrance of his cave, in my own limited speech, but as his idol I said "Thank you Speck." and left.

I became a vagabond after that. I was free from Caitlin, the need to return to her has never come back. She has never visited me since. She has never given any indication or acknowledgment of my survival. I am fine with it this way. I roamed around the States, sometimes on foot as a man, sometime as the wolf. I had an inkling of where Dylan and Louis were, and eventually drifted towards New York. I had never been removed as a chair-member for the companies there, so gathering the information I needed was quite easy. I found that he had married Cora, that Louis was growing into a fine young man. I had wanted to see him, to contact him, but his life had taken on a normalcy I was loath to interrupt. And I was scared of how he would feel about me, reject me. So I stayed away. The war came, but I did not go to join it.

I spent time at universities, libraries, trying to glean any information I could about Caitlin, what she is, if there is a way to fight her. For the time, this was information that was not readily available in America, I wrote to scholars in other parts of the world, gave them the bits and pieces that I knew, and asked if they had anything greater to add. It took some time, but I was able to glean something new. She's old, very old, she came from a race of people or gods called Fomorians that sprang up in Ireland thousands of years ago. They existed as some sort of monstrous primal counterpart to the Tuatha De Danann what would eventually be known as gods, elves, and all other manner of creature common to Irish Folklore. She was called Cethlenn, a seer, and wife to Balor, a warlike leader said to have an eye that would cause destruction with it's gaze. There was a great battle in which the Tuatha god Lugh, being also the grandchild of Cethlenn and Balor, slew Balor. This seemed to bring about the end of the Fomorians. Cethlenn was said to have caused extreme damage on her own against another god, and some account have her surviving, and another had her being slain shortly after. In short, the "good guys" won, and the "bad guys" lost. I do not know how much of that information I can use as being "true". I'm sure it was to those who told it, but for a long time, these stories were passed down from storyteller to storyteller by word of mouth. By the time they were written down, they could have gone through several iterations, any truth being conflated with falsehoods, or removed entirely. The important thing I took from these tales, is that these gods could die. Not only that, but they could be killed.

Years passed, I stayed the same. I watched Dylan become an old man. By the time my regrets got the better of me, I was too late. I paid a visit to his home, finally having the courage to face him after all that wasted time. Cora, now an old woman, answered the door, there was slight recognition in her, but as we were never close, and because I still looked young, it faded away. I told her my father had been an acquaintance to Dylan, asked if I might have a word with him for the sake of nostalgia. She said I was welcome to try it, but that his mind was not well anymore, some days he didn't recognize her, or his own son. She led me to a sun room in the back of their house. He sat, old and bent over, in a chair, a blanket over his lap. She loudly introduced me, but there was no response. Cora offered tea, I accepted, and she left to make it. I sat in front of him, I said his name. Caught his eye. For the briefest of moments his eyebrows raised in surprise, I could see him working inwardly, grasping at memories, something. He said my name, more out of caution and respect of being wrong about recognition. I smiled, I told him yes. It was good to see him. Sorry for taking so long. He waved the apology away, tears coming quickly. He reached out and I gave him my hand. He gave a good, healthy squeeze, and then he was gone. The recognition passed, his hand went limp and his eyes were empty. I said his name again, but nothing came. Cora returned, asked me to come with her. She led me into a kitchen, tea at the ready. She had heard, had seen, he said I had died, had been a wolf-man of sorts. She remembered strange things had happened there, but nothing as awful as the stories he told later. Had gone crazy with it in his journal. She let me see it, read it. So much confusion, fear, pain, he was right about so much, but in the dark as well. I was able to ascertain that Caitlin needed him for his bloodline. I thought it very likely that he, and then Louis, are descendants of the god Lugh. Fomorian, Tuatha, and eventually human lines all converging. The link, Caitlin needed to contact Balor, most likely resurrect him. We had prevented it, but what is a small collection of years to her? A new purpose had dawned on me. Louis could still be in trouble, Cora told me he had just had a child, a boy named Orwin, he and the mother were doing well. I made it my duty to protect them. Certain that Caitlin was biding her time again, her patience was near limitless.

I stayed nearer to them, Dylan passed away. I watched Louis flourish with his family. But I was not directly involved with him, I thought it safer if I watched from a distance as before, not learning my lesson with the lost time from Dylan. I had not seen Louis for some days, with my curiosity and concern building, I made inquiries and learned of what he planned. He had a strong lead ahead of me, I hoped I could make it to him in time to help. I did not know what to believe could happen to him. It is hard to transcribe human thought and emotion onto Caitlin. As I said, she looks like us, sounds like us, but she is not like us. Her mind is as alien to a human's as a human's is to a spider. I was too late. I could not save him. She would not allow me onto the land, would not allow me to find it even though I followed familiar paths. I found his belongings stored at an inn, I found the journal in his possessions, his entries, the unsent letter to his wife. I arranged to have it all shipped back to his family's home. I met with his wife, she was a modern, sensible woman. The fantasy her father-in-law had fallen into, that her husband had entertained, was not something for her. She would not accept my offers to stay and help, to guard and protect. Did not believe they needed it. I was happy to be proven wrong. I still stayed near, I watched them grow older, the baby turned to a child, the child turned to a man. The man started a family of his own, he had a son who did the same. How quickly this happened to me, it felt as though only a few days had passed. I was aware I was well over one hundred years old, but it was at the back of my mind, the miracle of longevity had taken a back seat amongst the horrors of my life.

And now its to you Ronan, being grown, being the one Caitlin had once again enacted plans for. She was ready for me, kept me delayed just long enough. The storm she raised to keep you and yours inside the land, she did as much to keep me within, disoriented, walking in circles. Any progress I made, she pulled it in further, increasing the size I was stuck in, but also narrowing what was left. By the time I made it through, began working my way up the mountain, I was too late. I arrived to see her with a hand over your face, to see the giant god Balor opening his evil eye over the bodies of the victims, somehow reawakening them in a painful undeath. Then he began to eat them, to grow, to regain his strength. But then there was an oddity, something I never expected. From where I was hidden, ready to reenact the events of almost one hundred years prior. Caitlin turned to me, the mass of goblins parted, making a path for me. She called me out of hiding. To come forward. I didn't understand. Bres, alive and well after all, began walking to where I was. She stopped him, and I heard her in my head, calm and serene. She told me to come, quickly, while Balor was distracted. And so I did. She gave you to me, you were out cold. She passed you over like an adult handing another their child.

You were the one later to explain to me, to theorize, that Lugh was her grandson, she tried to save him just as much as she tried to save Balor. Being a descendant of hers twice over, maybe there was such a thing as a familial bond within her. I understand the sentiment, from a human perspective. I will not entertain one from hers. The fact remains that she, and Balor, are creatures that are capable of committing what we can consider to be great acts of evil. To Balor, humans are likely little more than a food source. The dreams you have had in the years since, of him sleeping, gathering strength from the earth itself, we can agree, at this point are clearly more than just dreams. Your eye is his, his blood is your blood, there is such a link between the two of you. I think we can exploit it. We will figure this out. You were right, child. It has done me well to record this. Hard yes, but ultimately cathartic. Putting this out into the world is a dangerous game. It will draw them to us, knowledge of them brings destruction, ruin. They are secretive and protective of what they have. I suspect there will be retaliation. We need to be ready.

-End
Kit Gilmore, November 2023

-Acknowledgements-

Where would this book be without the help of family and friends? First and foremost is my wife, Danny, her love and support was of course paramount to the writing and completion of this book. Without her encouragement it would have been dead within the first ten pages. And also without her say so, the dog might not have lived to a nice happy old age. To the Underworld and Back.

Then, in no particular order but as they come to me.

Thank you to my fellow researcher Bob Alan, their availability at all times of the day and night concerning the workings of ancient languages, lore, and mythology were key to ideas and themes that went deeper into the earth than I originally planned.

Thank you to to my way-too-long-time-friend Kevin, for being my first reader. His input was well needed and well regarded. And to his father, for lending me his voice.

To my parents, who I reluctantly gave copies to, and for their amazing support and kind words.

To my circle of friends, who's personalities I stole, altered, and killed off in gruesome ways.

And to the artist, Erinthul for the amazing cover.

And of course, to you, dear reader.

Thank you again one and all. This would not have been possible otherwise.

About the Author

Kit is a lifelong story teller, tall-tales and otherwise. He lives way up high in the mountains spending his days sitting around the campfire telling stories to any of the woodland creatures who come his way.